THE PIT

DOCTOR WHO – THE NEW ADVENTURES

THE NEW DOCTOR WHO ADVENTURES

THE PIT

Neil Penswick

First published in 1993 by
Doctor Who Books
an imprint of Virgin Publishing Ltd
332 Ladbroke Grove
London W10 5AH

Cover illustration by Peter Elson
Typeset by Intype, London
Printed and bound in Great Britain by
Cox & Wyman Ltd, Reading

ISBN 0 426 20378 X

For my mum.

Thanks to Jane.

'How art thou fallen from Heaven,
O, Lucifer, son of the morning!
How art thou cut down to the ground,
Which didst weaken the nations!
For thou hast said in thine heart,
"I will ascend into heaven,
I will exalt my throne
Above the stars of God:
I will sit also upon the mount of the congregation,
In the sides of the north:
I will ascend above the heights of the clouds;
I will be like the most High."
Yet thou shalt be brought down to Hell,
To the sides of the pit.
'They that see thee,
Shall narrowly look upon thee
And consider thee, saying,
"Is this the man that made the earth to tremble,
That did shake kingdoms;
That made the world as a wilderness,
And destroyed the cities thereof;
That opened not the house of his prisoners?"
'All the kings of the nations,
Even all of them,
Lie in glory,
Every one in his own house.
But thou art cast out of thy grave like an abominable branch,
And as the raiment of those that are slain,
Thrust through with a sword,
That go down to the stones of the pit;
As a carcase trodden under feet.
'Thou shalt not be joined with them in burial,
Because thou hast destroyed thy land,
And slain thy people:
The seed of evildoers shall never be renowned.
Prepare slaughter for his children
For the iniquity of their fathers;
That they do not rise,
Nor possess the land,
Nor fill the face of the world with cities.'

ISAIAH 14: 12–21

Prologue

The night sky was dark and brooding. The clouds were moving quickly as if late for an appointment on the other side of the planet. Atraxi thought he saw shapes in the clouds. But there were no signs of a ship. He spent his time staring out of the window. And playing with the old amulet. He ran the chain through his hands and looked at the design.

Atraxi had waited. He hadn't slept for two days.

He sat in the detention room. Apart from the Capitol guards who had escorted him to the cell he had seen no-one since his return.

He coughed. His body ached and he had a high temperature.

He looked into the mirror. He saw an old man. His face had been burnt and his expression was that of a tortured soul.

The Eternal War was over. They had stood alone in the galaxy and they had won. He was the sole survivor. The armies had been annihilated. Even Liall a Mahajetsu, their great General, had died.

But legends would never grow about the warriors' heroic deeds, during the Dark Times. The Monsters were not dead.

He had returned to warn his people.

If it wasn't too late.

Gallifrey had changed.

Rassilon's single-minded will had transformed the world.

The warriors had been gone for over a thousand years. They had fought a war across the length of the galaxy. In that time religion had been abolished and rational science had been restored as the centre of their law.

He knew that it was a mistake.

As if science could explain away the Monsters. They had just appeared . . .

Science did not offer a glorious future. He had returned, expecting a hero's welcome. But the people had forgotten the warriors. The plague had ravaged Gallifrey. The scientists had done nothing to prevent it. Only a few survived. Many of the politicians, the law givers and the great leaders were dead.

He rushed over to the sink. He vomited again. The insides of his stomach were bleeding. The pain tormented him.

He had to see Rassilon.

They had to prepare.

The battle was over. But the war would continue. The Monsters would be back. One day.

He held the amulet and kissed it.

The pain . . .

He opened his eyes. He must have passed out. A figure stood over him. It wore a protective radiation cloak and mask to aid breathing. It had difficulty making itself understood. It was using a translator device developed, like much of their new science, to fight the bloodthirsty war with the Monsters. The figure towered over him and he felt no warmth or friendliness.

'I need to speak to Rassilon,' Atraxi said.

'Why?' the figure replied. A broken and sore voice.

'It isn't over.'

The machinery crackled. He couldn't make out the response.

'I am the only survivor,' Atraxi continued. It was so cold in the room. He could hardly breathe. 'He must listen to me. We fought a war; we won at great cost; we averted a threat far bigger than anyone had contemplated.' He lost the sense of his thoughts. 'I'm not thinking straight. I feel ill . . .'

'You are dying,' said the voice. 'Only death and destruction hold dominion in this realm.'

'Who are you?' Atraxi asked. He couldn't stand up.

The figure unwrapped a layer of cloth from around its mask. The mask was shattered and had been damaged beyond repair. The cloth kept it together and prevented unwanted bacteria and radioactive dust getting in. The figure slowly and painfully removed the mask.

The man stared.

It couldn't be. It couldn't possibly be.

He coughed up blood.

He shouted, 'Help!' There must be someone around to hear.

The figure knelt down beside him.

'You shall not die alone.'

Atraxi was shivering. He couldn't keep warm.

He couldn't grip anymore. The amulet fell from his hands.

'Please, give it back to me,' he begged. He needed it for protection.

His body began to shake uncontrollably. He stared at the figure's eyes. Eyes that had seen so much suffering.

The figure picked up the amulet, and ran his fingers over the design.

'Evil against Evil,' the figure said, clasping the amulet in his hand.

The figure held him tightly and began to utter a prayer.

Atraxi screamed. A long final howl of despair.

Part One

DAY THREE
18:00–24:00

Bernice sighed, sat down on the mahogany rocking chair and put her feet on the TARDIS console. The TARDIS hummed, a gentle purr like a pet cat. Although it was the product of a highly advanced race, the Time Lords, the machine was currently behaving in an erratic and temperamental manner.

The control room was sparsely furnished with the central console, a chair and a hatstand. The Doctor had at least three other hatstands dotted around the ship; he had at one time claimed to be collecting them.

'Doctor, are you playing?' she asked. It looked like she was going to win another game of chess.

'Yes. And you can act your age and put your feet down.' When the Doctor was annoyed, in his usual spluttering way, he talked too fast and everything came out in a drifting Scottish accent. He didn't like losing. He walked to the chessboard and stared at the black pieces surrounding his white king.

'Is it my move?' The Doctor was increasingly distant. His mind seemed to wander as she talked to him.

Twice recently she had found him standing in the TARDIS corridors, staring at the ceiling. She ordinarily took the Doctor with a pinch of salt when he was in a mood but this behaviour was strange, even for him. He had murmured to her about past experiences hanging about him. Bernice thought the Doctor was a lonely man, and when his mind dwelt on old friends he became unbearable.

Apparently without the Doctor noticing, Bernice had managed to move a pawn across the chessboard and promote it to a queen. He picked up her new queen, put it down, walked off and lay on the floor underneath the console.

'What are you doing, Doctor?'

He pulled the sonic screwdriver from his pocket and began to tamper with the TARDIS control mechanisms.

He ignored her question. 'Where do you want to go?'

'I'd like to finish this game of chess.'

'Chess?' He shouted at her, as if he'd forgotten they were in the middle of a game. She decided she would have won anyway, and if he was offering her the opportunity of choosing a destination she would make use of it.

'I'd like to go to the furthest reaches of the galaxy, to the dark places or the uncharted wilderness. I'd like to explore the unknown. I keep asking myself the same question, Doctor. Is this all there is?'

The Doctor looked irritated. 'But time travel is so exciting. You can travel to the cradles of civilization and see what really happened. How were women treated in those days? What did people do for money? As an archaeologist you must appreciate the potential?

'What about the beauty of the universe? The fiery suns, the spectral asteroid belts and the lone worlds bubbling with chemicals that will give birth to life. I could take you to Mars before mankind walked the Earth.'

'I'd like to go to the Seven Planets,' she said. He wasn't listening to her. 'Are you listening?'

'Yes, yes, Bernice. Could you pass me the weazle flirt.'

The what? She looked underneath the console. He was pulling out wires, putting them together and seeing if there was a spark. There was a loud bang and the Doctor shot out of his temporary workplace. His face was covered in soot.

'That's fine,' he said, standing up. He took a handkerchief out of his pocket and wiped his brow.

He smiled at her and raised his eyebrows. 'Bernice, wouldn't it be nice to stay at home, drink tea and read the papers. I'd like to do that but I can't.' He raised his voice on the final two words. He walked out of the console

8

room, whistling a tune which she recognized but couldn't place.

The Doctor was slightly over one and a half metres tall. He had a mop of curly brown hair and a cheeky grin. He wore checked trousers, invariably too big for him, a white shirt and red braces imprinted with question marks. He seemed like a circus performer and had a shuffling walk which gave the impression he was balancing on a tightrope swaying in the wind. She could trust the Doctor, unlike most men. He had taken her on many adventures. He was an old romantic and the universe had precious few of them.

'What are the Seven Planets?' The Doctor had walked in, having washed his face.

She had managed to interest the Doctor in her suggestion. Anything to escape from the TARDIS: there was something disturbing about it – not quite right.

'Fifty years before my time an entire solar system was destroyed,' Bernice said. 'I've always wondered what happened. Some say that it was a meteorite, others that it was a terrible civil war.'

'I've never heard of it.'

'Nicaea, 2400.'

He looked concerned. 'Why have I never heard of it?'

The star charts on the TARDIS had no record of the solar system but many of the Earth colony worlds would never have been charted before the colonists arrived. Bernice pointed out to the Doctor where the planets could be found. He programmed the TARDIS.

'I want to know why the TARDIS has no record of this system,' said the Doctor.

She smiled to herself and then began to wonder. Where had she heard of the Seven Planets? She thought, but all she knew was she'd always wanted to go there. She shook her head. What was she worrying about?

Suddenly the lights began to flicker and the sound of machines grinding to a halt interrupted their conversation.

'Doctor,' she said. The TARDIS was still playing up.

'This is most unusual,' he replied, running over to the

9

console. He pointed to a warning light, flashing on and off. 'Another TARDIS.' But the light quickly went out, as did all the lights on the ship's console.

'Complete all-systems breakdown,' the Doctor said. He looked underneath the console at his repairs and urgently tested various wires and microchips; when that didn't work, he kicked the console.

The ship darkened.

'Doctor?' She wasn't particularly worried. But sometimes it was necessary to make sure the Doctor hadn't been entranced by a hideous proposition which threatened a whole civilization but which he, temporarily, found interesting.

'Aren't you going to do anything?' she asked.

'Sometimes there isn't anything you can do. Let's wait and see,' the Doctor said, sitting on the chair and putting his feet on the console.

The funeral had been quick and efficient. Although death was not unusual on recently colonized worlds, Carlson always found the process of laying the body to rest unpleasant. He stood at the corner of the plot and watched the electronic pall bearers lower the coffin into the ground. The priest mumbled a lamentation.

The parents were distraught. The husband held on to his wife. She couldn't let her child go. She fell to her knees by the grave. She was begging for the Prime Mover, the Supreme Deity, to intervene and return their daughter. The priest was silent. He seemed embarrassed.

The assembled crowd started to sing, 'Shall We Gather At The River'.

The husband tried to calm her but she needed answers. 'Why?' She looked at the crowd. 'Why my child?'

' . . . the wonderful river of God . . .' The mourners sang on.

Carlson looked around. There were forty-three mourners. The deceased was a nineteen year old girl. She had started college, training to be an agricultural advisor; learning how to turn the virtually barren earth into fertile soil. She and her boyfriend had been talking about marriage. She was from a nice home and had everything to live for.

But it wasn't to be. Her badly mutilated body had been found by the side of a dirt track. It had taken days to identify her.

There had been no sexual attack. The injuries were not consistent with an attack by a Hunter or any other animal. Carlson could understand the uneasy silence at the funeral. The crowd was in shock. They couldn't explain what had happened to this beautiful girl.

He had searched her conapt. Other Justice Police officers had searched the parents' and the boyfriend's apartments. There had been no clues. He had come to the funeral to observe the mourners. Automatic cameras had scanned the crowd; later the information would be examined and cross-referenced.

Although Carlson only knew her from photographs and her possessions tidied away in her room, he felt the sadness and despair of the crowd. Life on a frontier world was like balancing on the edge of a precipice.

The hymn had finished.

The father held his wife tightly. Carlson knew that they were both believers. The Book told of the Eternal battle between the Prime Mover and the Form Manipulator. Would the girl's parents see this as a victory for Evil?

The mourners drifted away. The priest returned to the church. Carlson walked up to the parents. An electronic digger was filling the grave. There was an uneasy silence.

'Major,' said the father. 'Thank you for coming.'

'I'm sorry,' Carlson replied. He didn't know what else to say.

The mother looked at him. 'You bastard,' she screeched, slapping him across the face. She burst into tears again. The father muttered his apologies and pulled his wife from the grave side.

Carlson was left alone with his thoughts. The mother had to blame someone and why not him. There was no-one else.

11

He looked down into the pit. We all have to die sometime, he thought. If our lives have any significance then it comes from what we do whilst alive.

He spoke a quick prayer.

He felt strange, as if being watched. The temperature over the last few days had started to become unbearably hot and it was starting to affect his thought processes.

His throat was dry. He needed a drink. He would feel better after a drink.

At that distance, secure within the confines of the spaceship, Thomas took a great interest in the unfolding events on Nicaea.

His planet was about to erupt into civil war. Even watching the daily vidscreen broadcasts, where the elite talked about peace and there was no mention of the conflict between the Priesthood and the Academy, he knew that the war would be coming. The Military had been put on standby in their barracks even though there were concerns about which side the troops would fight on.

The Justice Police had been ordered to monitor and watch all unusual activities on the Seven Planets, and at the first sign of conflict all rebels, agitators and those suspected of being such would be . . . He didn't know. He was not privy to the machinations of his controllers.

Under the leadership of the main colony world, Nicaea, the six inhabited planets had recently gained independence from one of the major Earth corporations.

Thomas felt that he was safe from the conflict which raged across the Althosian star system.

The four Killer-type androids had reputations amongst the Justice Police for ruthlessly carrying out their programmed tasks. They had been hand-picked for the one-way journey.

'Getting nervous?' Marilyn asked.

'Yes,' he replied. 'They must know we'd come after them.'

Her eyes were staring at him. He tried to look away

but was forced to keep on sneaking a glance to see if her gaze had altered. She was two metres tall with cropped blonde hair and a muscular build. She stared at him with her cold blue eyes, like a snake trying to hypnotize its prey.

Suddenly there was a pain in his back. He had been kicked.

Spike screamed, 'Pay attention.'

Marilyn was still looking at him. She stood up and smiled. She was ridiculing him.

'What do you think you're playing at?' Spike looked at all three of them. 'Down there you'd all be dead now. You need to be constantly vigilant. What were you playing at?'

Marilyn turned her attention to him. 'Just testing lover boy out.'

Thomas now knew he couldn't trust her and he didn't like it. The group had to rely on each other, bury their personal differences and work together.

Perhaps it was a mistake to put four Killers on the same mission. Sometimes it was difficult to see what his controllers were trying to accomplish; they must have some hidden purpose and perhaps the conflict on board the ship was part of it.

Marilyn held two fingers up, in the shape of a gun, and pretended to shoot him. She mouthed the commander's words, 'Down there you're dead.'

Spike glared at her.

The dense foliage rendered the wildlife invisible. As Ell took off her clothes she stared into the trees, listening to the scuttling sounds of a multitude of small creatures. She wondered if there were any other intelligent life forms on this overgrown rainforest of a world. She found the thought disturbing, somehow. Part of her mind told her not to think it.

Her husband stood at the laboratory table in the middle of the glade. His test tubes and charts lay strewn over the table. A computerized microscope analysed the endless

13

stream of figures and results. He uttered occasional grunts of surprise.

The glade was next to the river. Ell had been swimming every day since their arrival on the planet. Although the water was a dirty grey colour, it kept her clean in the humid climate. She paused on the bank, looked at her husband and dived in.

It had been continuously light since they had arrived. The twin suns of the Althosian system meant that only every seven days was the planet plunged into darkness.

This was very different from her normal work, as a secretary for the State publishing company.

It was difficult earning enough money to cover the cost of basic food. At least her husband also brought home a wage. As a government scientist he worked more than the regulated three hours a day.

She spent most of her time looking after their conapt, cleaning it and making it seem like one of the homes featured on the afternoon vidscreen broadcasts.

She'd never thought that she would leave Nicaea again. Twenty-eight was too old to be discovering that she enjoyed adventure.

'Come on in,' Ell shouted to her husband.

'Don't drink any of it,' he replied, as if he hadn't heard what she had said. She splashed him with water. 'Stop it,' he muttered, not looking up as he continued to type his findings into the computer.

Huge black trees shadowed the clearing and the pool of water. She looked skywards but couldn't see the roof of the forest.

'This liquid isn't H_2O,' Jarak said. He looked around for her having forgotten, in a matter of seconds, where she was.

She clambered out of the water and picked up her towel. She walked over to Jarak and dripped over his charts and maps.

She looked at his receding hair-line and emaciated appearance.

'Put some clothes on,' he said.

'You've seen me like this before.' Although she taunted him she wasn't proud of her body. She was embarrassed about the effects of malnutrition; the planet's distance from the twin suns; and the chemical additives in the Nicaean water supply.

'Yes, but . . .'

'There's nobody else on the planet to see.'

He seemed dissatisfied with her words. His eyes flickered, nervously.

His mind switched again. 'Have you seen this?' He produced a glass slide and placed it in the microscope. 'Go on, look.'

She looked at a close-up of swirling patterns.

'What am I looking at?' she asked.

He produced another slide from the tangle of rubbish on his desk. She studied the new slide.

'There's nothing on this one.'

He nodded frantically. 'These are samples of river water taken two days apart. The first slide was taken this evening; the second slide was taken yesterday morning. Something's happening in the river.'

She lowered the towel to cover her body.

'Where have you been?' he asked.

'I've been swimming.'

'In that?'

'Yes.' Ell was used to his absent-mindedness.

Again she heard that noise. She could hear the sound of a machine in the upper atmosphere. But this is a banned world. There can't be any other visitors, she thought. I must remember that.

The TARDIS was silent and still. It hadn't moved for over an hour. It had stopped in time and space. According to the ship's monitors they were almost at their destination. They were in the Althosian planetary system. The Doctor was stretched out. His eyes were closed and he was snoring. His lack of interest in their plight made Bernice extremely angry. She walked up and down the console room thinking how terrifying it would be to spend

15

all eternity trapped, with her complacent companion, in deep space.

'Does nothing frighten you, Doctor?' she muttered underneath her breath.

'The lack of hope,' he replied, as if he had been wide awake all the time. He swung his legs around and looked at her. 'That point when there's no hope left.'

'You know, Doctor, I used to hate watching twentieth century films and seeing the words "The End",' she said. Although interactive holovids were the main source of home entertainment Bernice collected old movies and watched them repeatedly. 'What happens to the people after the film's finished? Those films were so . . .'

'Finite?'

'Yeah. Things can't be changed. I remember that I'd watch *The Great Escape* to see if other people would escape. I always got upset when Donald Pleasance was shot at the end. Why couldn't they do a version where he survives?'

'Because there's no justice. In real life good people die as well. But never give up hope. I fancy a jelly baby, I haven't had one for ages.'

Whenever he thought of something serious, Bernice thought, he would suddenly become frivolous.

He stood up, distracted. 'I wonder what *is* happening here. Why aren't we moving?'

The Doctor held up a moth-eaten red velvet jacket.

'I'm sure I put the jelly babies in here.' He rummaged through the pockets. 'Hmnn, nice jacket.'

Bernice sat on the floor.

'Doctor, are you never afraid of the monsters?'

'What monsters?' he replied, pulling out a felt hat from the jacket pocket.

'The monsters you meet on your travels: Cybermen, Daleks, you know.'

'They aren't monsters. They're alien races with their own agendas, plots and dreams.' His voice slowed. 'But there are monsters out there, very real monsters.

16

Monsters which shadow us; that are part of our imagination.'

He pulled out an empty sweet bag and looked disappointed. He kicked the console in irritation and the TARDIS groaned. It was impossible to know whether the Doctor had caused something to happen or if it was a coincidence, but the TARDIS began to make a wheezing sound, signalling that it was landing.

Bernice was thrown on to the floor and the Doctor followed, falling over his companion. The TARDIS was materializing.

The vidscreen projected a black and white hologram. It was of a small old man with black robes, shaven head and furious burning eyes. The chain of high office hung around his neck. This was the Archon, the supreme ruler of the Althosian system – the Seven Planets and the immeasurable asteroids that lay in-between.

The four androids waited to hear the message before they parachuted down to the planet. They knew that they were on a very special mission. They supported their leader without question and had all vowed to follow him to hell and back, if that ever proved to be necessary. Thomas prayed every night to the Prime Mover, for the survival and prosperity of the man who had ruled Nicaea, and its former colonial worlds, since the revolt against the Corporation three years ago. Thomas would lay his artificial life down for the great man.

'At a time like this our world needs your strengths here, and in the days ahead I will be thinking of you. What you do now is for the safety and security of our alliance. These criminals cannot be allowed to succeed. They must be annihilated. There can be no negotiation, no settlement with terrorists . . .' the line faded as if the Archon had been distracted back on the homeworld, ' . . . who would hold our whole way of life to ransom. Destroy, destroy! I say destroy their very existence. If anyone could achieve those results I know it is my shock troops.'

The Archon paused, looking away as if being addressed

17

by someone else in the room. The line began to crackle and the image of the old man disappeared. Just as quickly the hologram returned. The Archon was rushed and tried to hurry his prepared speech.

'You will not be returning, but you will live on in the memories of our entire race. You must carry out your mission. I now tell you that my order is irrevocable and under no circumstances must you default from the prime task. Destroy the missile, and wipe out the criminals and let our nation rejoice in your success.' The Archon nodded, probably to the vidcamera operator. The hologram receded.

Spike looked around the small task force. 'Let us pray for the success of the mission.'

The four knelt in silent prayer. Although prayer was a mere formality in military circles, Thomas had faith that the Prime Mover was a personal deity who would look after all believers.

'I serve.' Major Carlson entered the room. He moved his arm to his chest, saluting the Archon.

The vid equipment was being packed up by the technicians. The permanent studio, within Parliament, was being closed during the state of crisis. Various pieces of equipment were being moved to the Imperial Palace, in case it became necessary for the Archon to address his people directly.

Carlson shuffled. He was uneasy. He had been ordered to attend Parliament for a briefing session with General Kopyion, his commander.

He could still do with a drink.

The technicians finished packing and left the room.

The Archon was sitting on a box, listening to the general advising him about the current situation on the unnamed planet.

Kopyion stood in the corner of the room, in darkness. He was a military man, with a shock of white hair, a small beard around his mouth and an aristocratic pony tail. He had only one arm, gold teeth and a large facial wound:

all scars of battle. Tiredness seemed to hang around him as if the present conflict was too much of a burden for him.

The major could see that the secret police might have a new commander in the near future. Kopyion had been one of the first settlers and had created the Justice Police. He still owned Mirage Enterprises, the company which built the androids.

Carlson had been twenty-four when he had travelled out to the Althosian system. The Seven Planets were far from the usual trading routes and many years' travel from the nearest Earth colony. This was how they had managed to win their independence so easily from the Corporation.

He had been a security officer on one of the deep space freight lines. He had felt it was time to settle down and had chosen to stay on Nicaea. He applied for the Justice Police. He had been interviewed, selected and had proven his skills over the last decade. He had risen up the ranks and was now a deputy commander. His remit was to investigate internal crimes.

There were about seventy androids used by the Justice Police, but they were placed in the external defence force, the political section, or the smuggling and immigration section. He had no androids under his direct control.

Kopyion was a dictator. He told his four deputies as little as necessary for the implementation of his wishes.

'No-one will ever know about their mission, apart from the three of us in this room now. Misunderstandings would occur if our enemies were to find out about the theft of "Pandora's Box",' Kopyion said. 'This is the reason for sending androids, from my Justice Police.'

'We aren't able to trust the military at this moment in time,' the Archon said. 'Do we know any more about the criminals?'

'We've been unable to ascertain more information,' the major said.

Kopyion walked over to the Archon and handed him a file. 'We're writing on paper at the moment. Hackers are trying to break into the computer system.'

'Arrest them,' the Archon retorted.

'We are feeding them false information and monitoring the results of the disinformation. We can find out more and identify our enemies with greater certainty,' said the major.

Kopyion looked annoyed. He had told Carlson that he felt he was prone to reveal his hand too early. The major felt that the Archon should be told all information they had; he was the leader of the Federation, and all Justice officers swore an oath of allegiance directly to him.

Kopyion continued, 'The androids have the following information. Using recording equipment on the air base we have identified the criminals as Butler and Swarf, shapechangers who have been involved in mercenary and serious criminal activities on colony worlds elsewhere in the galaxy.'

'Shapechangers?' The Archon seemed puzzled.

'They appear to have a remarkable physiology which allows them to mutate at will into any shape or form of their choosing,' Kopyion said.

'I wouldn't have thought that was possible . . .' said the Archon. Kopyion shrugged.

' . . . although this means that we have nothing to worry about. These are simply criminals. We don't know why they took the missile but they are only criminals. It's not our enemies who have stolen this weapon.'

Kopyion walked around the gutted vidscreen studio. 'All our information would suggest that Butler and Swarf have always been hired by other people. They are simply criminals, but I am unable to tell who has employed them.'

The Archon sighed. 'I'm trying to save our civilization. We are about to enter a war none of us, I'm sure, wants. I need information. That weapon is the most devastating nuclear device ever created. We don't have it anymore and we don't know who does.'

Kopyion shrugged his shoulders. The Archon waved his hand. He had heard enough.

'My troops are ready to return you to the Imperial Palace,' said Kopyion.

'Thank you, but give me a few moments,' replied the Archon.

Kopyion bowed his head and left the room. The major saluted and followed his commander.

Kopyion seemed thoughtful.

The corridors of Parliament were empty and quiet. The hustle and bustle had stopped. Footsteps echoed around the halls as civil servants hurried by, carrying boxes of papers from dingy offices into waiting hover cars. Parliament seemed to have been abandoned.

'Sir, I haven't got any further with the murder,' Carlson said.

'No,' Kopyion replied.

Carlson had spent two days investigating the last few hours of the young victim. He hadn't been home and had managed only a quick phone call to his wife, last night. She was used to his job. But it was still a strain.

'You'd better go home,' said Kopyion.

Carlson smiled. Sometimes the commander seemed to read his mind. He would answer questions that had not yet been asked.

'Sir,' he said.

The Dragonslayer continued its circular path over the surface of the unknown world. The four androids were studying information being received from monitoring equipment on the exterior of the ship, trying to pin-point Butler and Swarf on the huge planet.

External microphones and heat sensors were pointed in the direction of the planet's surface.

The ship was the most technologically advanced machine built by their civilization. A civilization which invested much in military security. The Dragonslayer, with its stock of nuclear warheads, and chemical, biological and electronic weapons contained the kill power to pacify any class 3 type planet. It had flown over a dozen combat missions and had returned virtually unscathed.

The Dragonslayer class of interstellar gunships were based on insect models; they were seen as an ideal blueprint for fast-moving attack craft. Its shape was like a wasp's, with a smooth outer surface which felt like warm glass.

Inside the dark ship, strange substances recycled and gurgled through pipes around the androids' heads. A constant chatter of voices, from radio transmissions picked up from other planets, played over the loudspeakers; these were analysed and fed into the computer brain. Dust and rubbish lay strewn over the crew area; androids had no sense of cleanliness and wherever they were found there was also debris and waste.

The defence and attack modes of the craft could be launched with no animated life on board. There were environments in which it had been foreseen that even the android Killers would have difficulties functioning.

Androids had some of the senses of living creatures.

Thomas found the hum of the ship, and the incessant chatter from the loudspeakers extremely distracting. The air conditioning also made the craft too cold; sometimes it felt like standing in a wind tunnel.

He shivered, not with the cold but because of thoughts about what lay ahead of them, and because of the self doubt, always the self doubt, that he would not be able to serve his controllers as they so wished.

He thought the strict separation between those alive, and a second class, machines, sprang from sheer ignorance and he believed that the Prime Mover treated all life forms alike.

All four soldiers were now dressed in their battle armour. It was light-weight plastic, able to camouflage the wearer in a variety of situations; it also contained the in-built technological fire-power to respond to most emergencies.

The androids had originally been developed to fight insurrectionists and the occasional Hunter.

Hunters were aliens, apparently native to the Althosian system, who were able to survive in space. They dropped

22

into the outer colony worlds, hunting the inhabitants for food. They were one of the main reasons that this distant star system was not seen as prime colony material. The Hunters were very nasty beasts, with lots of teeth.

Thomas didn't have any fond memories of his last battle with one. He had been the only survivor of a ten man crew. Perhaps that was why he had been chosen for this mission.

Chaney handed him a set of photographs, taken from the external cameras. All Thomas could see was a set of concentric circles. There was a possible fault in the photographic equipment. Discordant images revealed an inadequacy in the gunship's technology.

'We have a problem,' Chaney stated the obvious. He was a large man, built like a gorilla and not renowned for his intelligence. 'I can't get any close-ups,' continued Chaney, not able to recognize when no-one was listening or interested. 'This machine is capable of taking highly detailed photos, up to a millimetre from deepest space, but I'm not getting anything. The machine is . . .' Chaney hit it, with considerable violence. He believed that brute force would win out in the end.

'Don't damage the equipment,' instructed Spike. He had an air of authority. This didn't come from his two and a half metre stature, or his shock of red hair, but from genetically created leadership qualities. All previous android models which had failed to display the right degree of superiority were destroyed prior to registration.

'Anything, lover boy?' Marilyn was still watching Thomas. He had control of the sound equipment, and had been trying to concentrate on the sounds of the planet. So little was known about this unnamed planet at the edge of the Althosian system.

'Not yet.'

Suddenly Thomas heard something. According to the computer analysis of the sounds, it was a creature moving through a jungle environment. Something which had been very still was careering through the undergrowth. The amplifiers echoed the sounds around the ship.

23

'I can't tell the size of it,' he admitted.

'Only one though?' the commander asked.

'Yes, I think so.'

'Right! Final stages, ready for the drop,' shouted Spike.

'I'm not sure,' Thomas tried to say.

Marilyn shook her head. 'Lover boy, you're going to have to do better.'

The loudspeakers played the sounds of branches being broken. The androids followed Spike's orders, putting their parachutes on quickly and efficiently. If things were going to go wrong on this mission, Thomas thought, it wouldn't be due to their failure to follow orders.

Chaney answered for all of them, 'Ready.'

Marilyn made a last check on their distance from the planet's surface. She was unable to specify what they were parachuting down to.

'Any other sign of life down there?' Spike asked.

'No,' Marilyn replied.

After a few moments' silence, Spike made the decision.

'Out. Remember, no radio contact.' Spike patted them all on the back, as they leapt from the gunship.

Down to the planet, below. Thomas felt the shrieking cold as he fell through the atmosphere. Would this be a silent death? He could see Spike in the hatchway of the ship, watching, turning his tracking control on, and throwing himself after his troops.

The Dragonslayer automatically closed its hatch and armed itself. 'Countdown 71 hours, 59 minutes, 50 seconds.'

Its orders were unusual. To deliver four androids to the Planet – the Planet without a name, on the border of the star system; a Planet that inter-planetary law forbids all life-forms having any contact with. Did the androids know what lurked down on the planet, waiting for them? The machine had no name in its memory banks. But it knew and the androids didn't. Not yet, anyway.

DAY FOUR
00:00–04:00

It was a dark world, full of ferocious half-glimpsed night-mares and strange dreams. In the twelve hours since they had landed on the planet Chopra had felt the strong presence of evil.

He had been brought on to the planet for his ability to read minds and foretell the future. However, this special talent was more of a curse.

Chopra looked at his fellow khthons. There were eleven of them. They were small wizened creatures, naked and hairless, with skin like ancient papyrus. No matter what their age they appeared, walked and talked like very old men. They were the original inhabitants of this planetary system. They were all deeply pessimistic, due to centuries of slavery and horrific maltreatment, most recently by the human colonists.

After the Seven Planets gained independence from the Corporation, the Academy had issued a decree which gave the khthons their freedom and equal status with the colonists. However, on the furthest reaches of the star system the khthons continued to be imprisoned and sold by slave-traders.

Nothing changes, thought Chopra.

The khthons had been brought to this unnamed planet by the shapechangers, Butler and Swarf.

The shapechangers were midgets. They wore small dark one-piece overalls, had round smiling faces, vast over-weight bellies and bald heads. They had a constipated walk and pig-like facial expressions. They appeared age-less and looked like contorted children's toys.

'Why are we here?' Chopra had asked.

'Drugs . . .' Swarf had replied.

They were not going to let him in on their plans; there would then be a possibility of him leading a mutiny.

Chopra sensed something monitoring them, in the upper atmosphere.

He watched four figures slip from the relative safety of the heavens down to the unknown dangers of this poisonous world. They would almost certainly die at the hands of the shapechangers, thought Chopra.

The parachutes opened and the figures slowed down in mid-air.

'They've tracked us down, Mr Swarf,' Butler said, in a squeaky high voice.

'Indeed, Mr Butler, but no surprises there,' the other dwarf calmly replied.

'Let's lose them,' Butler suggested.

Swarf shook his head to disagree.

'All right, I'll just keep an eye on them,' Butler continued, tittering to himself.

Butler indicated to the khthons that they should continue the journey. They picked up the metallic box and without speaking placed it across their shoulders. They were struggling. The coffin shaped object they carried was difficult to balance and walk with at the same time.

Chopra did not know why they had brought the warhead to the planet. He could not read the minds of the two shapechangers. Apart from some life forms which had a natural ability to protect their thoughts from those with psi ability, androids and a few enormously powerful individuals could deliberately cloud their minds and defend the deepest recesses of their consciousness.

Swarf walked to where Chopra knelt on the floor.

Chopra was exhausted; the power coming through him was causing him intense pain. He could feel a painful throbbing in his forehead.

He pulled the Stones out of a little pocket sack and held them tightly in his hands. The primitive twelve Stones had runic symbols chiselled into the rock. He shook the Stones, threw them on to the ground and looked at the patterns in front of him. He knew what the shapes would augur.

'What does it say?' the shapechanger asked.

'Death. For two weeks now it has been the same message, again and again, and it is getting stronger; death and destruction, the end of all things, Armageddon.'

Chopra began to cough, and felt blood and phlegm coming up from deep inside him. Swarf put his hand on the khthon's left shoulder, and tried to reassure him.

'But think of the money.'

Although it took him several moments to come to his senses, Thomas had survived the parachute drop.

The planet was horrific – worse than he had imagined. The jungle had a stench of rotting vegetables and was dark and unfriendly. The light from the twin suns, caught by the huge trees and their canopy of leaves, barely touched the planet's surface.

He folded the parachute and sprayed it with acid from his body armour, to erase any evidence of his arrival on the planet.

He was breathing through the armour's portable air supply. He checked the dials and found the atmosphere breathable, although a little high in nitrogen. He turned the machine off and took a few seconds to become used to the stale natural air.

The portable laser cannon was strapped to his back. He slid it out of its holster and made sure the firing mechanism was still in order.

The small dial on his wrist registered two androids within close proximity.

He set off walking but within a few moments found himself back where he had landed on the planet. He had walked in a circle.

It was going to be a struggle to wade through the undergrowth. The broken branches, his footprints on the grey volcanic earth, and the noise of his struggle through the undergrowth, would signal his location in the jungle.

He wondered how they were going to sneak up on the

shapechangers to carry out their mission and annihilate them.

And then he felt the barrel of a staser gun against the back of his head. Someone had sneaked up on him. He stood perfectly still, not able to tell if the owner's finger was tight against the trigger. If he sensed the gunman relaxing, he would turn at speed and disable him. It would be a matter of hundredths of a second. As long as he kept calm he could overcome the power and speed of a weapon.

'Hello lover boy,' Marilyn's voice whispered in his ear.

She had survived. He sensed her take a couple of steps back. He turned to face her; the staser still pointed at his forehead.

'Put it away. We've lost the commander,' Chaney muttered. He was checking the portable flamethrower. He looked at Thomas.

'Our weapons need to be totally reliable. Out here we won't have a second chance.'

Marilyn slid the hand weapon back into her body armour. She was carrying the heat seeking equipment and was armed with minimal offensive weaponry.

Thomas shivered. His fellow androids had managed to approach him, and he hadn't sensed them. They had also lost their commander, early in the mission.

If they saw Spike they would have to destroy him. He could be one of the shapechangers trying to infiltrate the small unit.

Thomas turned to his two companions. He realized that it might be too late and the shapechangers could already be in front of him.

'The air is particularly heavy tonight,' he said, waiting for the agreed answer. Both Chaney and Marilyn looked puzzled, but did reply.

'We are waiting for a thunderstorm.'

'The great bear has escaped from the zoo.'

They *were* his companions, although he felt far from safe with Marilyn at his side.

There was a very uncomfortable feeling in his guts, a

stretching pain. He dismissed it. He had an intellectual fascination with emotions and liked to pretend that he could also feel. However, the only purpose of their programming was to increase their ability to predict their enemies' behaviour. They were near perfect killing machines.

'We have to find the body,' said Thomas. 'Without it we can't be sure.'

'We don't need to know. It will only slow down the mission,' replied Chaney, in his matter-of-fact tone.

'I have another signal,' Marilyn reported. 'Two humanoid-sized life forms moving, slowly, about two kilometres to the west.'

Chaney started to move, certain that his companions would follow him.

The jungle sprawled for thousands of miles and, as far as she could see, the trees grew up to the sky. Bernice thought, this is what the ancient woods were like in the fairy stories her father read to her as a child.

She wouldn't have chosen to go there dressed in green combat trousers and T-shirt. She wouldn't describe herself as 'prettily dressed' but what the mud and sharp grasses were doing to her was unacceptable.

Where were they now? This was an uncharted planet according to the Doctor but, unusually for him, he had no further information about their present location.

The TARDIS had crash-landed on a planet on the fringes of the Althosian system, and all the electronic equipment had ceased to function. The Doctor had reasoned that it was not the erratic time machine which was at fault, or his bizarre repairs, but an unidentified power source on the planet.

Had he considered the sheer size of this planet, Bernice wondered.

'Doctor, wait up,' she said.

He stopped, turning on one foot. 'Hmnn?'

'Where are we going?'

'Looking to the future, you could as easily have asked, "where have we come from?",' the Doctor said.

The Doctor dangled a yo-yo to the ground but the toy refused to return to his hand. He had broken it. Bernice could get very impatient with her companion when he acted like a small child, played with his toys and beamed that idiotic grin.

'We'll know when we arrive,' he added.

'My feet are getting very muddy, and I'm awfully tired.' Bernice knew it was unlike her to complain but they had been walking for a couple of hours, with litle purpose and no change of scenery. 'Can't we go back to the TARDIS?'

She looked him over; his brown jacket, white straw hat, and paisley scarf. An umbrella hung from his breast pocket. He gave that innocent 'but aren't you enjoying yourself' look which she remembered Stan Laurel doing when caught out by his wife in *Sons of the Desert*. She liked old black and white comedies. She, and the Doctor, had gone to a 1980s Laurel and Hardy convention in Ulverstone, Lancashire. The Doctor had recited stories about his old friend Arthur Jefferson. The fans had thought the Doctor was in fancy dress. She'd given up trying to tell him how ridiculous he looked, not because he didn't listen to her but because she felt he did it deliberately to be different.

'Here.' He handed her the yo-yo. 'Wind it back. We'll need it later.'

She refused to take it from him.

She had a feeling about this planet. She couldn't describe it. She found it easier to moan about her companion. She was about to tell him that she wasn't his slave when suddenly the air was cut by a piercing scream. Bernice turned to the Doctor.

'I didn't hear that, did I?'

'Hear what? Come on, we need to keep walking.'

He held his hand out to help her along but she knocked it aside.

'I can walk.'

30

Ell heard the scream. It was the cry of one of the black birds. She had never seen one close up but had seen them swarm in their thousands, like phoenixes rising from some age-old ashes, clouding the sky as they flew overhead.

She had never shown much interest in nature.

She smiled to herself. At the time of the crisis threatening the Althosian system, they had come to this forbidden world, although there was a sentence of death on anyone who approached the planet, so that her husband could carry out tests on the water.

He never discussed his research with her, but the whole idea of coming to this inhospitable world struck her as the height of stupidity. She couldn't think why they had done it. She mustn't think.

The heat was unbearable and a purple haze was rising from the river. She sat down on the bank. She looked closely at the water. It seemed to be thickening. There was a red foam on the surface of the grey liquid.

'Jarak,' she called.

He eventually wandered over, his mind distracted with complicated thoughts and scenarios. She was embarrassed at interrupting him but thought he would want to see the state of the water.

'This is extraordinary, I didn't expect this yet,' he said to himself, apparently seeing this as further evidence to support his theories.

'What will the Academy say when we get back?' she asked, wondering how he would explain his visit to this world.

'I don't know.'

'Have you even thought about it?' she asked, although obviously he hadn't. 'You need to have an explanation ready. You'll have to explain why you came to this planet before they'll listen to anything else you have to say.'

He put his arm around her.

'Just be glad that I'm here to protect you.'

She shook his arm off her.

'I must have a sample,' he said, and returned to the tent to collect a test tube.

He smiled and knelt down to look closely at the water. There didn't seem to be any sound coming from the river. There was an unnatural silence.

The river looked a misty red colour. He lowered his hand towards the water. His hand went into the liquid.

He shot back up, screaming.

He lay on the ground in excruciating pain, crying and unable to keep still. He was writhing in agony. Ell moved towards him. There was a wound on his left hand, pulsating and throbbing.

'Help me,' he screamed.

She grabbed him by the right arm and pulled him from the water's edge.

He screamed.

Desperately, she looked around for the emergency medical supplies, eventually finding them in the tent.

Jarak wasn't moving. He had fainted. Pain was sending shockwaves through his body. Sores covered his skin, looking like the injuries of someone who had fallen into broken glass.

She stood over him and felt powerless to help.

His body seemed to petrify.

His eyes were staring at her. He was unable to shout.

She thought she could hear one of the animals, in the distance on this unspeakable planet, cackling and laughing to itself.

She screamed out: 'Shut up, just shut up!'

The jungle once again descended into silence.

Crash.

Bernice stopped. Although the light filtered through the trees it was a dark, shadowy world and the source of the noises, although its direction was impossible to locate, seemed to be coming closer all the time.

The Doctor kept on walking towards the sounds. He showed an increasing interest in the ground. He pointed out compressed grass, broken twigs and footprints formed in the soil. From this information he could apparently work out the size of the life-forms, their diet, sleeping patterns, how long since they had passed by and in what direction.

Bernice was surprised when they found the first evidence of life on the planet. She had imagined huge hairy creatures with large teeth and a nose for blood. But the little reptiles resembled the smaller dinosaurs which had once been extant on Earth; fast of foot, vegetarian and extremely docile. The creatures were eating leaves and berries from the ground-level plants. She approached them, and as they paid no attention to her she touched one, carefully, and felt the rough hide. The Doctor pulled her arm away.

'Be careful. Appearances can be deceptive. It may have parasites underneath the skin which would find your blood very tasty.' He was serious, and slowed his voice down in order to scare her. 'Beware the monsters . . .'

Movement through the jungle was slow. Although they had been trained for jungle warfare during survival courses on Nicaea, the well-designed simulations couldn't give an accurate feel of moving through a primeval forest.

Taking the strictest precautions, Marilyn walked in front with the heat-seeking equipment. Chaney and Thomas kept several metres behind her, watching for any sudden movement.

The shapechangers could be close by, behind the next tree or a nearby blade of grass.

Chaney spoke first, 'Lost one boy, bad mission.'

'No prisoners, he was told,' Marilyn reminded them.

Thomas could feel the casual cruelty of his comrades.

'No sign of Spike?' he had to ask. Marilyn shook her head but he had got away with asking; they didn't look at him as if he was weak.

'The creatures?' Chaney asked. Marilyn replied, 'No sign,' as if somehow they could be invisible.

'Those blips?' Chaney referred to the heat traces which they had been following for the last four hours.

'Just echoes, I think,' Marilyn said, doubting the machinery which they needed to protect their lives.

'How far, though?' Chaney needed something definite to go on.

'100 metres, north-west,' she estimated. 'But I'm sure they're not real. Just a product of our advanced technology.'

She stressed the word 'advanced' to indicate her contempt for the latest equipment.

'O.K. let's move,' decided Chaney. He had taken on the role of leader. Thomas realized that he was more frightened of his comrades than of what lurked in the jungle. He thought he would feel safer if Spike was with them.

But they would have to kill Spike if they found him alive. Just in case.

Ell had sat with her husband and watched him die. Here she was, alone, in a strange world, with the dead body of her husband.

The water was no longer moving. It was as if the river had frozen.

It reminded her of a vidscreen documentary she had seen. She remembered seeing the petrified remains of victims of a volcanic eruption. The molten ash had fallen over their bodies, had caught them unexpectedly. They remained frozen in time.

She began to laugh.

Chopra turned quickly. He had sensed death. He gasped and tried to breathe rapidly to take control of this terrible feeling. He then felt a great warmth and the feeling of the other body's journey was lost to him.

'I feel pain.' He needed to express the dark unknown dwelling inside him. He stood against a tree to stop himself collapsing.

The struggle through the forest was proving difficult and Butler had taken to shouting at the khthons.

The khthons were on edge due to the darkness and

the sounds of this strange world. They were superstitious creatures who lived in a half-way state between the real world and that of superstition and dread. They could accept Chopra's visions as much as they could accept the nature of the trees and vegetation around them.

The khthons had been complaining in despair about their mission. They were frightened.

They regarded Butler and Swarf with some distrust and although they allowed them to share in their food and drink, they would not share their thoughts.

Chopra had heard Butler telling Swarf that he wanted to kill a khthon as an example to the others of the results of anything less than strict obedience. Swarf said that the rocks they had seen on the ground indicated that they were close to the edge of the jungle. Then the journey would begin to get easier.

Neither Butler nor Swarf showed any interest in the parachutists.

'Soon it will be too late for them to interfere. Don't worry, Mr Chopra.' Butler had tried to reassure him.

'I do worry. This is a bad place,' replied Chopra, fighting off the small mites which seemed to be trying to drink his blood. 'I have cast the stones.'

'Superstition. I hope you won't allow childish fears to interfere with your work. Mr Swarf wouldn't like that.'

'You know the history of this planet – '

Before he could finish Butler grabbed hold of him and lifted him several inches off the ground. He felt pain, sheer excruciating pain. Butler spoke to him in a low murmur and although he could barely hear he knew what the shapechanger was telling him.

Swarf was smiling, appreciating the pain, and watching for any unrest amongst the dozen khthons.

'I could destroy you, but not yet,' said Butler.

'A diversion perhaps, Mr Butler,' said Swarf.

Butler also smiled and threw Chopra to the ground. Chopra sank to his knees, coughing and gasping for breath.

'Would you like to see some real magic?' Butler asked.

Chopra looked up as he heard the sound of cracking bones. It wasn't an illusion. The dwarf was changing shape. His face was elongating, narrowing around the mouth and thickening on the forehead. Bulbous horns were growing out of his face; thick brown hair was breaking out on the surface of his body. His clothes ripped as the dwarf grew into a three metre giant. Teeth protruded from the skin around his mouth, hooves erupted in place of his hands and feet, a scaly tail grew out of the base of his back and the creature fell on to all fours. This was a Chakras which had once roamed the planet Szabo, attacking and butchering the first colonists. Its foul breath polluted the air, its hide stank and it moved closer to lick Chopra's face. He felt sick and retched over the ground.

The apparition stood in front of them. Breathing, stinking, perspiring.

The shapechangers enjoyed terrifying weaker life forms.

Chopra felt frightened. The shapechangers did not understand. They were blind to the true purpose of their deeds.

Butler raised its front legs into the air, halting its hooves before they stamped down on Chopra's body. It roared deep into the jungle, a howling animal cry.

DAY FOUR
04:00–08:00

The music of Leonard Cohen drifted around the room. Academician Brown always thought of his first girlfriend and her love of oranges when listening to the twentieth-century singer. Her skin always smelt of fresh citrus fruit. He had met her on Earth when they were both studying Politics. His specialism was the local conflicts of the early twenty-first century, between the different nationalisms and religious groupings. How his mind wandered. The choice of the music had not been his but that of General Kopyion.

The supreme commander of the Justice Police sat opposite him. Kopyion's shattered figure remained carefully erect to avoid the pain which followed every movement of his body. The frontier conflicts, and colonization of worlds, had left many physically and psychologically wounded. Kopyion was a reminder to those in the Academy who were tempted to forget the wilderness that Nicaea had been before colonization, and the many that had perished building the new world.

Although a friend, Brown rarely saw Kopyion smile. He was not allowed access to the secrets in the military commander's mind – the plans and strategies needed to monitor the enemies of the state.

Kopyion always dressed in black and tended to skulk in the shadows. He reminded Brown of a spider spinning its web.

They usually met once a week to drink and listen to Earth music till the early hours.

They took it in turns to cook. Brown loved preparing Chinese cooking whilst the General tended to fry up rare

Lokan grasses in exquisite vegetarian sauces. The simple things of life.

Brown again began to think of his first girlfriend. Cohen's music always had that melancholic effect on him. He wasn't in the mood for socializing tonight. Too many thoughts going round his head.

'Your mind is elsewhere, old friend,' Kopyion said, sipping his wine.

'I was thinking of the past. Do you mind if I change the music?'

Kopyion nodded. Brown stood and moved over to the music centre.

Confidential briefing papers still lay sealed awaiting his attention. They contained the latest reports on the conflict which was enveloping their star system. As one of the most vocal opponents of the current regime he received numerous documents and unofficial reports on the social unrest enveloping the Althosian system. Brown felt that events were overtaking them all too quickly.

The Academy was due to meet in thirty-six hours, with calls for the supreme decision making body to be temporarily suspended until calm had been restored on the planet. The Academy was the government of Nicaea – a body of philosophers, priests and military personnel who debated the great issues of the day, and tried to govern the planet and its lesser worlds. The military had openly talked about a council of war. Overnight more riots had been reported over the face of the colony world of Trieste, and the government controlled vidscreen channels there had stopped broadcasting.

Brown turned the music off and returned to the game.

Snakes and ladders had replaced chess as the game of the elite. Intellectuals reasoned that, with its ups and downs and reliance on chance, it reflected life better than the skilful but empty chess. A dice is thrown, and following the score a number of moves are made across the board. If a player lands on a ladder then he climbs up the board; if a player lands on a snake then he descends to the pit. A world of chance.

He looked around his apartment. It was sparsely furnished. He had few antiques. Colony worlds treated old Earth products as collectable items, and the elite competed to own rarer and more obsolete items. In pride of place was an original Decca recording of the Rolling Stones' 'Sympathy for the Devil'.

Kopyion rolled the dice and moved his counter two squares up the board.

'Tell me about "Pandora's Box".' Brown knew he would be expected to ask.

Although he tried to keep work separate from their friendship, he had been asked to find out the circumstances of its abduction, and the potential risks if it were to be used. The Justice Police had tried to keep the missile's existence, and theft, a closely guarded secret.

Kopyion did not look surprised at the question. 'It is the most powerful thermo-nuclear device ever created. Its destructive capacity is monumental. Two shapechangers, Butler and Swarf, broke into a top secret military establishment and removed it. Their purpose was unknown.'

Kopyion could be annoyingly matter of fact. Although Brown had known him for several years – they shared an interest in the classics – Kopyion had never expressed any emotion.

'I think the Academy would be more interested in why it was developed, and why they weren't consulted.' Brown realized the irony of his words, with his world about to be plunged into a new dark ages.

'It was a doomsday device. The corporations aren't happy about the Nicaean Declaration of Independence. We're expecting a full scale attack from the mother world. The weapon would have prevented them from succeeding in their attempts to recapture Nicaea.'

'War. That's all the military mind can see. The Academy has been negotiating . . .'

' . . . with a corporation. You can't negotiate away freedom,' Kopyion interrupted. 'Sanctions have contributed to the unrest on Nicaea. If we can't feed the population then they're susceptible to the forces of anarchy and ill-reason. Enemies have used the discussions and ponderings to create unrest.'

Brown moved his counter up the board, and drank some more red wine. Kopyion was right. They had come to this world to set up a paradise and they had so wanted it to be different from Earth.

He thought again about his first girlfriend, how they had married and she had died of cancer.

Science had developed but they still had no cure for death. He looked around the room, and knew how much it reminded him of her.

'Do you believe in the Prime Mover?' Brown asked. Kopyion didn't answer. 'I just wonder about the future. Will there be any beauty, or is there just aching, longing loneliness?'

Kopyion shook the dice and carried on moving his counter up the board, landing one square before a snake.

Bulbir Singh Mann looked up at the Church of the Fallen Man. Nicaea had many Churches. Although it was not his religion, he felt the Churches were magnificent. They resembled the dark cathedrals which had once stretched out over Mediaeval Europe with their gothic architecture and gargoyles staring down at the insect-like population.

Out here in deepest space the gargoyles were real. The Hunters lived in the upper atmosphere of Nicaea, and flew across space to attack other colony worlds and small space freighters. The vidscreens were full of stories of their attacks on isolated encampments and their kidnappings of small children and animals.

Mann was extremely hot. His red turban and thick beard were stained with his sweat.

He walked through the streets of the capital and saw long queues for government hand-outs of food. He saw the military patrolling the streets. And he saw the priests on street corners calling for the Academy to act and launch an all-out war on the Hunters. In the last few days Mann had noticed more people gathered around the priests. People starving and seeking simple solutions.

He was heading for the blocks of flats which had been built when the first colonists had arrived on Nicaea. They had become a no-go area, but he had some new deliveries to pick up.

Annalisa was one of his contacts. She could arrange with various smugglers to bring items in on the legitimate shipping. Black market traders thrived at times of uncertainty, and his goods were in constant demand from the elite. The old Earth products, which he specialized in, could retail for a high price. And in this batch he had something very special.

Nicaea was a bare world. There were a few towns and some isolated villages, but little vegetation and greenery. Generally, the atmosphere produced enough oxygen to keep the population of several million people alive. At certain times, however, when the volcanoes on the other side of the world became more active, it became difficult to breathe and numerous people ended up in hospital or collapsed on the streets.

The colony's smaller worlds, Trieste and Byzantine, were much more hostile. Mann had no wish to risk his life and visit the off-world colonies. He had heard enough to frighten him away from travelling away from Nicaea. And his small business was doing very well.

Earlier, he thought he'd heard a couple of shots. He had heard sirens from ambulances and fire engines moving across the city.

People were nervous. Standing around like scared animals.

Although he tried to move quickly through the streets, he found it increasingly difficult due to the crowds gathering around the priests. The largest crowd had taken over Washington Square, named after the American leader who had won independence from the imperial British. A priest stood berating the gathered masses.

All the priests wore brown monks' robes and a cowl, hiding their faces and flesh and making them identical. The priests talked about it being Judgment Day, and how they had to fight the last battle, the War against the

Hunters. And then the chosen ones would be provided for, and the others would be cast down to the eternal pit.

Mann couldn't hear what the priest was screaming but the crown was becoming increasingly unfriendly. He carried on to the market.

He wasn't a student of Earth history. His occupation of 'antique dealer' always implied that he had an education. But the only education he'd received was on the space docks of Glasson Minor.

The huge planet sized ship-building stations were the modern day equivalent of Amsterdam or Shanghai on Earth. Travellers and vagrants swelled the small populations of these commercial worlds as colonists were shipped across the galaxy. He had started out as a rat catcher – the rodents had a knack of invading new worlds as soon as man had laid claim to them – but had turned his hand to a more profitable sideline.

Stealing items from the warehouses was punishable by summary execution. However, many of the private security guards would turn a blind eye in return for a financial reward. He had never worked with the youth gangs or the mobsters but had managed to earn enough to buy a one-way passage out to Nicaea and the new life. He had learnt the value of the smallest of items. Someone's rubbish was another person's treasure. And people were prepared to pay huge sums of money.

He had arrived at the Mikhail Gorbachov conapt. The block of flats was seedy. From the main thoroughfare he turned left down a narrow street, and arrived at downtown Riotsville. Barbed wire, broken glass and graffiti marked the walls. Dogs barked and fought battles with the rats. There was no military presence on the streets in this part of town.

Children hung round the corners selling chemically induced nightmares. They openly carried small hand weapons. He walked past them. They were mainly young men, sweating, and following him with beady eyes. Trying to be cool and macho, they just about coped with the illegal chemicals they stuffed inside their bodies.

'Meester,' a ten year old shouted. 'Catcha monkee?'

Mann tried to ignore the street scum with their Riotsville lingo and threatening behaviour. He knew that they might just shoot him; he gambled that it was too early for most of the druggies and the hustlers. Riotsville came alive at night. A seven year old girl rattled some chains; Mann didn't know whether this was a warning or an invitation.

He entered the conapt. The security doors were broken. The individual flats were secure with computer identification providing the only means of access. He had lived aboard interstellar freighters, but this place had an air of aggression and vice which would rival the worst human ports. The stench of urine and faeces was overpowering.

He felt that the world was changing. There had always been some rough areas, but those places had been inhabited by characters. By funny and sad people, the lost, and the fighters down on their luck. You couldn't trust them but they'd share their food. He'd had some great times. But not anymore. He couldn't trust anyone.

He knocked on her door. He noticed that the security system had been broken. It might have been the Justice Police. They were the only ones with the technology. But they wouldn't venture into Riotsville. He thought long and hard before deciding whether to go into her flat.

He pushed the door and it creaked.

'Hello, Annalisa,' he shouted, looking into the flat. He didn't admit to himself that there would be no reply.

The place had been turned upside down. The chairs had been thrown against the walls, cupboards ransacked and the small safe broken into. He entered the room. The electronic monitoring equipment, the vidscreen and the phone all remained in their place in the flat. It had obviously not been thieves, trying to burgle the place.

The flat was empty. The bedroom was in a similar state and had no occupant. He didn't bother looking in the bathroom. He mustn't know what was in there. Annalisa wasn't here. Someone had been, though. He mustn't ask himself who.

Perhaps they had wanted the package. Perhaps someone else had it. He realized that if they hadn't found what they were looking for, and were still watching the flat, then his life was in danger. Time to leave.

And then he saw it. The book was on the table. Whoever had broken into the flat had no interest in William Ashbless's poetry. He smiled. If only they realized how much it was worth. If only . . .

I must concentrate, I must concentrate. He had almost let the barriers down.

Specially trained psi operatives were employed by the security police, corporations and criminal organizations. They could have read his mind. He had to concentrate. He was an antique book dealer. Concentrate.

He picked up the book. He felt it in his hands. A most valuable purchase. He smiled again. I am an antique book dealer. I have never been here. I have never been here.

He slipped the book into his pocket and left.

Sunset hadn't happened.

Bernice had expected the world to be plunged into darkness but the twin suns continued to shine. The jungle floor was a shadowy world and her imagination conjured up a host of surprises in the half light.

They had walked for several hours but the Doctor showed no sign of tiredness. He carried on with a single-minded dedication. He would occasionally hold out his umbrella, point it to the left or right and then yell out: 'Forward'. Bernice thought they were actually heading deeper into the jungle and had remonstrated with the Doctor a number of times. He smiled, winked at her and carried on.

'What else do you know about the planet Nicaea?' he asked her. Bernice didn't know what concerned him more, that he had never heard of the planet or that she apparently knew more than him.

'Nothing. All I know is that at this time, many former

Earth colony worlds were fighting for independence from the mighty Earth corporations. Many were in half-forgotten places spread across the galaxy. Some succeeded. But when the threat of renewed Dalek attack came, the planets returned to the fold. They needed each other. And then it was discovered that Nicaea and her entire system were gone, destroyed. A few rocks and some debris were all that remained. It was a mystery.'

Little insects flew around them. They seemed to sing and chase each other like children playing. Bernice was reminded of the fairy stories of her childhood, of the wonderful forests and the little creatures who helped humans, and the malevolent goblins and sprites who caused mischief and harm. One of the insects seemed to follow them shining with a bright incandescence. She called it Tinkerbell.

As she walked she found some words entering her head; a memory of her life before the Daleks had taken away her parents. A long time before she had joined the Doctor on his travels.

'On the first morning Eden saw play,' she said to the Doctor. He hadn't heard her.

'Yes.' The Doctor was thinking. He stopped. 'Bernice, we aren't alone on this planet.' The Doctor pointed his umbrella up to the sky. She looked up and saw a parachutist hanging from a tree above them. He looked dead.

Bernice usually enjoyed climbing trees, but this one was different. The dark trunk pointed towards the heavens. In the stygian gloom of the forest, and behind the bark, scuttled little spiders. The spiders' webs brushed against her face, cold and clammy, sticking around her eyes. She brushed them aside and clambered up the tree. A rat was perched on an outstretched branch. It had been trying to climb over to the dangling figure. It hissed at her and ran back into the shadows.

She leant over and tried to take a closer look at the man. She could see little apart from the green khaki military uniform. And the size. This was a giant. He looked over two metres tall. The only way to get the body down seemed cruel and unthinking. But there was no choice. Bernice cut the parachute straps and the body fell through the air on to the floor of the jungle down below.

'They've stopped,' Chaney said.

'They were moving fast through the jungle,' Thomas added.

'We're catching up. They're less than twenty-five metres away.'

'Action soon, lover boy,' said Marilyn, smiling in a threatening and hostile manner.

'Moving towards us,' said Chaney. 'Quickly. Arm yourselves.'

The three Killers fell to their knees and formed a tight circle. They armed their hand weapons. The blips on Chaney's monitoring equipment were heading directly towards them.

And then it appeared. Bursting through the jungle growth, it ran straight at them. Marilyn started to fire first, erratically, with few bullets hitting their target. The combined fire power of their weaponry eventually felled the creature. A wingless bird that had been startled by their movements and had tried to escape in a blind panic. Its corpse lay torn apart on the ground.

Thomas looked at the other two androids. They'd now given their position away. The gunfire could be heard for kilometres over the jungle. He looked at Marilyn. And remembered Spike's words to them.

'Down there, you'd be dead.'

The khthons stopped. They had heard the gunfire. It was a long way back into the jungle. But they knew that they were being followed and those in pursuit would not stop until they had caught up with them.

Chopra felt nothing. He could sense other visitors to the planet, but the gunfire had not been aimed at any sentient life form.

'They are just letting us know that they are here,' he suggested to the shapechangers.

46

'A challenge?' said Butler. He had returned to his original form. The shapechangers could only transform for short periods of time.

They had reached the end of the jungle. They stood on the edge of an escarpment. Chopra looked out over the rest of the planet. A river cut across an uninviting dark muddy plain. This was why they couldn't have landed any closer, Chopra thought. The interstellar freighter would have been swallowed up in the mud holes.

Standing guard over the plain were three ashen black trees, without leaves but with branches outstretched. Chopra seemed to sense that the skeletal trees were sculpted from bone and stood witch-like guarding an entrance to the spirit world.

In the distance he could see the lightless silhouette of their final destination. A chill ran down his back. Places had memories. And the Black Castle had more than most. He had never been here before, but the image was on fortune telling cards throughout the universe. The mythology of many races told of the cataclysmic war between the Old Ones and the distant warriors.

'You've stopped,' said Swarf.

'The Tower,' Chopra replied. 'There is horror within those walls.'

Swarf nodded. 'How many are now on the Planet?'

'I sense two women, on their own. And three androids,' replied Chopra, trying to turn his attention away from the symbol of destruction.

'Who is the other?' Swarf asked.

'The woman whose husband has died. In her mind I sense a partition, but I cannot read it. Perhaps the distance . . . The other is unknown to me. She is tired. They are moving closer.'

Butler listened carefully to the khthon.

'It's time for the hunt,' Swarf said.

'Yes,' Butler smiled. 'Carry on. I will return. After a bit of fun.'

The shapechangers started to giggle.

'And what do we like?' Swarf asked.

47

They both said together: 'A bit of fun.'

Their laughter was like that of small children. Chopra knew how dangerous they were, though. Their casual cruelty could be unleashed on anything that stood in their way.

Butler shuffled into the jungle belching loudly and spitting at the small animals running from his path.

The khthons picked up the coffin and continued on their journey.

The space hopper had been their means of getting from Nicaea to this jungle world. Ell left it, carrying the main medical supplies. She was in a panic. Her husband had died. But they must have something which would bring him back. There must be something which could help: a shot of atrophine, the kiss of life, a bandage. She knew this was irrational. Tears rolled down her cheeks and she found her movements clumsy and difficult. Where is the clearing, Goddamn you! Why was it taking so long to get back?

Arrival. She was back. Her husband's body lay on the floor of the clearing.

Opening the medical supplies she began to search for something which would give her time. All she needed was time.

She moved towards Jarak and then shrieked.

The grass around her husband had turned a deep scarlet colour. The blood red seemed to be seeping, like a dye, from the river to the surrounding jungle. The trees and bushes closest to the river were no longer moving.

A deathly silence inhabited the clearing.

Her thoughts were desperate and confused.

'Is he dead?' Bernice asked the Doctor.

The Doctor replied with a noncommittal grunt. He was measuring the body with his umbrella. The giant lay on the floor while the two travellers examined him. The Doctor took the knife from Bernice and started to cut the clothes off the giant's chest.

48

'Just what I suspected,' the Doctor said, pointing at the giant's shoulder. Bernice looked closely. There was a tattoo.

'Mirage Enterprises,' read Bernice. 'What does that mean?'

'It means our friend is an android, an extremely advanced one.' The Doctor looked momentarily troubled.

'Is. You mean he's still alive?' she asked.

'No, it's never been alive. It's a machine. Created by man to perform various slave functions, too onerous or dangerous for your own race.'

'Is it dead?' she asked again.

'We could have a long discussion about the nature of life, and what distinguishes the living from the dead. But the answer I think you want is that the android is still functioning.'

The Doctor rattled on as she felt the texture of the skin.

'It feels real,' she commented.

The Doctor took a deep breath. 'Well, again, what is the nature of reality? If we look at what Augustine said on the subject . . .'

The android moved very quickly, its hands snaking out and grabbing Bernice by the throat.

'Doctor!' she shouted, wrestling with the machine that was trying to strangle her. As the Doctor moved forward, Bernice suddenly found herself thrown several metres across the jungle into a tree. The breath was knocked out of her. The android sat up and pointed a gun at her.

'One move, you're dead,' it said in a deep, gruff voice. 'You are both my prisoners.' It began to cough. Bernice reckoned its machinery must have been damaged by the fall to the ground. The Doctor was negotiating with the machine.

'My good man. You see . . .'

'Silence,' it replied with considerable strain. 'I am Spike, commander of the Fourth Tactical Wing of the Justice Police of Nicaea. You are both my prisoners.'

'I see,' said the Doctor. He seemed to turn away but

49

with a quick parry with the umbrella he knocked the gun out of the android's hand. He grabbed Bernice by the hand and ran.

They crashed through the dense jungle.

'Go,' he shouted, holding on to his hat.

Bernice kept ducking in case the android had found its gun and planned to shoot her in the back of the head.

After a few minutes they stopped and she looked back. She couldn't see anything but, with the density of the jungle and the darkness on the surface of the world, the android may well have been only a few metres behind them.

She could hear. Heavy breathing, panting, branches being broken. The android was moving towards her. The sounds were becoming louder. Trying to find her. The Doctor tugged at her arm.

'Come on. Don't stand still.'

Bernice followed him. They arrived at a clearing. He walked in front of her, in a straight line. He turned to face her and put two thumbs up.

And he disappeared.

One moment he stood in front of her. And then he was gone. She ran to where the Time Lord had been, waving her arms trying to find him or discover how he had disappeared.

'Doctor, Doctor!' she shouted.

Spike had followed them. He was puzzled by their present body shapes. Why would the shapechangers transform into a young woman and a – he searched his memory banks for an appropriate word – clown? It had to be trickery. He had to be on his guard. Now he had been separated from the three other androids he was alone on this planet.

He knew that this was a banned world, but not why, and he knew that Butler and Swarf had brought 'Pandora's Box' here, but again not why. However, his job was not to find answers but simply to kill the two criminals and retrieve the weapon.

He would pursue the two fugitives across this miserable planet, even in his damaged state. His internal monitors registered that his power supply and his motor neurons were badly damaged. He had sixty hours before he would cease to function.

He followed them. They made a lot of noise. He kept at a distance of ten metres and moved in diagonal lines to make it impossible to predict his movements. As they were shapechangers, he expected them to leave traps or to transform into smaller creatures and reappear behind him.

He caught up with the woman. She was standing by a tree, shouting out for 'the Doctor'. The name that the other shapechanger was answering to. But the other shapechanger was not around. The woman walked as if there was some invisible object in front of her. Another trap? Perhaps the shapechanger was disguised as the tree.

Spike moved up behind her, grabbed her head in an arm lock and put a gun to her temple.

Systems override. Power failure. Spike began to overbalance. He couldn't see or hear. He felt himself collapse and he hit the ground. He blacked out.

'One of the signals has suddenly gone off the screen.'

The three Killers had followed the signals on their machines. The planet itself seemed to be causing interference on their equipment. Electrical emissions, perhaps from storms raging on the other side of the world, distorted their figures and information.

Thomas felt closer to Marilyn. Four individuals working together for the first time always created conflict, as they took time to learn each other's strengths and weaknesses.

Marilyn stopped and pointed ahead. There were two figures. A young woman and their commander. The commander lay propped up against a tree. The young woman stood over him. There could be no option but to annihilate both of them. He had a slight twinge of sadness. He would have liked to have known.

Chaney moved forward, followed by the other two androids. They were about five metres from their targets. The weaponry they carried was lined up, swiftly and silently and aimed at the figures. Thomas looked at his two compatriots. This would be a lot easier than he had originally thought.

'Fire,' shouted Chaney.

And the guns started repeatedly firing.

DAY FOUR
08:00–12:00

Carlson lay on the bed. He had closed his eyes but couldn't sleep. His wife had left a bowl of chilli out for him. He had reheated it and eaten it. As he tossed and turned on the bed a mild stomach ache began to trouble him. The indigestion was his fault. It wasn't the food. He worried too much.

Melanie had left a note. She was going shopping. This was her usual behaviour when she didn't want to talk to him. She was angry. He'd read the note and thrown it into the waste disposer; it wasn't working. He saw an ant crawl over the waste. Around the pipe-head there were a dozen of the ants. He'd have to call the vermin control. Ants swarmed. It they were not dealt with quickly the apartment block would be infested with the creatures. But then again, he thought, someone else would report them. If he had noticed them other residents must also be having problems.

A couple of beers would make the situation better.

They didn't.

He wanted another couple of beers.

He didn't believe in taking tablets. Sleepers could give him three or four hours rest, but he wouldn't feel like sleeping the next day. He turned the vidscreen on. The usual platitudes about colonial life off Nicaea.

He couldn't imagine anyone was taken in by these documentaries. Everything appeared too harmonious and peaceful in the outer worlds. He thought back to the scene at the grave side. The desperate parents. What was he supposed to do?

It had shaken him. He couldn't understand why anyone would want to do that to the young woman. Didn't they know the effects that their behaviour would have? He'd investigated enough crimes. What was much more harmful was the ripple effect. The unknown and unknowable effects on everyone else.

Bernice reacted at a lightning pace. She didn't have the time to wonder whether those shooting at her were lousy shots. She was out of the clearing, heading for the nearest bolt-hole. The android kept up with her. The jungle was like barbed wire, scratching her face and hands. She kept moving. The only other option was death by firing squad. Back into the darkness of the foliage.

She thought of the Doctor and his mysterious disappearance. She hadn't looked for hidden traps or animal snares below the surface of the clearing. She would have to return and find him. Although this thought gave her confidence, she knew that she wouldn't be able to find her way to any specific place in this maze of death.

The android pushed her. His punches struck her back and irritated her. She turned to scream at the mechanical man. He lay on the floor. He hadn't been punching her but trying to grab her to stop himself falling.

She glanced into the jungle. The androids didn't seem to be pursuing them.

She started to walk away and then stopped.

'Are you all right?' she asked the android.

'I am terminal. Less than sixty hours before I cease to function.'

'Oh,' she said, lost for words. 'I can't leave you here.'

She stared into the jungle. Still no sign of the androids.

'Trickery,' Spike replied, in a matter of fact manner. 'I don't know what you are trying to do. It will serve no purpose to play your games. I will kill you and resume control of the missile.'

'Yes,' she said. 'But they want to kill you as much as they want to kill me. I suppose we have something in common.'

'You must take me to the missile.' The android stared at her, calculating its next move. 'We have nothing in common. Those pursuing us are my troops. They will not rest until you and the other shapechanger are destroyed. If that means they must terminate my life then so be it. I serve.'

'Right,' Bernice muttered, wondering why she had bothered to return for this over-sized toaster. The metal man stood. His gun still in his hand. She realized it had been pointed towards her all the time she had been offering to help him.

'Where is your companion?' the android asked.

'I don't know,' she replied. She wanted to know the answer to that as well.

The man's eyes opened. He was obviously trying to focus when the monkey launched itself at him. The monkey screeched, a blood curdling scream, and bared its myriad teeth.

The watcher, sitting in the corner of the cave, had seen a number of these gladiatorial contests between the marmoset type creatures and their victims. The marmosets always won. He had seen one fight between five of the creatures and a lion whose back legs had been removed prior to the contest. He just watched. He was still uncertain as to the whereabouts of his place of capture. There were no other English speakers in this hellhole. He had originally thought he was on a desert island, in the South Seas, the captive of Spanish buccaneers. But that wouldn't explain how he'd got here.

He had been visiting Cambridge, the Year of the Lord 1811, to talk to a group of people about his poetry. It was a cold January night and he'd gone out for a breath of fresh air. He hadn't felt right. He'd had visions ever since he was a child, seeing angels watching him on trees, but nothing had ever occurred like this. He'd been walking, then felt himself falling. He'd found himself in a desert, collapsed, and must have been brought to this cave. Five days he'd been here. Starving. Nothing had happened to him. The creatures fought their battles and three grotesque, pig-like creatures argued and bet small

55

coins on which contestant would survive the conflict. The Cun, whose name he'd deciphered after hours of listening to their incessant one-sided conversation, seemed half blind and screwed up their faces to view the bloodshed. They ate the losers. He didn't expect the stranger to last long.

The small scraggy man was having problems standing with the monkey balanced on his back trying to shove its fingers into his eyes.

The Cun were in apoplexy, throwing coins into the midst of the fight.

The small fires, burning in the sordid smelling cave, were the only illumination in the arena. Dust from the floor was whipped up by the two fighting figures. Slowly, as the contest continued, both gladiators were rendered into formless shapes and silhouettes. The sounds of the fight were drowned out by the screeches of the marmosets and the inane cackling of the Cun. The watcher was reminded of the sound of wild dogs gathering around the kill.

He sat back. The stranger would be dead soon.

Marilyn and Thomas scanned the jungle. Their bullets had missed. Chaney was checking the electronic sights and automatic heat-seeking pellets.

'Useless.' He shook his head and threw the ammunition on the floor.

'What's causing the failure of the weaponry?' Thomas asked.

'It must be something about the planet. Something we're unable to identify. The machines are functioning.'

'But we do know that they are Butler and Swarf,' Marilyn said. 'We don't have to concern ourselves about an attack from behind. We simply follow the two shape-changers and, in our own time, we pick them off.'

Chaney nodded, picking up the bullets from the ground.

The paralysis was spreading across the clearing. Over a

metre had fallen to its malign influence in the last hour. There was an unearthly silence from the infected area. Even the wind had stopped breathing life on the grass in the clearing.

She had thrown a stone towards the petrified body of her husband. The stone had hung in mid-air, without falling to the ground.

She had to return to the hopper.

The hopper fitted two. It had been devised for colonists moving 'short hops' from second stage colony worlds to primary frontier territory.

Her husband had chosen the hopper. It was old and had been purchased on the black market. She opened the heavyweight door. Various papers lay strewn over the ship. She sat down and closed the door. The width of the inside of the ship was two metres and the length was double that. It was a tight squeeze.

She had to think what to do next. The paralysis was infesting the planet. That was unexpected.

She couldn't stay in the space craft.

They were depending on her.

But she would never make it. Her husband had been the expert on the rough terrain. She wouldn't be able to survive on her own.

There had to be an answer.

She began to cry.

This was not the way it was meant to be.

Bernice was trying to understand the artificial man. He had vowed to kill her but hadn't done so yet. She concluded that the return of 'Pandora's Box' was more important than her death. At least she had someone with her who had some information about the planet; with that she could perhaps find her way back to the Doctor and then the TARDIS. Perhaps it was 'Pandora's Box' or the shapechanging aliens or the androids that had caused the TARDIS to cease functioning. Come into my parlour, said the spider to the fly.

They continued to walk. Spike's pace was unvarying.

He didn't talk but made small movements to indicate he was listening, or looking out for things just beyond her perception. He occasionally reminded her of a guard dog sensing approaching danger and taking steps to protect itself. They were still being followed. She suspected those pursuing them, if they were also androids, were moving at the same programmed pace.

'Where is "Pandora's Box"?' he asked.

She pointed ahead and indicated that the Doctor was with the missile.

'Is it out of the jungle?' he inquired gruffly, waving his gun in her direction.

She nodded and replied: 'Just beyond.'

Although the jungle vegetation seemed to be thinning, this was the first evidence she had that the jungle didn't cover the surface of the planet.

She had tried to be funny with him. Her attempts at caustic wit rarely left men with favourable impressions of her; they thought of her as intellectual or difficult. But she never learnt.

Spike ignored her comparisons between him and various household objects; and her comments about him not having a lifetime guarantee.

She hated the military. And this machine, with its single-minded purpose, just bored her rigid. And why were men always in charge?

She could see what was happening. Every time she met someone, every problem she ever had, or was likely to have, ended up being that person's fault. She was starting to wind herself up.

'We are coming to the river. Did you travel down the river?' Spike asked.

What was she supposed to say?

'No, I didn't think the river was safe.'

Spike stared at her. His mind was elsewhere. 'Safe?'

'Yes. You know. Deep enough.'

He nodded. 'We will travel down the river. It is the only means of moving quickly across the surface of this world. Walking would take too many days and is fraught with dangers. Your friend, for instance. If your companion has not taken the river route then we will overtake him.'

She smiled a sarcastic you-know-best smile. She thought of telling the machine of its mistake in believing that she and the Doctor were shapechanging villains, but she suspected the machine would then dispose of her, like unnecessary baggage. It did prove the android was not infallible. The toaster carried on heading for the river.

The man was not a fighter. He lay unconscious and bloodied at the watcher's feet. A most uninspired conflict, with the marmoset winning within a few seconds. Some of the matches had been relatively entertaining, but this had been dull. The watcher had dragged the apparently dead body from the arena. He was looking to see if there was anything he could use in the body's pockets. When he discovered the man was still alive he decided it was not decent to rob him. The watcher looked more closely at him. There was something noble about him. The face had a mysterious quality he had seen in Roman busts on display in the British Museum. A Roman nose. Long forehead, distinctive chin. But there was the hair, looking as if it had been stuck on.

'My hat, my hat.' The stranger started to stir. He moved his arm in a circular movement, trying to find his hat. Finally, the man opened his eyes.

'Hello, you haven't seen my hat?'

'No,' the watcher said, realizing the other man was speaking English.

'Hmmn. That is a problem.' He then seemed to startle and looked around quickly. 'What happened?'

'Good news and bad news. The good news is that the Cun decided to eat the winner of the fight you lost.'

The stranger looked down at his torn clothes. 'Pretty one-sided?'

'Yes. The bad news is that you are still alive.'

The stranger pulled out a clothes brush and dusted his clothes. 'Nothing a needle and thread couldn't fix.' He pulled out a needle and piece of cotton from another pocket and started to sew his jacket. The light was dim but he moved with an assured hand. It reminded the watcher of a Jewish tailor in Soho who had a magical touch with men's outfits.

Putting the needle in his mouth the stranger said, 'By the way, I'm the Doctor.'

'My name is Blake. William Blake.'

The Doctor stopped. 'The poet? "Tyger, Tyger, Burning Bright, In the Forests of the Night"?'

'I am pleased you know my work. Yes.'

'My granddaughter loved your work.'

The Doctor held out his hand and seemed genuinely pleased to meet Blake. 'I'm sure things can't be as bad as you think they are. Where are we?'

The Doctor continued sewing as Blake visibly breathed in. Blake would make the most of this. 'We are in the deepest bowels of hell.'

'It could be worse. Waterloo station in the rush hour, for instance. I'd never find my hat there.'

The Milkbar was usually a heaving mass of people listening to jazz, drinking illegal alcohol and reading poetry. There were regular fights over the merits of various political systems and the strengths and weaknesses of the government. The atmosphere was good. Cheap drink and decent food were also readily available. Mann liked it. He wouldn't touch alcohol, but the milkshakes were tasty.

At midday he had closed the shop. The vidscreens had announced government restrictions on movement through various parts of Nicaea and a nightly curfew. The penalty for breaching either of these military commands was summary execution.

The Milkbar was virtually empty. The civil unrest was starting to have repercussions.

He ordered a brussels sprout dish with a cool yogurt sauce and sat down.

The music was the same but the heart had gone out of the place. Even the food didn't taste right. He looked around. A plastic bar, green and white colour scheme, bright lights and smiling cheerless bar staff. What had he seen in this place?

'Bulbir, my friend,' said a figure, moving up to him. He didn't know her name. They met here, smoked rotweed and talked about how life used to be before they had come to Nicaea. She was in her sixties, and was a character. She had been a nurse on the ice world of Cosgon during the uprising there. She'd run her own hospital wards on various colonial worlds. They'd once spent a night together when they'd started by comparing scars and finished with an arm wrestling contest, which she'd won.

'My friend, sit down,' he said to her. He bought her a whisky which she drank with relish.

'Hair of the dog,' she said. She bought another one. 'What do you know, Bulbir?'

'I have something very valuable being delivered today.' He rolled a rotweed joint. He took some back and shared it with her.

'What have you got?' she asked.

'A book of poetry by William Ashbless.'

'It's not real. You know Ashbless never existed. They say his stuff was written by Samuel Coleridge.' Her questions disturbed him.

'It's a very valuable book. Someone in the Academy has asked for it, and will pay good money.'

Mann was pleased that he had managed to obtain the book. It had taken a lot of research and had been his most difficult acquisition. He concentrated on thinking that. There was so much he mustn't remember.

'Don't trust the Academy, Bulbir. It isn't safe.'

As the drinks went down she began to gesticulate and shout to people at the other end of the bar.

He felt warm and comfortable. The rotweed always made him feel safe and protected. It was as if he was back in the womb. He had been smoking large quantities of the drug recently.

'None of us feel safe at the moment,' he said to her.

'But I know something which, if you knew it, would end your faith in the perfect system. I know something.'

It was the drugs talking. As he smoked more he couldn't care about the rest of the world. He was happy. His life went on and he supplied people with what they asked for. This is beautiful, the best experience in my life. He wanted to smoke even more. Why did he have to do anything but smoke forever?

'Don't be stupid,' she shouted at him. He couldn't remember what they were talking about. He couldn't think straight when he had smoked rotweed. And he always tended to forget that she would get drunk and start a scene. He would limp off back to the shop, and what could have been a great afternoon would be another one of those humdrum days.

And he had to be extra careful. He couldn't let his defences down.

'Don't be stupid.' She stood up, shouting for all to hear around the bar.

She was right. But not in the way she thought. He should not have taken the drugs. He had to concentrate.

He walked off. Life is so miserable.

He looked back at his friend. A Justice Police officer approached her; tall, muscular, blonde and Aryan. It was talking to her and she was shaking her head. They got everywhere, but he hadn't expected to find one here.

The level of monitoring made him sober up.

He was right to be careful. He could get very paranoid coming out of rotweed high. It was better not to worry too much about what people were saying, or what he thought he had seen. He remembered once that he thought the whole town was following him along a deserted street. The more he turned round and saw no-one the more he knew that they were hiding from him. It was a bad scene.

He'd have to give up on drugs. He walked home determined not to touch them ever again.

He would phone his contact and tell him that he had his

purchase. The vidphone showed the signs of atmospheric storms and took time to connect.

The phone was answered. A tall lean man, in his mid-forties, stared at him. He had a hungry look about him. This was Academician Brown.

'Mr Mann,' said the opposition leader.

'Sir. I have the William Ashbless poetry.'

'Good.' Brown smiled. 'Is it safe?'

'Of course. It's a very valuable book.'

Brown nodded. 'Yes. We must arrange to meet.'

DAY FOUR
12:00–16:00

Thomas felt the bush move as if the wind had suddenly caught the shrub and was trying to tug it to the heavens. He wondered if this was the start of a whirlwind. The atmospheric conditions on the planet were unknown to him. He shivered. Was this because of the sudden drop in temperature, or because of a sense of danger?

He looked at Marilyn. She was staring at him.

They had followed the twisted grass and the broken branches, keeping behind the shapechangers. But he didn't think it *was* the shapechangers. Their behaviour was too predictable.

'What are you thinking, lover boy?' Marilyn asked.

'I don't think it's the shapechangers in front of us.' Thomas hoped his answer would quieten her down. She had been taunting him even more since their failed contact with the shapechangers. Somehow, it was his fault.

'There's nothing on the screen now. Everything's quiet,' Chaney added.

'Well, lover boy, what are we going to do now?' she asked.

'Listen,' he said.

He heard a branch snap. He was sure there was something out there. He held up his arm to try to silence the other androids. Marilyn smiled and looked at him as if he was a fool.

Thomas had been listening for some time. It was behind them, perhaps twenty metres south-east. It was trying to conceal itself and wasn't moving in any rhythmic pattern. But it was there. Quietly stalking them. He guessed there was only one of them. It wasn't close enough to be watching them. Perhaps it was waiting for the right moment to attack. He thought it more likely to be playing a game. Not only was it not disguising its presence, but it wanted them to know it was following.

'There is something out there,' he repeated to them. Chaney ignored him and carried on walking.

Suddenly Thomas started to shoot into the jungle. Blazing fire into the foliage. Chaney threw himself on to the ground. Marilyn grabbed the laser rifle from him.

'What are you doing?' she shouted.

'Listen,' he repeated. She stood, still.

He heard the sound of another branch snapping and then a dull thud.

He shivered.

The path of the river took the headstrong waters over savage cutting rocks. The river was screaming.

Bernice borrowed Spike's binoculars to look at the other shore. She estimated the river was nine kilometres across. On the other side of the river there was a similar formidable forest, but shrouded in a thin layer of mist. The forest was a purple colour. At that distance all colours ran into each other. The more she stared, the more indistinguishable the shapes and shades of the planet were to her tired eyes.

Between them and the other shore various islands, and clumps of mud and tree, sailed down river to an unknown destination.

Spike had hacked down two tree trunks and then wrapped them together with vines, to build a small raft. Bernice didn't fancy travelling down the river. She sat and watched him. Earlier she had mixed together various plants he'd collected, to create a glue to bind the logs.

Although he knew what he was doing, twice he had to stop and lie on the ground. She wondered if this meant he was closer to termination. She'd asked how he was, but he'd ignored her and carried on as if she hadn't spoken. He didn't trust her.

'Why did you come to this planet?' she asked.

'To retrieve the missile.'

'Yes, but why did they send androids?'

'This is a dangerous world. Interplanetary law forbids any sentient life-form from having contact with this planet. It is not safe for sentient life,' Spike replied.

'But if it's safe for you,' she asked, 'what's so dangerous about this place for everyone else?'

'Data unknown.'

The raft was almost complete. Spike had found a long branch to guide the raft down the river.

He was quite a man. If he had been human she could have quite gone for him. But she wasn't going to form any attachment to a machine. Spike fell to his knees and gestured that she should follow him. She did.

'Prime Mover, who guides our every step, praise be to you and protect us on this our last mission. Spare your thoughts to protect the Archon and the people of Nicaea. I serve. Amen.'

She hadn't prayed but had watched the android. She hadn't prayed for a long time. Since she was a child, when the universe had been a lot simpler.

'Why do you pray?' she asked as he pushed the raft into the river. He appeared to be genuinely surprised.

'Do you not?'

'No.'

He shook his head and jumped on to the raft. He held out his arm for her. For a moment she thought about the Doctor and how her travels were now taking her further from him. She knocked Spike's arm away and jumped on to the raft. She landed on her backside, and it smarted. But she had got on herself. Spike pushed on the branch and the raft moved away from the shoreline. Soon they were caught up in the currents and were sailing down the river.

He had watched the ants swarm. There were hundreds of them, enveloping the waste.

Carlson hadn't heard anything from his wife. She had been gone over six hours. He wouldn't usually worry, but the city centre had been sealed off by the military. There were reports of shots being fired. There was even some indication that tanks had been moved out of their bases and towards George Washington Square.

He had been in touch with Police Headquarters. They could give him little information.

He wished that he could relax. He'd turned the vidscreen off. He sat silently. The stomach ache still troubled him. He couldn't wind down from work.

The phone call came as a relief.

A second body had been found. Same injuries. Should they keep in touch? No, he replied. He would come in.

He was worried. Where was his wife? This wasn't like her.

He'd asked the name of the victim.

Annalisa Sellen.

At least . . .

But there'd be more relatives. And he'd have to look at that expression again.

The horror, the horror.

The Doctor was whistling. He seemed happy and grinned at Blake. Blake sat in the corner of the cave. He couldn't tell how long they'd been there. He had lost his sense of time. They might have been there for hours or even days. He seemed to have lost interest. The dark cave, with the flickering shadows on the wall, didn't change. Blake remembered that the Greek philosopher Plato had argued that the nature of reality was unknown and all that was perceived were shadows cast on to the wall of a cave. The stench of animals caused his thoughts to return to his predicament. He didn't want to move; perhaps sunk too deep in despair.

'I've been thinking,' said the Doctor. 'We've either been plucked out of space and time, or we've both fallen through holes in the space-time continuum.'

'I don't understand,' said Blake.

'It doesn't really matter, apart from helping us to answer two questions. Are we invited guests? And if so, to whose party?'

The Doctor put his restitched jacket on and continued whistling that tune. Blake was losing his patience.

'This is just a vision. I am sure that I am presently in my friend's study in Cambridge, dreaming this nightmare. I wasn't feeling well. I remember that. I must have a fever. You know, I think there are great untapped parts of the human brain which we can explore at times of illness or stress.'

'Sigmund Freud, a dreadful man with a big beard, once argued that as well. You've heard of Freud?'

'No. Is he a Prussian?'

'Yes. I mean no, he isn't born for another fifty years. It depends whether we judge time on your scale or mine. What are years when you walk in eternity?'

Blake was having difficulties following the train of the Doctor's thoughts. The Doctor leaned over and whispered, 'I think we should get out of here.'

'You will tell me more about Freud?'

'He tried to explain existence in terms of mere cause and effect. What about the mystery?'

Blake was puzzled.

'I've been looking at these bones,' said the Doctor. 'I recognize ogrons, terrileptals and human skeletal remains. There are many I don't recognize. But they've all been eaten. I suspect this fate awaits us, soon.'

Blake had never considered that he might be a meal for the Cun.

The Doctor continued. 'I don't know where we are. You may well be right that we're in hell. What did Dante say? "Abandon all hope you who enter". There's something about this place which is having an effect on our central nervous systems.'

The Doctor stood. 'We must go.' Blake didn't move.

'I'm not asking you, I'm telling you. We must go,' the Doctor said. 'Do you remember anything about your arrival in this land?'

Blake thought. 'I have the memory of a desert. And a huge black nothingness, a hole standing in the middle of a barren wasteland. There were demons.'

'Demons?' the Doctor asked.

Blake was helped to his feet. It had been some time since he'd stood. He felt unbalanced and unco-ordinated. He was drunk. Perhaps he was lying under a tree in Cambridge hallucinating all of this. He knew he wanted to lie on the ground until he gained his breath. The Doctor held his shoulders and forcibly walked him through the cave.

'Get off,' Blake said, struggling against the stranger's greater strength. He would have taken a swing against the Doctor if his arms hadn't been pinned in an arm lock. He looked around. Remains of bodies lay in the arena. Dried pools of blood stained the ground. The Cun had gone, for now, but he knew they would return for food. He couldn't see any other creatures in the cave. He realized that the stranger had been correct. He would have been the next victim.

'Walk,' the Doctor instructed, pushing him harder.

The entrance to the cave was only about twenty feet from where he had been lying, and there'd been no-one keeping him a prisoner.

Outside was a small town perched in the middle of a desert. The buildings reminded him of Bible stories he'd heard when a child. White buildings excavated from rock. Windows and doors hammered out. The town was silent. There was no wind or movement. He looked at the sky and could see no sun, clouds or stars.

The Doctor wasn't holding the poet any more, but marching out in front. He was walking towards the buildings.

The Doctor poked his head in the first rock dwelling he came to, shook his head and carried on. Blake also looked in. A few blankets, some strange metallic objects, and that rancid smell of animal flesh.

One of the other buildings was full of hundreds of the monkey-type creatures, most apparently asleep. One of the monkeys paced nervously around the window. It saw them, spat, and exhibited its savage teeth. Others of the creatures moaned in pain having been wounded in fights.

Two or three seemed to be in sexual ecstasy, dancing around each other in a weird courtship ritual.

Blake followed the Doctor away from this inhuman zoo.

Suddenly the Doctor stopped and indicated for Blake to listen. Blake initially couldn't hear anything. But then he did. Drums; discordant, different pitches and out of sequence.

As the travellers walked, they came to a larger building. The noises were coming from in there. The banging. Footsteps trampling.

'Are we going in there?' Blake asked.

The Doctor shook his head. 'No.'

The Doctor wandered around. A number of horses were tethered at the side of the meeting hall. But they weren't the sort of horses Blake had seen before. They had stripes, heads like tigers and were twice the height of a normal horse. He couldn't imagine they were like the placid creatures he had ridden outside London. They had saddles and were obviously meant to be ridden. The Doctor pointed. He went over to one and tried to stroke its head. It tried to bite him and he pulled his hand away quickly.

'They're bapputchin. They're pack animals but relatively safe to ride. Come on,' said the Doctor.

Both he and Blake untethered and then clambered on to a bapputchin. The creatures moaned. Blake had tried to go for the most docile looking one.

'Gee up. Go on Neddy,' the Doctor shouted, to no great effect. He smiled at Blake and then kicked the creature with both feet. It moved down the street and out into the wasteland. Against his better judgment Blake repeated the Doctor's actions and was soon alongside him. The creatures swayed as they moved. Blake found that he not only had to hold on with his legs but had to grasp the sweaty hair on the creature's back.

'Just like riding a camel,' the Doctor said, looking decidedly nervous.

'Where are we going?' Blake asked.

70

'Out there,' replied the Doctor.

Although he'd only met him recently, Blake could tell that the man was stupid.

They found themselves precariously balanced on the bapputchin and moving at a considerable pace. Outside the village there was a flat scorched desert which went on as far as the eye could see.

There was no temperature. It wasn't hot or cold. Blake couldn't describe the sensation other than as dream-like. Events seemed to have their own internal logic. And Blake was caught up in an unravelling maelstrom.

He tried to wake himself up but the nightmare continued.

After about five miles they came to the first signs of life. People wandering around aimlessly, crying out. Their faces were hidden, although parts of their legs and stomachs were uncovered. They moved in an erratic, stumbling way with arms outstretched. They were blind. Many had the unmistakable signs of leprosy. Although they spoke different tongues they cried the same thing: 'Help me.'

'What are they?' Blake asked.

The Doctor ignored him and pointed out five creatures flying above them. Blake thought they looked like demons. Bat-like wings flapping loudly, horns, extended faces finishing in savage teeth, piercing yellow eyes, claws, long tails and skeletal bodies. As they came closer, long fork-like tongues could be seen protruding out of their mouths. Their bodies were hairless and seemed to be composed of brown reptilian hide. They screeched and flew down closer to the two travellers.

'We are indeed in hell,' shouted Blake.

There was a bite to the air. Bernice had sat on the raft and felt the water working up to a frenzy. Spike stood like the Statue of Liberty, impervious to the wind and rain, offering his protection to the huddled masses. He gently guided the raft down the river, pushing the branch and steering the craft away from swirling whirlpools which

71

suddenly appeared on the water's surface. He had real strength.

She had seen things in the water she couldn't clearly describe. Some were like giant jellyfish. Huge sacs of an opaque shapeless substance with tendrils that drifted across the water's surface to catch their food. She hoped visitors to the planet weren't part of the diet of the jellyfish creatures. The creatures, however, appeared to be harmless, moving little and keeping their distance.

As the travellers carried on down the river the water became rougher and the colour of the jellyfish changed to a pale sickly colour. Bernice occasionally saw bubbles rising from the river bed and presumed these came from other forms of life which lived at greater depths.

She was worried. Something seemed to be happening to the river. Perhaps it was the gravitational pull of the twin suns or an effect of the geography of the planet. But she didn't think so.

'Listen. You know we're not supposed to be here?'

'Yes,' Spike replied.

'Well who says?' Bernice thought she'd asked a good question.

'The Academy.'

Bernice was none the wiser. 'Who precisely are the Academy?'

'The parliament of the Nicaean Federation. In the early days, when this system was first colonized, many spaceships disappeared or were destroyed in the vicinity of this planet. For the safety of the colonists, and the peoples of the Federation, this planet was officially declared a banned world.'

Bernice thought the android's reply seemed more like a speech than an explanation.

'What did the survivors say? What happened?'

'There were no survivors. No-one has ever returned from this planet.'

'Until now,' said Bernice.

The android shook his head. 'Do not forget that I will

72

kill you. That is my purpose. And whilst there is life in my body I will seek you out and obliterate you.'

Merry Christmas to you as well, Bernice thought. This is exactly what I needed. A cruise down the river, with good company, haute cuisine, excellent service and all the luxuries necessary for a quiet holiday. She lay down on the raft, wondering where the Doctor was and whether he was enjoying the visit to the planet any more than she was.

The antique shop seemed to be from another era. It contained skeletons, lizard skins, cages, dust and strange things behind glass. The window was full of second-hand books and bizarre inventions. Mann was a collector of bric-a-brac.

He had stood at his shop door for an hour, drinking synthetic coffee. There were no customers. The vidscreen was on in the shop, but all it did was preach about the wonders of colonial life and tell how paradise could be found by emigrating to the smaller planets of the Althosian system. Government propaganda sold Nicaea as a cradle of civilization. Adverts displayed luxury items and claimed that they were available for purchase in the state-run stores. Although the vidscreen broadcasts were a huge lie, Mann didn't mind. He could supply many of the items they mentioned for a resounding personal profit.

The vidscreen had temporarily stopped transmitting earlier in the day. The first time the state-run broadcast station had ever stopped spewing out its propaganda and lies. This was the strongest message yet to the rebels, and the people, that the almighty military state could be toppled.

He looked at his watch and returned to the back of the shop. He sat in his shop with no customers, and the sounds of gunshots and police sirens wailing in the distance. Most of the other shops had put up closed signs and the shopkeepers returned to their homes. Public transport had apparently ground to a halt. This not only stopped shoppers but also prevented workers from reaching their destinations. The city was at a standstill.

He heard an explosion and ran to the door. Smoke was rising over the rooftops from the city centre. He couldn't tell whether it was the military using their armoured carriers to control a radical band, or another terrorist bombing. He could hear screams. People had been injured. Another explosion, followed by the sound of repeated gunfire.

'There's something out there,' Chaney said.

'Perhaps they've doubled back on us,' Marilyn suggested.

Thomas felt that rational argument was not a means to defeat the shapechangers. The planet had a mechanism to prevent their sensory equipment functioning at 100 per cent level. They couldn't trust their technology. They were on their own. The creature was out there, and watching them.

'We must be unpredictable,' Thomas said. 'It's expecting us to behave in a pattern. Its intention is to make us believe that we're trapped. We'd be psychologically at its mercy. I suggest we ignore it until we have further information. We carry on walking. If it meant to attack us it would already have done so.'

Marilyn stroked her short hair. 'You're prepared to sacrifice one of us simply to see if the shapechanger is playing a game?'

'Yes,' he replied. 'If an attack does come then we must ignore our companion and launch a massive and total counter-offensive. Attack the creature when it lunges forward.'

Chaney started to flame the jungle. He scorched the shrubbery over a radius of ten metres. He concentrated on the ground. Although the shapechangers could turn into huge monsters, the androids felt it more likely that they would be approached by small insects crawling on the jungle floor. The smell of burning and the whispers of smoke drifted through the jungle. Thomas looked at this clear signpost of their location, realizing that they had again unnecessarily given away one of their few advantages over the enemy.

The cavalcade of police hovercars moved quickly through the city. The centre was virtually empty apart from armoured carriers positioned at strategic points and army units patrolling the abandoned streets.

The major's journey from the Justice Police Headquarters to the mercantile area of the capital took less time than usual. The military wandered around looking lost, and pointing their guns towards the ground. The cavalcade had avoided the central square where reports indicated that various unidentified infantrymen were shooting at each other. Earlier reports had stated ten people were dead following explosions at the space docks.

'Sir, we are approaching the antique shop,' his driver said. He nodded and took out his staser. He checked it was working. The power pack was at maximum.

There had been no news about his wife. There were some reports about injured persons lying in the road outside one of the shopping centres, but they had turned out to be department store mannequins.

The hovercars pulled up outside the shop. Mann stood outside. He seemed to have been entranced by the flashing lights and screaming sirens.

'What do you want?' Mann shouted.

Two of the Justice Police officers grabbed him and slammed him against a wall. Electric handcuffs were placed over his wrists and he was bundled to a car. He struggled and tried to punch the androids.

'Bulbir Singh Mann, I am arresting you for the murder of Annalisa Sellen. Anything that you say can and will be taken down and possibly used as evidence against you. Get him out of here,' the major barked at his men as they bundled the prisoner into the car.

They were sure they had arrested the murderer.

The major entered the shop. The Justice Police officers were tearing it apart, searching for evidence. Books flew in different directions and the vidscreen was broken in order to check if there were any weapons hidden behind the monitor.

As the police car drove away, Mann pressed his face against the window.

'It's my life's work,' he muttered to himself.

Darkness was falling. In the upper atmosphere, small specks were riding the air currents, falling thousands of metres, unfolding their wings and rising back up. Cracks of thunder and stabs of lightning illuminated the sky and the devilish shapes of the Hunters. The storms raging across Nicaea failed to produce any rain. There seemed to be an electrical charge in the air which kept people on edge.

Major Carlson had left the interrogation room for a breath of fresh air. Although brightly lit, and made with the most modern building materials, the cramped cells below the Justice Police HQ were like mediaeval dungeons.

Carlson looked at the police vehicles forming a roadblock a kilometre from the building. Surveillance equipment and crowd control units were in place to monitor all approaches to their HQ. Although this would probably prevent suicide bombers, or civilian mobs, he thought it unlikely to defend them for long against the army.

There were about thirty Hunters hovering above the building. They seemed to be laughing and chasing each other's tails. He wondered if they were oblivious of the riots and chaos on Nicaea or whether they were the cause of the self-destruction laying waste to the Federation.

There was no news yet of his wife.

He returned to the interview room. Two young police officers had been interviewing the suspect. Mann was stripped to the waist and kneeling on the floor.

A khthon, a psi operative, sat in the corner of the room, trying to read the prisoner's thoughts.

One of the police officers saluted him. 'I serve.'

The major returned his salute.

The heat was affecting them all. The air conditioning down here barely worked at the best of times. The main power supply had cut off twice in the last hour, although only for a few seconds each time. The emergency generators were on, but they only maintained the security apparatus and the lighting. It was becoming increasingly hot and stuffy.

The major picked up the photographs from the table and asked the khthon, 'Have you picked anything up?'

The psi operative shook his head. 'He is blocking his thoughts.'

The photographs were of Annalisa Sellen. Her body had been found, in her conapt, over six hours ago. She had been crucified. Her body had been spread-eagled and nailed to the floor. She had been alive when this happened, as her hands and feet had rips and tears where she had tried to pull herself free.

'I've done nothing wrong. Please let me go,' Mann said.

He wore a red turban, had a dignified beard and unsettling, deep blue eyes. He was fifty years old. His clothes were cotton. Mann was ostensibly well off.

Mann had been seen, walking in the so-called Riotsville area of town. He had been followed and seen entering the Mikhail Gorbachov conapt.

'You were seen entering her apartment. We have fingerprints and traces of your clothing that prove you were there,' the major said.

The arrested man remained silent. The Justice Police records revealed that Mann was a known black market dealer, but there was no information on the woman.

'Why? Why?' Carlson waved the photographs in the prisoner's face. The mother of the first victim had asked the same question of the priest.

'I did nothing,' Mann said.

The major nodded to one of the officers. He didn't think there was much more he could achieve. He would report to the general on his progress.

'Is he a liar?' the major asked the psi operative.

'Yes.' The khthon nodded his head. 'He is lying even to himself. But I cannot tell you the truth. He is not frightened. Not of you. He has been trained to conceal his thoughts, to prevent his mind being read.'

'By whom?'

'I do not know,' replied the khthon.

Carlson was puzzled. It was a horrendous crime. Perhaps we are dealing with a psychopath, he thought. The intense loneliness of the journeys to the stars had upset many hitherto stable minds. There was something else about this double murder which he didn't like. Something else, something intangible which he couldn't latch on to.

Deep in the bowels of the building were the Justice Police records, their monitoring equipment and General Kopyion's office. Carlson had been ordered to report to Kopyion once the interview was over.

The general's own android guard patrolled the corridors. The major was stopped, searched, and disarmed. He was then allowed into Kopyion's office.

Kopyion was watching the vidscreen on his desk. As Carlson entered, he turned it off. The major thought his commander had visibly aged over the last seven days. This man, who had run the Justice Police since anyone could remember, seemed to be under a terrible strain.

The Justice Police had apparently done very little during the current disturbances.

'I serve,' Carlson saluted.

Kopyion remained seated. 'What have you to report?'

'He's not saying anything. My officers have interviewed him for over two hours.'

Kopyion nodded.

The major read out a summary from the file:

'The neighbours reported an argument in the apartment. A fight. Screaming, silence, and then a voice shouting the "days are eerie". Even residents from this seedy downtown apartment block were disturbed enough to call the security police. We were called to investigate a crime in what is generally considered to be a no-go area of the city. The witnesses talked about inhuman screams.'

'This isn't an ordinary killing. Have you discovered any connection between this and the other murder?' Kopyion asked.

'They were both women, and both victims were killed in some form of bizarre ritual. The first victim was a student, whilst the second victim was a prostitute,' Carlson said.

'What makes you think that?' Kopyion asked.

'She'd lived there only a few weeks. The neighbours say they rarely saw her. She seems to have ventured out only at night.'

Kopyion sat back in his chair. His eyes seemed to stare. He inhabited a dark, shadowy world.

'What do you think of her last words?' Kopyion asked.

'The days are eerie . . .'

'No. Did you ever study Latin?' Kopyion asked.

Carlson shook his head.

'I think we'd find her last words were in fact "Deus Irae". The God of Wrath.' Kopyion picked up a date from a little container in front of him. He put it in his mouth, chewing it slowly.

The major saluted.

'Carry on the investigation,' said Kopyion.

'I serve.' Carlson turned to leave the room. As he did, Kopyion signalled with his hand, as if he had remembered something.

'Your wife has returned home,' Kopyion said.

'Sir?' Carlson was puzzled. 'I didn't tell anyone that she was missing.'

'No?' Kopyion shrugged. 'I wonder how I knew.'

Carlson saluted his commander. He was more concerned about where his wife had been, and if she was all right, than about finding out how the general had known she was missing.

Bernice sat on the side of the raft thinking what to write in her diary. She remembered the Hans Christian Andersen

80

stories that her father used to read to her as a child. She couldn't remember much about her father but would always remember the feeling of being scared by the weird world of the fairy stories. As they drifted down the river, the forest looked like it might contain, away from the light of the day, the little shoemaker's cottage or the old witch's toffee house. Spike was like the woodcutter come with his axe to chop the tree down.

Her mind was wandering. Back into her past. Her combat trousers became a short skirt as she stood on the river's edge, skimming stones across the surface of the water. She was giggling as she tried to beat her father by throwing the stone and hitting a rock in the middle of the river. Her mother had prepared sandwiches. This was her favourite memory.

She didn't want to write in her diary. She wanted to have stayed at home, with her parents, as a child. Why did things have to end? Why did she have to grow up?

About twenty metres from the raft the river was starting to bubble. A shape was moving towards them. A jellyfish broke the surface with a splash, and lay on top of the water. The creature was ten metres long with a grey body and black spots. There were no signs of sensory organs. Bernice guessed that it experienced the outside world through its tentacles. The tentacles seemed to be stretching beneath the water and towards the raft. As she looked, she wondered if this was an intelligent life-form or another parasitical creature surviving off the smaller marine life. It had a beautiful –

The creature exploded. Parts of its body erupted in a white flash. The sound of gunfire. Screams from the jellyfish. It was in great pain. A black life-force was seeping out of the screeching beast. Bernice smelt burning and turned to Spike. He stood with a laser rifle over his shoulder. He blasted the creature once more. She stared at him. He was calm, and indifferent to any suffering he may have caused. The creature was scattered over the river. There was no sound from it anymore.

'We cannot take any chances. It may have been your friend.' He slung the rifle over his shoulder.

'What would happen if I told you that I wasn't one of the shapechangers? That you've made a mistake and they're both still out there.' She was angry at the unnecessary slaughter.

Spike smiled. 'And who are you?'

'My name is Bernice Summerfield. 'I'm an archaeologist.'

He obviously did not believe her. 'And what are you doing here?'

'I came here with my friend, the Doctor.'

'Why?'

She realized that she couldn't tell him any more. She could hardly tell him that they were time travellers who had come here to discover what was going to destroy the Nicaean star system, any time now.

'Oh, forget it. You wouldn't believe me.'

Spike continued to smile at her.

'And don't patronize me. I don't want to be here either.'

'You are trying to trick me. I laugh at your vain efforts.' She sat down forcefully and found herself almost falling off the raft. Spike pushed at the branch and continued to navigate their way down the river.

About an hour later he pointed up ahead. Bernice made a show of being bored and turning ever so slowly to look. Whatever he pointed out, she was going to say, 'Oh yeah. So what?'

Somewhere upstream a hue radiated out over the trees. The glow must have been thirty metres above the jungle. She wondered what caused the effect. And then realized that it was the first sign of other sentient life on the planet. This must be their destination.

'So what?' she said.

'I estimate that we are two days away. But we have just seen the end of our journey.'

'Oh yeah.' She lay on the raft, pretending that she was writing in her diary.

The journey continued. Blake had watched the black demons flying above them, and had seen them disappear. A cobbled road lay in front of them. The bapputchin, by habit or instinct, headed on to the path. The Doctor seemed to be enjoying the ride. Blake hated it. It made him feel distinctly unwell.

It reminded him of one night on the Thames when he had drunk a flagon of beer, borrowed a row boat and tried to get home on the river. It had seemed to be a good idea, but then most things do when drunk. He laughed to himself, remembering that he had dipped his face into the cold water as he tried to sober up. He had ended up going for a midnight swim. He had felt exactly like he did now the next day, but there had been the pleasure of the night before. There was no pleasure to go with this present experience.

His body ached. It was not surprising. He was getting on in years. He was fifty-four and led a sedentary life. When he was inspired he had to take himself away from all social life. He had to wander around. Pace around the house. He couldn't explain creativity. There was a muse which visited and communicated something to him. Something he had to struggle with and tell the world. There wasn't much physical exercise in being a poet and artist.

His stomach rumbled. He realized that he was hungry. He liked his food. He could do with goose and boiled potatoes. How long would this journey go on for? He needed feeding.

'Doctor, where are we going?'

'I'm trying to find some way of us returning back to our universe.' The Doctor pointed in front of them. Somewhere in the distance rose a thick column of smoke. 'There.'

'Do you think it's the Cun?' Blake asked.

'I don't know,' replied the Doctor. He looked very serious, contemplating some thought that had entered into his mind. 'Let's carry on.'

The bapputchin were able to move faster on the stone track. Their speed rivalled the race horses that Blake had seen outside London. They had no problems keeping up the pace, did not tire, and didn't need to stop for water.

'What were you working on?' the Doctor asked.

'I don't understand.'

'You were a poet and artist,' said the Doctor.

'What do you mean, I was?' Blake retorted.

'Yes,' the Doctor seemed uncertain about what to say next.

Blake stared at him, appalled by his casual remark.

'Are you frightened of death?' The Doctor seemed surprised.

'No.' Blake wasn't sure. The older he became, the more accepting he was of his eventual fate. It wouldn't be too bad a thing. He would miss people. But he believed there was something after. Death wasn't the end. There was always a small part of him which believed he was immortal, that he wouldn't die. That he would be the first person to live forever. He knew it wasn't true. And now this strange man had told him that he wouldn't continue on and on. At life's end there would be lots of things he'd never done, he thought.

'Company,' the Doctor said, pointing once again to the sky. There were seven objects heading towards them. Were the demons returning? As they came closer he realized that these creatures moved in a different way. They were twice the size of the demons, with huge beaks and wings larger than his house. Their outstretched claws alone were larger than the bapputchin.

'Pterodactyls!' the Doctor shouted as the creatures dived towards him.

'What are they?' Blake asked.

'Dinosaurs. They existed on your planet millions of years before mankind.'

'What do you mean, my planet?' Blake was mystified by the traveller's incoherent conversation.

Suddenly there was an explosion. Blake fell face forward on to the ground. Another explosion! White acrid smoke billowed around them. The Doctor remained on his bapputchin. The pterodactyls' wings were flapping dangerously close to them. Blake heard a loud bang. The ground erupted around him, spraying him with sand. He rubbed his eyes. They were stinging. He tried to look into the sky. When he did, he saw people actually riding the pterodactyls. Women!

Their bodies were painted a dirty blue colour. Blake could see they were half naked and had parts of their bodies missing. Some had absent limbs, others' faces had been re-arranged.

And these women were throwing bombs at them; small pots which were thrown on to the ground, smashed and then exploded. Another bomb was thrown, this time landing only feet from the Doctor.

An explosion. Amidst the smoke Blake saw the traveller slipping from his mount. The Doctor's head hit a stone and he lay, not moving, on the ground.

The door opened automatically. He had travelled across the city. Melanie smiled at him. She was dressed in her grey overcoat, her head covered in a similar coloured scarf. She had been packing two suitcases. She placed her perfumes and soaps on the luggage.

She had tidied up the room.

'John,' she said.

'What have you been doing? Where have you been? I've been worried about you,' he said.

'I'm leaving,' she replied.

'You are what?'

'I've had enough. I can't cope with not knowing what you're up to,' she shrugged.

'I love you,' he said. He walked up to her and held her shoulders.

'Don't be stupid,' she said, knocking his arms away.

'I'm not.' He didn't know what to say.

'We've given it a go. We've tried,' she said.

'Don't go,' he said.

'It's too late.' She shook her head.

'Where are you going?'

'I'll be all right. I'll be in touch.'

He couldn't cope with this. He needed her. She needed him, he was sure. They had been together for four years.

She'd been a nurse. They'd met after he'd been beaten-up by two Riotsville thugs. She'd stitched his wounds. He'd asked her to come out for a drink. They'd had a good time.

But he needed to drink. He had to soften the horrors of his job. The nightly scenes of violence. And the dreams. He couldn't cope. They both knew he couldn't cope.

But at least he had a job. They were well off. Not rich. But they survived. And he loved her. She was everything.

He heard the hovertaxi arrive. The taxi driver carried her cases to the car.

Carlson shouted at her, begged her to stay. He said he would crack up without her. He wouldn't be able to cope.

'Please stay,' he shouted, as the taxi disappeared down the road.

The androids' movement through the vegetation was slow. The jungle around them had been decimated by the flame-thrower. Ashes marked their path for over a kilometre.

Caution about the location of the shapechangers occasionally led them to stop suddenly in response to a half-glimpsed movement or a sound heard in the surrounding jungle.

They had been trained in jungle warfare by the legendary Brian Parsons. A veteran of many of Earth's most notorious space conflicts, he had been dead for over two centuries. However, his methods were still programmed into the android Killers. As part of their practical training, they were transported into hostile territory where they had to survive and retrieve a chosen item. The androids that returned were classified as 'Killers' and put into action on the frontiers. Thomas remembered – he and eight other novices were placed on a shipwrecked moon transporter, in an airless world, against a simulated Dalek task force.

Parsons concentrated on the 'Najake' concept. 'Najake' was a word which didn't have an exact meaning. Parsons translated it as 'neither here nor there'. He spoke of the enemy as constantly using trickery, and of the dangers of trusting perception.

Thomas still felt the dangers on this mission were more from his fellow androids than the two shapechangers. He had considered that there might not be any shapechangers, and this mission might be another training exercise. Would he and the others end up terminating each other without there being a real enemy on this planet? This would explain why his controllers had sent four different personalities on the same mission. It was an experiment and they were being watched to see if they failed.

'It hasn't attacked,' Marilyn said, stating the obvious.

'No,' replied Thomas.

'You know, I think it's scared of us,' said Chaney.

The ashes around him began to move as if caught by a strong wind. A black residue had begun to congeal around Chaney's feet. And then suddenly the ashes appeared to stand. The shape of a man stood before them. It waved its arms and laughed.

Thomas and Marilyn lined their weapons up. This time they wouldn't miss. The bullets and lasers ripped into the amorphous form. Their weapons cut into the body. The ashes reassembled into the same shifting shape. The form moved over to Chaney and enveloped him.

'No!' he screamed.

He was struggling. It was as if he was fighting with his own shadow. Then there was no more movement and his lifeless corpse fell to the ground. The shape turned towards the other androids.

'You're next,' it whispered.

The ashes fell back to the earth. Thomas and Marilyn were alone. And they knew they were the hunted.

The khthons had taken over ten hours to climb down the

87

escarpment. The box had to be kept upright and steady. The warhead was armed and any accident could set off an explosion the size of a star going nova. They lowered the missile down to the plain using ropes and levers. Swarf had watched the manoeuvre and occasionally broken into a squawk if it appeared the khthons were mishandling the missile.

Chopra felt something was growing inside him. A feeling, which he couldn't explain, was slowly taking possession of him. He felt sick but it was not a virus. It was something outside of his body. He sensed one woman travelling down an expanse of water and another trapped in a small space. Both were a great distance away. He couldn't feel the presence of the androids. Butler was about ten kilometres away, deep in the jungle. There was also a darkness on the planet. Close to the shapechanger he felt an emptiness, the like of which he had never experienced before, throbbing and growing.

'Careful,' shouted Swarf. Chopra looked up. A khthon was falling down to the earth. He felt no surprise or pain. Life and Death were mapped out. There were no accidents, no free will. Only the impersonal machinations of the Gods.

There was a nasty thud. The body was badly broken but there was still life. Chopra knelt over the dying man. He held his hand.

Near the body Chopra noticed a scorpion. Its stinger was swinging to and fro as if it was about to let loose a deadly poison.

The khthon pulled himself up to Chopra's face and whispered, 'They're back.' His body shuddered and he was dead.

Chopra turned in panic.

Bernice stirred. She had fallen asleep. Spike sat on the other side of the raft, his eyes scanning the surrounding jungle as the raft headed down river. He looked across at her. She smiled. He looked away.

She was sure she had heard something out of place

which had woken her from her sleep. The sound of horses' hooves. She couldn't remember what she had been dreaming. She listened to the sounds around her. She could hear the water lapping around the raft. But no horses. It was ridiculous. The galloping horses must have been in her dream. She closed her eyes and lay back on the raft.

DAY FOUR
20:00–24:00

The universe seemed such a small place. Spike was watching Nicaea slowly rise over the horizon. He wondered whether anyone would mourn his passing. In thirty-two hours he would be terminal and never again be able to look at the stars and the heavens. The Prime Mover had claimed his life from the darkness, created him from spirit, and soon would return him to his eternal breast.

Spike clasped his hands and prayed. It wasn't a prayer for him, but again an intercession request for the people of the Federation. If only the Prime Mover could be merciful.

Spike knew that his task was vital and that the hopes of the people lay with the four androids. The Archon had spoken to them directly, giving the irrevocable order that they must lay down their lives.

He looked over the planet. Whose hand lay in its creation? The cosmos was a primeval battle between the forces of good and evil. The Book told of the Form Manipulator being scattered throughout the universe by the explosion which wrenched the cosmos apart. However, even in this primitive world Spike felt the hand of the Prime Mover.

His life's work had been to destroy the Hunters. Although they were not mentioned in the Book, the priests explained that the parasitical creatures were living representatives of the Form Manipulator. Carrying out his work, terrorizing and abducting the most pure and holy believers, out here in the midst of his realm.

Spike had never noticed the Hunters to be choosy.

90

They attacked young and old, pure and corrupt, without any sense of divine intervention.

He glanced at the sleeping woman. He wondered about her, and how she appeared helpful and even innocent. He could hear her breathe, a slight exhalation of air. The ripple of facial muscles and the stirring of her body. Her dark, short hair had fallen across her face. He could just break her neck while she slept, or strangle the life-force out of her. He had been called to do this many times. He was not programmed for morality, only to serve his controllers.

The river journey would continue until they arrived at their destination. He checked his gun and held it close to his chest. He said quietly to himself, 'I serve.'

The drink had made little difference. The beers had gone down easily but they couldn't take his thoughts away. He desperately needed Melanie. He could hear her talking to him. He would start a conversation with her. He needed her. He loved her.

She had been right. The job was screwing him up and destroying their relationship. Every time he thought of her his mind would wander off to worries about his job, and the murders. The scene at the grave side. The distraught parents. Someone had to care. That was it. It was caring. He couldn't turn off. The unhappiness. The pain. It had burnt him out. He was next to useless. But he was better than the androids. The cold, expressionless machines. A spark still burnt inside him. He suffered from terrible stomach pains, he had headaches. But he kept going. Pushing his body.

His work had enveloped their relationship. He hadn't meant it to happen. The job meant that there were places he couldn't go, people he couldn't talk to. He didn't feel that this was home. The conapt had become a prison.

Melanie knew. She had tried to talk to him about it.

He couldn't give an answer. He didn't know why he kept working. He didn't think it was due to something in his past. He didn't feel he had been chosen for a special task by the Prime Mover. Other people's battles. The dead, the dispossessed. Perhaps they were more important than him. But were any of them more important than Melanie?

He shook his disposable can. It was empty. There was no more. He'd tried to order a takeaway earlier but had been told that until further notice deliveries had ceased.

The conapt was a mess. The heat had started to make the pile of waste smell, an unpleasant and sickly odour. This would only encourage the rats.

He had to return to work. He couldn't stay here on his own. He had a mystery to solve.

Why had she left him?

He felt sick.

Blake had a headache. The explosions had possibly damaged his eardrums. His jacket was covered in dust, and he had swallowed a mouthful of sand when he had hit the ground. He could also taste blood in his mouth. He really could do with a drink.

The Doctor lay where he had fallen. He had not moved.

The pterodactyls had landed and their riders had dismounted. There were four mutant women and all wore blue skin-paint. They had black greasy hair cascading down their backs and yellowing nails. They wore shell necklaces and dirty animal-hide skirts. They walked like the monkeys he had seen battle in the arena.

'Acu tasha,' said one of their number. This was obviously their leader.

'My friend, he is hurt,' Blake said, hoping to divert their attention from him. Blake didn't like the look of the pterodactyls. Although he had seen them fed plant roots by the women, this didn't mean that they didn't eat meat. And they were three or four times larger than the bapputchin.

'Acu tara tash,' the leader shouted, presumably working on the assumption that the louder one shouts the more easy it is to be understood.

Blake shrugged his shoulders. 'I don't understand.'

The leader bared her teeth and made a sound with her tongue pushed to the side of her mouth. Blake couldn't tell whether this was a challenge to fight.

'Doctor,' he shouted to the unmoving stranger. He couldn't cope with this much longer. Feeling in a panic, he walked past the women to the senseless Doctor, bent over and shook him.

The Doctor stirred and opened his eyes. 'We really should stop meeting like this.'

'Mooqier chan lai tash,' said the leader to her fellow mutants. They sat down and faced the two travellers.

The Doctor looked puzzled, almost frightened.

'Tan a'k'ai,' the leader said.

The Doctor pulled out his handkerchief to wipe his face. He signalled Blake to follow him and moved over to face the women.

They both sat down.

The Doctor bowed. 'Acu tarash.'

Blake looked surprised. 'You can speak the language.'

'Yes,' said the Doctor.

'How?' Blake asked.

The Doctor seemed to ignore the question. 'Unless I'm much mistaken, they want to trade.'

'Trade what?' Blake asked.

'They'll let us live if we give them something they regard as of equal value.' The Doctor smiled. 'Empty your pockets.'

Blake searched his pockets. A handkerchief, some tobacco, a flint and some paper. The contents of the Doctor's pockets were strewn out in front of him. Half-eaten apple, bits of machinery, cards in a wallet, some money, and a child's toy carriage. The leader of the mutants picked the toy.

'Acu,' she said, bowing to the Doctor. He returned the compliment. The mutants returned to the pterodactyls, bickering excitedly over the toy. The pterodactyls flapped their wings and returned to the skies.

'What was it?' Blake asked.

'A batmobile,' replied the Doctor.

'Oh,' said Blake. Was it worth asking the stranger any questions? He was never any better informed when he'd heard the answers. 'Tell me, how could you understand their language?'

The Doctor looked nervous. 'It was Ancient Gallifreyan, the early language of my people.'

'I don't understand,' said Blake.

The Doctor shook his head. 'I wish I did. There's something quite terrifying happening here. We must get away.'

'You know it's dark on Nicaea,' said Thomas.

'Time,' Marilyn replied. 'Time is running out.'

They reviewed their strategy. It was difficult when the shapechanger might be next to them, listening to their every word. The last plan had been to draw the shapechangers into the open. It had worked, but they had been faced with something they could not defeat. Thomas thought of their commander and wondered if he had survived.

The Parsons theory examined how a guerrilla enemy would run until it felt it didn't have to run any more. The advantage of the androids was that their programming offered no opportunity to give up. An android would happily spend its lifespan making sure an enemy was destroyed. It would not make assumptions, or offer mercy, or be distracted by beauty or poetry, it just killed.

We must keep on moving, Thomas thought.

In the distance there were loud explosions, accompanied by the screams of injured souls. The desert disappeared over the horizon and, as far as Blake could see, there was nothing else within a few hours' walk. He and the Doctor had continued their journey by foot after the bapputchin had run off. The Doctor walked on merrily, whistling that infuriating tune. Blake was hungry but there was still no sign of food.

He wondered about the stranger. He seemed to be walking as if he knew were he was heading. The Doctor said that they had to find the origin of the noises. This could be the location of the exit from the desert land.

'Where are you from?' Blake asked.

'Gallifrey,' said the Doctor.

'Where's that?'

'It's a planet in the constellation of Kasteborus. Go to the centre of the universe and veer left.'

Blake would have doubted a few days before that a man could travel to the stars, but that was before he had been transported to hell.

'Have you been to Earth?' Blake asked.

The Doctor nodded.

'What is the future of mankind?' Blake asked.

The Doctor looked pensive, as if wondering whether to tell Blake some pertinent fact.

Blake said, 'I foresee a glorious tomorrow for humanity. In the last twenty years forces have been unleashed which will transform the civilizations of the world. The Americas rebelled against British tyranny and stood up for truth and justice; the French overthrew their aristocratic heirs, destroyed the Bastille and the common man took his rightful place as the arbiter of his own destiny. There is an excitement of the old times being replaced by a new democratic movement.' Blake unleashed his wisdom to anyone who would listen. He remembered a number of dinner parties descending into argument, and one into fisticuffs, when he argued about the corruption of the British aristocracy.

The Doctor looked at him. 'The future of mankind? Remember these words – Auschwitz, Stalingrad, Hiroshima and Nagasaki. Just words. Gladys Aylward, Mother Theresa, Albert Schweitzer. Just names. Somewhere between the words and the names lies the future of mankind.'

Blake was mystified. 'I don't understand.'

The Doctor stopped walking. 'No, neither do I.'

The walk continued on in silence.

Blake couldn't tell how many hours had passed. Time had

no meaning in this world. Later, sometime, they saw further signs of life in the desert. Hundreds of people crucified, stretched out in a line of wooden crosses. They were dressed in white robes and nailed to the blood-drenched emblems. All were screaming in pain. Blake was horrified at the pain of the dying.

The Cun were gathered around the scene, excitedly running around, betting on the length of time it would take for the injured to die. There were forty of the pig-like creatures. They were fighting and lashing out with their teeth if their money was seized too early when there was still life in the victims. The Cun were not interested in the two travellers. The inhuman attitude of these creatures.

Blake heard a strange sound and touched his face. He was sobbing. The Doctor walked up to him. He offered his handkerchief to Blake. It was dirty. Blake wiped his eyes.

'I'm sorry,' Blake said. His comment wasn't aimed at the Doctor, but at the frail figures hanging before him. For a moment he thought that he would kill the Cun, free the injured and nurse the dying. He didn't. He knew that he was totally powerless in this place.

'If only,' he said.

The Doctor shook his head.

'Why?' Blake asked. He looked at the Doctor. 'If you only answer me one question, star traveller, answer this one. I need to know. You have travelled across many times, been to many places . . .'

'Yes,' replied the Doctor.

'Is there a God?'

'Carry on walking. I'll answer your question, as best I can.'

The travellers continued away from the carnage and the slaughter.

They passed by a small child. A boy of about seven. He was naked and hairless. He sat looking at a flower growing in the desert. It appeared to be a red rose. He was crying, and his tears watered the flower.

'Help me,' he begged them.

The Doctor carried on walking.

The child spoke. 'Doctor, don't turn your back on me.'

The Doctor turned to face the child. 'You know me.'

'We have been expecting you.'

'Who are you?' The Doctor looked pale, as if he'd seen a ghost.

'I am innocence.'

Before their eyes the flower began to wilt, and the boy began to transform. First he was an old man, with neck length grey hair, then a middle-aged man with a mop of black hair. The changes were quick. Each time the figure seemed to be more weighed down by age. Although the size and build of the figure altered, Blake felt this was the same man. The final transformation was from a fat jolly fellow, wearing a multicoloured coat, to a mirror image of the star traveller standing before him. The voice was still that of the child.

'Do you ever feel, with all the pain and suffering you have experienced and seen, that there is no hope?'

The Doctor didn't answer.

Blake asked, 'Who are you?'

'I am Legion.'

The image of the child returned. It stuck out a long tongue which hung unnaturally over its chin. It licked its lips and snarled.

The child faded into nothingness. The real Doctor stood looking at the dead flower.

'What was that about?' Blake asked.

'I don't know. A long time ago . . .' The Doctor seemed confused. 'We must get out of here.'

'I thought that was what we were doing,' said Blake.

'You don't understand.' The Doctor was speaking quickly and Blake thought he caught the hint of an accent. 'We don't belong here. We must go now.'

The remainder of the journey was uneventful. The Doctor seemed different. Thoughtful. Hours seemed to go by as they continued in the direction of the explosions. The Doctor said that it sounded like machinery. Blake had no understanding of what the Doctor was talking about, and his attempt to explain the use of steam, levers and pulleys left the poet confused.

Blake found it difficult to take his mind off the sights of this world, and the small child. He could feel that the future of the human race was indeed unexpected, and that there was much which was unknown to him which would be familiar to tomorrow's generations. He wondered if the nature of humanity changed, and whether they would return to Eden. The Doctor knew much, had travelled far and wide, and potentially had answers which would satisfy the poet's curiosity.

'Doctor. You promised to tell me. Is there a God?'

The Doctor stopped and looked at Blake. 'It's not up to me to say whether there is or isn't a God. It's about faith. If there is a God then you must find that out yourself.'

The Doctor paused. 'The most holy person I ever met was in Africa in 1956. He was a French Jesuit palaeontologist. He felt that all humanity was developing towards a cosmic unity, which would be as one with God. That human consciousness would be one being. I can't tell you if there is a supernatural deity, or whether all we see are the workings of the inhabitants of the universe. A divine plan, or impersonal cause and effect. But I believe, as we wander the emptiness of space, that we must have the faith to believe that for each of us, that for all of mankind, there is a purpose.'

Blake listened and thought before replying. 'If there is a God then how could he allow the pain and suffering we have seen here?'

'I don't know. Sometimes I wonder if it's a test,' the Doctor said quietly.

'I am working on a poem called Jerusalem. It's about the Fall. How Man, seeking to walk alongside God, was banished from the Garden of Eden. How Man sought knowledge and was eternally punished for that act. I need to know why.'

The journey continued quietly. Within an hour they

arrived at the place where Blake had first set foot in this universe, a large black hole stretching from the ground into the air. The hole appeared to be a still pool of darkness. A doorway back to their world.

Around the doorway there were clustered about thirty of the flying demons. The Doctor pushed Blake past them towards the hole. The demons leapt and flew around them. The creatures were about four foot high. They were curious about the strangers. They tried to feel their clothes and touch the travellers' skin.

'Carry on,' said the Doctor.

The yellow eyes of the demons stared at them. Their forked tongues seemed too excited.

Blake watched one of the creatures take off. Its wings flapped, creating a sound like a whip cracking. The demons were starting to swarm, with more and more of them taking to the air, flying perilously close to the travellers. It was like being caught up in a flock of birds.

The travellers were at the hole.

'We have to walk through,' said the Doctor. 'I'll follow you.'

'Back to Cambridge, 1811?' Blake asked.

'Just walk,' the Doctor instructed.

Blake stared at the scruffy looking man. Although the Doctor was an idiot, Blake wondered if he'd see him again.

The poet walked forwards, turned for a last look at the Doctor, and felt himself tumbling into the depths of the black hole.

DAY FIVE
00:00–04:00

The spaceship was claustrophobic. Desperately, Ell tried to think of an answer. She searched through her husband's papers, finding it difficult to breathe and concentrate.

She thought of her husband. He had been so unappreciated on the planet. He had been rejected and spurned. Their anger had grown. Their hatred for everyone else had grown.

This had been the only way.

Her hands were shaking. It was panic. The last few hours of her life. There was no outside monitor so she couldn't check the progress of the red weed. She glanced at the papers. Perhaps somewhere there was a solution to her problem.

EXCERPT FROM THE SCIENTIFIC PAPERS OF
JARAK S. ROMER

We have been on the planet for 24 hours. Initial chemical analysis reveals that the composition of the air is extremely high in nitrogen, and the water is not water but a form of dilute acid. I have been unable to do more detailed tests, as the planet appears to be a cauldron of unstable chemical elements. I have no knowledge of a number of the basic elements. I cannot in the time given me draw a more complex analysis. I cannot see that it is possible for any form of life, as we understand it, to exist on this planet. I have been concentrating on the water, and this seems to be changing in its form and content even in the short time we have been here. Obviously I am unable to tell if this is cyclical or even a response to our presence on this planet. I need to spend more time checking the plant forms. I suspect that at least some of them are releasing hallucinogenic substances into the atmosphere. This would explain various illusions that I have been experiencing.

When we first arrived I had the impression that we had landed in the Garden of Eden. It appeared to be the doorway to paradise. But on basic tests, and twenty-four hours later, I could only say that I am extremely puzzled by what I have discovered. I need much more time than I have been allotted to make further tests.

Ell had looked at the reams of notes that her husband kept, marking his chemical analysis on graphs and adding unreadable comments alongside results which he had found of interest. There were ten or twenty sheets of confusing data which needed a scientific mind to unravel and explain. She didn't understand the information.

She again read the document which gave them authorization to visit this world:

THE GRAND COUNCIL OF THE ACADEMY OF THE FEDERATION OF NICAEA

This order takes precedence over all previous edicts. This authorizes Jarak Romer on behalf of the Academy to enter forbidden space and journey for scientific purposes to the planet, code number XIX.

Brown
Chair, Scientific Committee

The document had a wax seal planted where the signature would normally be found. It didn't indicate why her husband had come to the prohibited world on behalf of the Academy, although she knew that. She also knew why they had had no problems acquiring the hopper and survey items and travelling through military-patrolled space to this godforsaken place.

But her husband should not have died. That was not part of the plan.

It was all up to her now.

Ell had to control her thoughts. But she didn't care. Within a few hours the red weed would be surrounding the escape craft. There was nothing which would help her escape from her closeness to death.

She felt her hands again start to shake uncontrollably.

DAY FIVE
04:00–08:00

Spike clung desperately to the raft as it was buckled and thrown by the increasingly wild river. He had again collapsed. He had been fighting to breathe when the raft had hit the white water rapids. They were coming off the escarpment. This part of the river journey could endanger the mission.

The young woman was actually enjoying the stormy waters, laughing and thrusting her arms into the air. The water drowned her face and hair. She looked like a newly born baby, with a freshness and energy he hadn't seen before. Her clothes were dripping wet, and her body took a clear shape through the soaking top and trousers. He could see muscles.

'I love this,' she shouted across to him. She did not appear to have any difficulty in remaining standing, and whilst he lay struggling with his failing circuits she steered their path through the jutting rocks.

'You know, I used to do this with my dad. We used to go fishing, when I was younger,' she screamed into the torrent raging around them.

The water had turned from a dull grey to a fierce white, spitting and spurting out its venom. Spike held out his gun to protect himself from the shapechanger. He did not believe, he couldn't believe, she wasn't the nightmare shapechanger. It had to be a trick, an attack on his mind.

The young woman laughed and sang with the roar of the waters. He wanted to kill her. He had to destroy her before she destroyed him. He aimed the gun and pulled the trigger. She shook her head.

'I disarmed the weapon when you collapsed earlier.

Don't be frightened of me. I'm not the enemy. Enjoy yourself.' She returned the battery pack to him.

The raft dipped into the crest of a wave. Without her skill – navigating them around the rocks, avoiding the floating islands – the raft would have been destroyed.

'Why didn't you terminate me?' he asked.

She looked surprised. 'I said before. I need you.'

'You have succeeded. My life functions have a limited span of existence. I will soon be no more. What plans has the Form Manipulator for my Earthly existence?'

'Who?' she asked.

'You are not religious?'

'No. I got all the bilge at school . . .'

'You do not believe that this universe is purgatory, where sinners do penance. We are already dead, paying atonement for our past.'

'I'm a scientist. There's no scientific evidence for this mythology. I do believe that we go this way once, and we have to make the most of our journey.' She paused. 'Perhaps there is something else; out there or in here. But it's irrelevant. Life is about choice. We make a choice about how we wish to live our lives.'

'But you must believe in a future life. Is there no-one you miss, that you want someday to meet again?'

A raw nerve.

'What a stupid point. What do you know? I can't believe this. Here I am travelling down this river, having an argument with a toaster about philosophy. I'll tell you what *is* real. The Daleks destroying worlds, killing and enslaving. That's real. Me, I'm a survivor. Now shut up.'

The young woman was angry.

Spike tried to explain. 'What if I told you the Daleks are not real. They are creations of our shadow side; nemeses that we create to haunt us. What is real is the relationship we have with our family and our loved ones. This universe is a test.'

She was quiet, as if distracted by some odd thoughts, but this only lasted a few seconds before her anger rose again.

'I said I'm a survivor. That's me, metal man.'

Spike was a machine. He had one purpose: to defend the colony worlds of Nicaea from all threats. His was a second rate life. He didn't know what his test was in life. Had there been one action which he had already taken which would now lead him to heaven?

'One day I will walk with the angels.'

He felt his body slowing down, circuits burning out, memories going from his mind. It wouldn't be long now.

They had sailed out of the jungle. The woman had navigated them to the plain. They were closer to their destination. She had a strength in her and an inner power.

He looked up to the sky. The planet of Nicaea was rising over this world. The Ancient Egyptians on Earth believed that the rising and waning of their sun was due to a scarab beetle pushing a ball of fire across the sky. What superstition had guided even the most enlightened races of mankind? They had known, however, of the eternal battle between good and evil. This girl knew nothing.

Chaney's inert body lay where it had fallen. This was a reminder of the fate awaiting them. They had walked in a circle. After four hours they found they had returned to where the android had been terminated.

Marilyn held her laser gun tightly to her chest. Any movement would result in a lightning response which would save one of them. If they wounded the shapechanger then that would prevent or slow down his ability to metamorphose. They had no way to fight an enemy which had no form or characteristic movement. They could not plan for an unpredictable attack. At least they knew they were being watched. They were the prey.

Thomas looked at his dead colleague. He felt his eyes were playing tricks. The unexplored jungle directly in front of him appeared to be a dark red colour. If they hadn't become lost they would have walked straight into the red hue. He looked behind. The forest looked different. He couldn't explain why.

Things were not going according to plan.

And then Marilyn saw it. The legs were the size of the tree trunks. The body towered above the tree line. A spider, over a hundred metres high, was moving towards them. It had two protruding molars, and a body covered in matted hair which concealed its sensory organs.

'Shee-it,' said Marilyn.

She started to shoot at the spider but the energy beams bounced off without causing any visible irritation.

'Fire,' she screamed at Thomas.

He held his two laser pistols and started to unleash their fire power at the approaching horror. The screaming of the weaponry polluted the air, but the spider carried on moving towards them. Thomas had a number of high energy grenades, for use in emergencies. He would have to wait until the creature came closer.

The spider made a clicking sound as it advanced. Its legs thundered down, making large prints as they slammed on to the ground. Thomas thought there was a balletic quality to the movement, almost as if the spider was doing a dance of death.

'It's trying to scare us,' shouted Marilyn. 'It needs an audience.'

Thomas nodded. Its behaviour was ostentatious. They had no weaponry to even irritate it, never mind terminate it.

The ground shook under its weight.

The head moved towards them. The mouth opened and closed, trying to grab Thomas in its teeth. He was transfixed, but suddenly felt himself falling. Marilyn had pushed him out of the way.

'The grenades,' she shouted.

He grabbed two grenades, pulled out the safety mechanisms and threw them into the mouth of the creature. The spider sounded like it was screeching, and moved its head backwards. There was an explosion. Blood splattered out of the wounded beast and over the jungle floor. The spider retreated from the two androids and disappeared from view. The sound of its movement through the jungle ceased.

Marilyn looked at him. Thomas was lying on the ground. She stood triumphantly over him, like a victorious gladiator.

'Lover boy, you let the side down.'

He stood and looked into the jungle. There was a definite crimson hue to the land in front of them.

'Shall we follow?' he asked.

She stared at him.

'You know, lover boy, I have a dream.'

He looked puzzled.

'I know androids aren't supposed to dream. But I dream of living this one out.'

'That isn't a dream, that's hope,' he replied.

'No, lover boy, this time it is a dream.'

She kissed her laser rifle. The jungle seemed quiet. He couldn't hear the natural sounds of the planet. Thomas could feel it, the quiet before the storm.

'What's happening?' he asked.

She turned and smiled. Suddenly her expression changed into blind panic. She screamed and dropped her gun.

Desperately, Thomas looked around. There was nothing between them and the forest, over fifty metres away. There was nothing above them in the sky.

Above them!

He looked down, at the jungle floor. A tentacle had broken through, grabbed Marilyn's feet and was pulling her body into the depths of the earth. Her legs had completely disappeared. Her arms grabbed for the sides of the hole, but even with her strength she was unable to fight the power of the shapechanger. Thomas couldn't grab her arms or he would have been pulled down.

She mouthed, 'Help me', then her face and hair were gone, dragged into the hole.

Her hands remained, clawing for survival.

For a few seconds.

The hole was sealed up.

He ran for his life. He could hear his breath as his body powered its way away from where his two companions had been killed. He ran swiftly to the jungle. His mind was unable to grasp the fundamental fact that the shape-changers could be anywhere, in any disguise. How could he destroy this enemy? How could he survive to complete his mission?

He approached the forest. There was something wrong. The forest in front of him was a strange colour. It was as if the trees were bleeding. It wasn't only the colour. The jungle was still and silent. There were no signs of life or movement. Even the wind had stopped. The forest was petrified.

He stopped.

He couldn't go any further. He sensed that whatever had happened to the jungle was extremely dangerous.

He looked behind. There was nothing there. There was no sign of the shapechanger. And then he noticed. A shadow which didn't seem to be cast by any object. A shadow moving after him, creeping across the ground.

He still held his guns tightly in his hands. He started to shoot. Dull thuds hitting the leaves. The shadow stopped, about four metres from him. A black shape rose from the ground, and changed into a decaying skeleton. The thing smiled at him.

'We've won,' it said in a high, squeaky tone. It continued moving towards him. Thomas held his gun at shoulder height and blasted away. Scorch marks appeared on the skeleton but had no effect on its forward movement. The bones clicked in and out of joint. He could smell the putrid body advancing at him. It smelt like food that had gone off. It chuckled and held out its arms to squeeze the life out of Thomas's body.

It was a few metres from him. Closer and closer.

Thomas walked backwards, towards the jungle. He was less than a metre away. He knelt down.

The skeleton lunged at him. He sidestepped and knocked the creature forwards.

The shapechanger landed face down in the blood red vegetation. It slowly turned.

Thomas lay in the clearing waiting for the creature to finish him off.

The shapechanger tried to scream. There was no sound. It couldn't move. It tried to transform. Halfway between its present form, a human skeleton, and its natural appearance, a hideous dwarf, its body failed to respond any further. The mutation was taken over by the red weed. In front of the android the inside-out creature turned into stone. The organs and the life fluid crystallized. Thomas saw the death of his enemy. In unnatural silence. The struggling movements slowed and came to a halt. The shapechanger seemed frozen in death.

Thomas backed off. The red paralysis was annihilating the jungle in front of him. He picked up a twig and threw it into the petrified forest. It stopped in mid-air.

'Shee-it,' he said.

The red weed was advancing over the artificial clearing towards him. He turned. Chaney lay where he had been killed. There was no clue as to where Marilyn's body would be found. Thomas glanced again at the red weed. It was now only a few metres from him. He knelt down.

'May the Prime Mover protect your eternal souls.' He looked at Nicaea, hanging in the sky. He pulled his arm across his chest. 'I serve.'

He stood and walked away. He had a mission to complete. The other shapechanger was still alive and 'Pandora's Box' had to be destroyed.

He would walk parallel to the weed.

The red weed extended for kilometres across the planet. During his walk he discovered a number of small creatures which had been caught in the grip of the red death. He passed a rat. The back half of the rat had been enveloped by the red death; the other half struggled to escape in the light of day. It shrieked and whimpered. And then was fully possessed by the terrible paralysis. No flying creatures passed overhead. Thomas wondered if the red death affected only those life-forms which touched its deadly spores. It was the stillness that made him feel uncomfortable. The stopping of time, the end of all things.

After about three hours – time felt so different alongside the paralysis – he saw a man-made object. A space hopper.

It wasn't the shapechangers' craft. The hoppers could fit only two humanoids. But there shouldn't be any other life-forms on the planet. This was a banned world.

He thought that on the ship there might be a clue as to why the shapechangers had come to this planet, or there might be tools or weapons which he could use to defeat them. He had to make the most of the opportunities open to him. Although the hoppers were not armed he wasn't going to take any chances. They did have external vidmonitors. He swiftly approached the craft.

There were no signs of life.

He considered the options. He had superior strength, but that did not give him the power to tear the doors off space craft. The hatch was in front of him. It was closed.

He shrugged his shoulders and banged on the hatchway.

'Anybody in there? Open up.'

The ship remained silent.

Blake shivered. It was late evening and a pea-souper fog hung over London. He was glad to be home but found it difficult to see where he had arrived. The Thames was obviously close by, as he had heard the sound of sirens from the river, warning other traffic to keep at a distance. He had stood for a couple of hours, waiting for the Doctor; he hadn't arrived. Blake thought that the Doctor must have either decided to remain behind or been caught by the demons. He couldn't wait much longer. It was so cold and he was still starving. He decided to buy something to eat from one of the street traders he was sure he would find nearby. He had a little money on him. A shilling in King George pennies. He wished he had a farthing. Traders would be unlikely to have the change.

The London streets seemed different. The only illumi-

110

nation came from the full moon trying to break through the fog. He must be near the Palace. He passed a couple of women who looked at him and giggled.

He saw a welcoming fire. A trader was selling roasted chestnuts. He walked over.

'I am glad to see you. What is the cost of the food?'

He was told a farthing. This seemed to be expensive. Beggars can't be choosers, he thought. The trader shovelled a few chestnuts into paper.

Blake asked, 'Where am I? I became lost in the fog.'

'Whitechapel, mate.'

The East End of London. No wonder he hadn't recognized the sights. He was close to the docklands. Although he had never been here, he was aware of its reputation for street crime. Blake handed a penny over. The trader looked at him.

'Who you kidding mate? This ain't no good.'

'What?' Blake replied. 'I am starving. I haven't eaten since—'

'I don't care. This won't do you any good around here. Now get away or I'll sort you out, hear!'

The trader threw the penny at him. Blake wasn't going to argue. This was a rough area. He needed to find the way home.

He continued to walk. He couldn't find the spot where he had returned from hell. How was he going to meet the stranger? He heard shouting. A news vendor selling the *Evening News*. He went over to look at a copy of the paper.

There had been some terrible mistake. No wonder the Doctor hadn't arrived.

The date on the newspaper was the thirtieth of September, 1888.

He had been gone over seventy years. He didn't have a home to return to, and he was alone in the most dangerous area of London.

He read the headline.

'Whitechapel Murders. Jack the Ripper strikes again.'

He would have much to say to the Doctor if he saw

111

him again. This was out of the frying pan and into the fire.

'Doctor,' Blake shouted, into the fog.

Part Two

DAY FIVE
08:00–12:00

Blake continued to walk through the fog-shrouded streets. The moon provided little illumination. Women stood at the corners of buildings, dressed in wide, bright dresses and adorned with garish make-up. They were touting for trade, crying out 'Want some business?' or 'Want some love?' at the men and groups walking through the fog. He didn't fancy asking the street prostitutes for directions out of Whitechapel. A few of the men were dressed in quality suits with top hats and canes; they moved quickly, keeping their faces to the ground. Blake's slow walk appeared to unnerve them.

It was an eerie atmosphere. Apart from the occasional siren from the boats on the Thames, Blake could only hear the sounds of footsteps on the cobbled steps. In the distance he could hear a woman's heels catching on the cobbles as she ran to keep an appointment. He stood listening to the footsteps coming closer to him. He couldn't tell direction in the fog. It was as if the sounds were rising and falling with a supernatural air current.

He heard a scream, some distance away. He stopped and walked forward. A sailor appeared in front of him, holding two women in his arms. The sailor had a scar across his face. His arms were muscular and adorned with Chinese tattoos. He was out for a good time, which might well involve finishing the evening with a fight. One of the women screamed. They were drunk.

'Watcha mate,' said the sailor.

Blake realized he was standing in their way.

'I'm sorry,' he replied, moving over to the gutter. Both women laughed at him.

'Just watch it,' the sailor warned, threatening the poet.

Blake moved to the side. He was swallowed up in the fog. He couldn't clearly see the buildings or tell how things had changed since he was last in London. The fog covered everything with a layer of mystery and fate.

There were taverns with dozens of people singing loudly. The people looked like thieves and liars. These places were to be avoided. The windows, smudged and grimy, let out a little light. The bars seemed like candles attracting moths from the dark. Blake felt the money in his pocket. He needed to be somewhere warm. He needed to eat some food.

He had seen a number of figures dressed in blue, patrolling the streets. He thought they were the local militia. He asked a street trader, who said they were the police, London based law officers. They were trying to catch Jack the Ripper.

He obtained directions on how to leave Whitechapel.

And then Blake heard something.

It was a whistle. That damn tune!

The stranger had arrived in this world.

'Doctor!' he shouted. There was no reply and the whistling continued. Blake screwed up his eyes, trying to peer through the fog. He couldn't tell whether the whistler was moving away from or towards him.

Blake moved from the Old Nag's Head, through a courtyard, and found himself in a long alley. He thought he could see a figure moving in front of him. The figure turned left. Blake followed. Another alley. The figure seemed to be speeding up. Not running though.

'Doctor, stop!' Blake shouted.

A right turn, and then another left. Labyrinthian alleyways crisscrossing and intersecting. They were narrow, high-walled and difficult for two people to pass in. Somewhere in the distance he could hear the infuriating whistle. But he'd lost sight of the figure. At one point Blake found himself on a main street and saw two policemen outside a baker's shop.

He needed to find the stranger.

Up an alleyway. He might have been here before. He

stopped. There was something else in the alley. He heard the scuffle of feet. Was that breathing? Although the fog played tricks, he was sure there was someone close by, trying to control their breath.

He was about to shout 'Doctor' when it dawned on him. He was alone, in a deserted alley, with someone or something unknown. He gulped and felt sweat falling down his brow.

The breathing was steadier.

Blake was unable to move. His eyes were becoming accustomed to the dark. He couldn't see anybody in the alley. But there was a glint! Something was reflecting the half-light in the alley. It was a knife!

'Oi!' a voice broke the silence. A policeman was standing at the other end of the alley. 'Stop!'

Blake looked. He saw a figure moving towards him, and felt himself pushed, with great force, into a wall. The policeman was blowing a shrill whistle. The sound of footsteps receded into the fog.

Blake had been pushed to the floor. The policeman stood over him.

'What happened?'

'I don't know,' replied Blake. 'He had a knife.'

'Jack?'

'I was trying to find a friend,' Blake explained.

'I see. And what's your name, sir, and where are you from?'

'My name's Blake, William Blake. I'm from Piccadilly.'

'I dare say, sir, that you could find a "friend" in Piccadilly.'

'What? No, you don't understand.'

'I understand very well, and may I suggest that you return to Piccadilly. I think you've had enough excitement for one night.'

'Yes.' Blake thought this seemed to be a good suggestion. He could do with a warm bed.

The policeman carried on walking, following the figure. Blake dusted his coat and returned to the main alleyway.

117

The Old Nag's Head. He hadn't gone far. He would like a drink. Perhaps they would accept his old currency.

He entered the bar. Solid wooden door. The place was heaving. People of all shapes and sizes. Numerous sailors, East Europeans, Chinese, ladies of the night, various thugs and drunkards. The bar quietened. Blake felt that everyone was looking at him. He moved through the crowd as the noise restarted. Shouting, arguments and a young woman singing 'Daisy'.

He went to the bar. Coloured glasses stood on the shelves. A man with a Lancashire accent served him.

'What can I do for you, sir?'

Although the bar didn't strike Blake as a place where the customers would be called 'sir' he thought they recognized a gentleman.

'I have a problem with money. Is this any good?'

A few men at the bar were watching him and seemed to be laughing at him.

'Sir's money is good here,' the barman said, glancing at the coins. 'What would sir like?'

The group of men were finding this even funnier.

'Beer.'

The barman walked away and filled a tankard. Blake was content for the first time in days. The barman returned, smiled, and threw the liquid over his face.

'Would sir like another drink?'

The men found this uproariously funny.

Blake glimpsed the looking glass behind the bar and saw what they found amusing. His clothes were filthy, covered in dirt and blood. His hands, face and hair were stained with a peculiar sand. It looked like he hadn't washed for months, and had deliberately slept in the worst hovels every night. He didn't want to contemplate what he smelt like. This was why they had all been calling him 'sir'. He looked like the worst kind of tramp.

He took out his watch to show the barman.

'I am desperate for a meal and a drink. Will this cover the cost?'

'Are you stupid? Give it here.' The barman seized the

watch. 'There's so many bobbies out there. Who did you rob for this?'

'It's my watch,' Blake protested.

'Yes.' The barman gave the watch a cursory glance. 'It's old. I'll give you half a tankard of beer and some bread.'

'Fine,' Blake replied. The barman seemed surprised.

Blake sat down on his own at a small table. The bread contained flour maggots but it was food. The drink tasted like ambrosia. Blake couldn't remember the last time he had sat down. He was very tired.

As he sat he felt he was falling into a deep slumber. The characters in the bar seemed to be moving with slow jarring motions. The tavern was silent. The customers were carrying on their conversations. There was a figure, standing at the door. It had a top hat, cape and medical bag. Blake couldn't see the face. The figure walked through the crowd. They couldn't see him. He was holding a knife! It was glinting. Blake couldn't move. He tried to prise himself off the chair, as the figure moved towards him.

Blake heard laughter. A tart at the bar. She was carrying drinks. She was going to walk into the figure. It turned and snarled. The blade flashed up and down. The drinks fell. Glasses smashed. A red liquid oozed over the floor.

No-one else in the tavern noticed. Blake tried to shout. He could only hear the distant sound of police whistles, screaming for help.

'The Ripper has struck again. She's dead.'

Blake opened his eyes. A woman stood at the tavern door, shouting at the crowd. There was a mixture of panic and curiosity. Part of the pub's clientele stood and then didn't move; others ran outside to the scene of the murder. There was no-one singing now. An awed hush had swept the tavern. Even those remaining were listening to the drama unfolding outside the hostelry. Blake drunk the last drops of his beer and left.

The woman, undoubtedly a common prostitute, was

sitting on the floor. She was shaking and crying. 'It's terrible.'

Blake walked past her.

There was chaos outside, with people milling around the dead body. A policeman ran past the poet trying to get to the crowd before it became an unruly mob. Blake could feel the anger. There were cries of 'Hang the bastard'. But it was all show. Even the men were frightened of Jack the Ripper. Smash! A stone was hurled and broke a window.

'Let's get him!'

Blake was shoved. A fight had broken out.

Berner Street. The police were trying to keep people away from the body, but they were outnumbered and the crowd jostled to get a look. There were thirty or forty people with more arriving all the time. Blake tried to see but the people had formed a barrier preventing him from seeing what was on the ground. What he glimpsed appeared to be a body covered with a blanket.

And then he heard a voice.

'Out of the way, out of the way, I'm a Doctor.' The Scottish accent seemed to come from the other side of the crowd. And then he saw a folded umbrella, pointed into the air, moving into the centre of the chaos. Light brown jacket, question mark shirt, without a hat. It was that idiotic man from hell! Blake had to talk to him. Why had Blake arrived seventy years later than planned, and how was he going to return home?

A hush descended over the crowd. The Doctor had pulled the blanket off the body. A woman screamed, another fainted.

'My God,' said a drunken sailor, sobering up quickly.

The body lay in a bizarre position. Its arms were outstretched and its legs laid neatly together. It looked like it had been crucified. Although it wore a dress, the person was unrecognizable as the face had been skinned.

He could hear the Doctor explaining the injuries to a policeman. The Doctor looked fascinated, explaining the nature of the injuries and the implements which could have caused them.

'There are parts of this body missing,' the Doctor said, finishing the medical examination. 'Sorry I couldn't have been more help.'

The Doctor started to walk away. The policeman's hand fell on to his shoulder. 'Sir, I think you could still be of assistance. If you could come with us.'

'I can't. You know how it is. Plane goes in ninety minutes. Have to book in.'

The policeman had not let go of the stranger.

'Unhand me.' The Doctor was raising his voice. 'I am a personal friend of Queen Victoria.'

Another scuffle broke out and the crowd started to shove and fight. Someone fell over and others collapsed on top. Blake glanced at the policeman. His arm was outstretched but the Doctor had gone. The policeman was amazed, looking excitedly around him. From the back of the crowd, Blake could see the shuffling figure of the stranger walking down the street. The stranger was swinging his umbrella and whistling that infuriating tune.

Blake began to follow him.

The raft was moored by the side of the river. It had been badly damaged in the rapids. Bernice and Spike had left the jungle. In front of them lay marshlands. At the edge of the marshes four tall trees stretched up to the heavens.

Spike decided that they should continue on foot. He could repair the craft but said he was unwilling to do so.

Bernice sat by the raft. Her clothes had been wet through. She had taken them off and Spike had squeezed the water from them. The extra power in his mechanized hands had acted like a mangle. The clothes were creased but were now dry. Although aware he was an android, she had thought for a few seconds before removing her clothes. But it was the same as drying her hair in the nude, with an electric hair dryer. The mechanical man had shown no interest in her body. She appreciated the lack of prejudice about her being a woman.

121

His body was suffering. Although he showed no pain, Bernice could tell that his strength was seeping away. He was having problems raising his left arm and he couldn't twist his head. They had stopped because of his need for rest. Bernice couldn't see what he thought he would be able to do even if they did catch up with the shapechangers.

He stood. It was time to go. His periods of rest were growing longer. He indicated for her to stand. She cried out. She had been bitten. Two ants were attached by their pincers to her left arm. Their bodies throbbed.

'Get them off me, get them off!' she shouted, in extreme pain. Spike grabbed both ants with his fingers and squeezed the heads until the bodies fell away. The pincers remained stuck to the skin.

'They need to be cauterized,' Spike said calmly. He pulled out a small laser from his belt. 'This will hurt.'

She nodded. He moved the flame to her arm. It burned. She flinched. The pincers fell off. Burn marks remained on her arm.

She had been watching the legion of black ants moving along the plain. There were thousands of them, each about five millimetres long. They had large savage pincers protruding from their mouths. They moved as one, with different mutations on each side of the army and another type, at the head of the travelling mass, to clear away obstacles.

She looked at her arm.

'Any poison will have been destroyed. Do not worry.'

'Thanks,' she said.

'We must move.'

She watched the ants attack a small shrew, moving with one mind to overpower and strip it of its flesh. The opening assault resulted in the destruction of the advance unit but they kept attacking in waves until their purpose was achieved.

'Why do they throw their lives away? Do you think they know that they're going to die?' Bernice asked, as the ants swarmed over their prey.

'They are a whole being. They are not concerned for their individual lives. The words life and death have no meaning for them. They will carry on moving, adapting and surviving as one single-minded being,' Spike replied.

'Is that what it's like to be a mechanical man?' Bernice asked.

'No. You are right in that we serve. Our life has no meaning other than serving our controllers. We are perfect machines built to defend colonists on frontier worlds. But this existence is unimportant. When our life systems are terminated we will again return to the Prime Mover. That is what distinguishes our lives from those of insects.'

Spike held a foot above the insect army and stamped down on to the ants. He killed hundreds of them. Bernice could see mangled bodies, struggling and dying. The army kept on moving.

'When they swarm they destroy all in their way. They must be wiped out, exterminated, before they can destroy us. Come, let us go,' Spike said.

Spike walked on top of the ants whilst Bernice tried to avoid stepping on them.

'They are parasites. Ignore them,' he said.

She wondered if Spike had saved her life. She was his enemy yet he had helped her. Machines! She didn't understand them.

'Hold on!' Bernice shouted. Spike was moving further away. 'Come on, wait for me.'

The banging continued. Ell wasn't going to answer. Perhaps it was the military. If so, answering the door was a dangerous option indeed.

If she believed in the Prime Mover she would be praying. But she didn't.

She closed her eyes.

After a few minutes she opened them again. She couldn't fall asleep. She looked around the hopper. The charts and the paperwork lay scattered around.

She had to think of an answer. She couldn't stay here. She must find . . .

She controlled her thoughts. She couldn't let them into her mind.

She looked again at the hopper's clock. She had been inside for a day. The red death probably surrounded the ship. There had been no sound outside for ten minutes. They might have gone.

If they hadn't, perhaps they would help her.

No. They would be suspicious of her.

Unless . . .

She smiled.

A bomb!

Ell, control your thoughts!

Perhaps . . .

She slid over to the control panel. There was a self-destruct mechanism on the craft.

She laughed.

DAY FIVE
12:00–16:00

The door opened.

Ell jumped as the hopper was consumed in a huge fireball. Flames were all about her and all she could see was a harsh yellow light. She had gone blind. And then a sound, as if she had been standing next to a huge thunderclap. She knew she had to keep moving, but she lay on the ground where she had landed. The unbearable heat; she felt her clothes and her hair on fire. Could it be worth this pain?

'Help me,' she whimpered.

As she screamed, she felt arms grab hold of her and pick her up off the floor. Arms she hadn't let herself expect. It had worked. She was being carried.

She closed her eyes and passed out.

The Imperial Palace symbolized the freedom and unity of the Nicaean Federation. It was situated several kilometres outside the city and sprawled across three hundred acres. The white marble, turrets, and drawbridges were an elaborate and picturesque disguise for the most secure, well-defended building in the Althosian system. Justice Police officers guarded the approaches and overflew the barren land between the main road and the palace. Since the civil disobedience began, the palace had also been surrounded by armoured carriers and remote crowd-control vehicles.

The Archon had retreated behind the security apparatus. Although nominally in charge, control was slipping from his grasp. He was now preparing his speech to the Academy, due to meet in eight hours' time at the behest of the military.

Although unfounded rumours were circulating that the military planned to declare martial law, Carlson knew a full scale military conflict was already unfolding on Byzantine. Initial reports indicated hundreds had been killed when a military unit had been stoned by a hungry and unruly mob.

The Archon's speech could be the last breath of civilization and order.

The motorcade journey from the capital had been quiet. Motor scooters had flanked General Kopyion's hovercar. The security police had also blocked off the streets in the downtown area of the city. Kopyion's car was the third car. The major, in the fourth car, was trying to see his wife. There was no-one around. He could just see boxes, litter blowing in the wind and rats scavenging for food.

Suddenly, there was an explosion. The lead car was on fire. It veered out of control, swerved across the road and crashed into a shop front. Carlson could hear machine gun fire rattling outside; although antiques the weapons were still able to kill and maim.

He picked up the radio handset. The radio crackled.

'This is Major Carlson. Keep on moving. Do not stop. Outriders three and four pull out and await reinforcements. This is Carlson to Security HQ. The motorcade is under attack. Car one, I repeat, car one has been hit. Unable to tell whether it was a primitive missile or a land mine. We are carrying on.'

As they sped away, Carlson could see three or four figures around the car, shooting automatic guns into the flaming vehicle.

He sat back.

The capital was soon behind them. They arrived at their destination. The automatic barriers rose up and the cavalcade swept through to the Palace.

The radio reported that when the back-up unit had arrived the block of shops was on fire. The Fire Brigade had been dispatched. There were no signs of the terrorists, although a house to house search would be initiated.

The two Justice Police officers travelling in the ambushed car were dead.

The chaos was spreading.

Carlson had never been permitted to visit the Palace before.

He entered.

The androids had to wait outside.

The corridors seemed to run for miles. But like much on Nicaea, appearances could be deceptive.

He didn't know why General Kopyion had asked him to attend the meeting with the Archon. The civil unrest was not his department. He had nothing to contribute to the discussion. Kopyion was quiet, his thoughts elsewhere.

Carlson thought of his wife. He had used the police computer network and discovered his wife had volunteered for nursing duty. The stupid bitch! Why didn't she stay out of this. It was not going to be safe out on the streets. She could find herself shot. A quick movement, a phrase uttered out of line. He should be with her.

Kopyion looked at him. A look which frightened Carlson. It seemed the general was reading his mind.

'You're worried about your wife?' Kopyion asked.

Carlson nodded. 'Yes, but how did you know?'

'There's no mystery. You checked her whereabouts on the computer.'

Carlson sighed. 'She's volunteered for nursing duties. She's staffing a volunteer ambulance, driving round the city, responding to situations.'

'Is that a problem?' Kopyion asked.

'She might be injured.'

'Yes,' Kopyion said. Carlson didn't feel that this was the best way to end a conversation. He would have preferred reassurance that she'd be safe. Kopyion never understood. He seemed incapable of basic pleasantries. He wouldn't understand why his deputy was upset.

They entered the throne room.

Around the Golden Throne was a mural depicting a magnificent sun sending its rays across the heavens.

Carlson thought about how the heart of the Nicaean Federation was a fake. This whole building was merely a hologram. Nicaea and the Federation worlds were bankrupt. The majority of public spending went on the security apparatus.

The Archon was talking to his daughter. She was about nine years old, with shoulder length black hair and wearing a pale nightdress. She sucked her thumb.

The Archon saw them enter. He kissed his daughter on the cheek. She left the room after a vague promise he would see her later.

'Kopyion,' the Archon said, walking over to the police officers. Kopyion bowed his head and the major saluted.

'I serve,' said Carlson.

The Archon ignored him.

'What have you found out?' the supreme ruler asked.

'Nothing,' Kopyion replied.

'He has friends in high places . . .'

The major was puzzled. What were they talking about?

' . . . I have received an official request from the Grand Council for the antique dealer to be freed,' the Archon continued.

'Who is it signed by?' Kopyion asked.

'Your friend – Academician Brown.'

Kopyion nodded.

'Do you have enough evidence to hold him?'

Carlson looked at Kopyion. The antique dealer? Had they come out here to talk about the murders? That would explain why he had been invited, but there was a revolution going on. Was no-one interested?

'We have nothing,' Carlson said.

'I understand you knew the second victim, Annalisa Sellen.' The Archon stared at the general. 'She was a member of your Justice Police and involved in a security operation at the time of her death. Is this true?'

Kopyion shrugged his shoulders.

Carlson was astonished. He hadn't known this. There was much he was not aware of in security operations, but the general had placed him in charge of the inquiry. He had interrogated the suspect. Yet he hadn't been told this highly relevant fact.

'You must let him go,' the Archon instructed. 'I have also received complaints about the damage caused to his shop by your bully-boys. General, you must temper your men's enthusiasm.'

Kopyion nodded.

'In only three hours I will be delivering the most difficult speech of my life. Our Federation's survival depends on diplomacy. If the military or those dark-age fools were to take the initiative, we would be doomed.'

The Archon returned to sit on his throne. He was tired. People seemed to be living on the edge of their nerves. The major had seen many walking around with blank stares, communicating in monosyllables.

'I have also received communication from your friend Brown.' He stressed *your friend*. 'He intends to ask me about "Pandora's Box" in the Assembly. How did he find out?'

Kopyion didn't reply and the Archon continued talking.

'Is there any progress on retrieving the missile?'

'No,' Kopyion said.

The Archon looked furious but the general had no more to tell him. At the best of times, General Kopyion was not informative; he did not trust people, and gave away as little information as possible.

Kopyion turned to walk out.

'Kopyion, I have not dismissed you,' the Archon stated. The general stopped. 'I want the antique dealer freed today. Your energies would be better employed in concentrating on the riots and the panic unfolding on this planet.'

The general asked, 'May I go now?', then walked off, not waiting for an answer.

'I serve,' the major said, saluting the supreme ruler of the Nicaean Federation. The Archon ignored him, stood up and shouted at the disappearing figure.

'You will never make Archon.'

The major followed his commanding officer down the corridor.

The marshland was barren with little vegetation and no visible life-forms. The soil was dry and firm underfoot. They passed by a series of layered rocks. Bernice was fascinated by rock formations. They were unusually powerful visions of the natural beauty of the universe, and they acted as a reminder of her place in the cosmos. She was thirty-one; they were millions of years old.

Spike was ahead of her.

'Come on, will you,' she muttered. 'How did I get into this, Doctor?' She frowned. She was talking to herself again. She remembered wandering around a boyfriend's house talking to herself, and then discovering him sitting in the lounge. He must have thought she was mad.

'Mind you, sometimes *I* think I'm mad,' she said.

She couldn't see Spike. He'd crossed over the rocks. In her way there was a pool of mud. She didn't have time to walk around it. She stepped forward and couldn't move. The mud was up to her knees. She struggled. She was sinking. It was quicksand.

'Calm down and think. Now remember Benny, the more you struggle the sooner you'll be swallowed up,' she said to herself. There was nothing to grab on to. She couldn't stretch out and touch the sides. There was only one thing for it. Bernice Summerfield needed the metal man.

'Spike, Spike!' she shouted.

She waited a few seconds and shouted louder.

'If you don't come I'm going to start panicking.' She had sunk to her waist. She would drown within a few minutes. She could no longer feel her legs.

'Help me, metal man!' She was anxious. Her throat would never produce a sound again if she shouted any louder. 'Help!'

She heard a sound. He was standing behind her. She turned. 'Get me out . . .'

It wasn't Spike. A figure stood in front of her. Her eyes

130

were dazzled. She couldn't make out his features. He seemed to be wearing a dark-coloured suit.

'May I help?' He spoke without a trace of an accent.

'No, it's all right. I'm quite happy. I do this sort of thing for relaxation.'

He seemed to be smiling. 'If you're sure?'

The mud was half way up her chest and her arms were waving in the air.

'Help!' She shouted for Spike. Where was the toaster when you needed him?

'He can't hear you,' said the man. 'If someone doesn't help you in a few minutes you will die.'

She wasn't making it easy for him to rescue her. But she wasn't into strange men suddenly appearing and offering to save her life. What did he want in return?

Suddenly she felt a jolt and her body was submerged underneath the mud. She couldn't see, and her mouth and nose were covered by the slimy, cold substance. Her arms stuck into the air, waving goodbye to the world. Why did she have to be so difficult?

'For God's sake, get me out of here,' she tried to shout, but ended up with a sound like blowing bubbles in the bath.

She felt her arm being grabbed, and slowly she was pulled from the quicksand. She coughed, and tried to wipe the mud from her face.

'You took your time. Not seen anyone drowning before?' Stop it. Stop it, Benny. Give the man a chance.

He handed her a survival bottle of water. She poured its contents over her head.

'Sorry. I don't come within an inch of losing my life every day. It's done funny things to my head. Thanks.' She couldn't see the stranger's face. The light behind him blinded her.

'Who are you?' she asked.

'You should not be here, child,' he replied.

She stood up. Grief! She was covered in mud. She looked a mess.

'Now you tell me!' Bernice replied.

131

'What are you doing here?' he asked.

'The sixty-four thousand dollar question. It's an old Earth programme. Never mind. What am I doing here? First of all the Earth cooled, and then along came these little amoeba, then there were the dinosaurs . . .' She stopped. Her facetiousness was not going to win her any friends. 'As I said, the mud has messed up my mind. Our ship, the TARDIS, isn't working. It stopped, ceased to function. We crash-landed here. The Doctor and I were trying to discover why.'

'The Doctor?'

'Yes. He disappeared. We were walking through the forest. One moment he was there and then . . .'

'He was gone.'

She tried to look at his features. 'I don't want to be rude, but who are you? I don't let any Tom, Dick or Harry save my life. What are you doing here?'

She had to work on her politeness. The Doctor had told her that many times. You don't have to aggravate people.

She could hear a voice, calling her.

'Where are you?' It was Spike's voice. He was looking for her.

'I'm here, over here,' she shouted. Bernice turned to the man. 'It's my . . . friend.' The man stood there. She turned away to shout to the android.

'Remember . . . the Empire that Never Ended,' the man said. She looked back to ask what he was talking about. He had disappeared. She had been talking to him only a few seconds before, but he was gone. It wasn't possible for him to have vanished like that.

Second time this week, she thought. This world has got some answering to do.

Brown sat at his desk. He was preparing a detailed set of reference papers for the emergency session of the Academy. He expected the Archon to make a rousing speech, denouncing the forces of ill-reason and pleading for a suspension of the conflict, pending negotiations. But it would all be lies. The military were firmly in control of the government, and the Freedom parties would not be allowed a voice in any discussions. Ever since the Seven Planets had become an independent Federation, the smaller planets had been struggling to break away from Nicaea.

The men in power continued to bleed the Federation dry. People were desperate for food, yet the Academy had done nothing to help. Brown was becoming angry. His doctor had warned him about his heart. He needed to keep calm.

The vidphone flashed an incoming message. He switched the machine on to receiver mode. The screen wavered. The state of the infrastructure was exceedingly poor. Roads, communications and power were government dominated monopolies, and failed to provide the necessary service. The picture cleared. It was the antique dealer. He had been arrested by the Justice Police and his shop had been virtually destroyed by the security officers.

'Brown?' the antique dealer asked.

'Yes, Mr Mann.'

'Can I speak?'

'Yes, it isn't an open line. Our conversation will be electronically scrambled.'

'I was phoning to thank you for getting me out of police headquarters.'

'Yes,' replied Brown.

'I think General Kopyion knows.'

'Knows what?'

'About the conspiracy,' Mann said.

'I realize that charade of tearing your shop apart was to discover if you had "friends". But we're both suspects. Me, a known Freedom Party sympathiser and you, a black marketeer.'

'But no-one has been arrested. We were expecting most of the main opposition leaders to have been imprisoned,' Mann stated the obvious. He was nervous. Brown couldn't tell whether it was from the day spent in police custody or the general tension electrifying the population.

'I think you're overestimating Kopyion. General Bourbollon's troops are gathering around the capital; he's prepared to cross the Rubicon. Even if the Academy is "allowed" to meet, we'll find ourselves under house arrest.'

'The people would rise up,' Mann said excitedly.

'No. If the military could provide them with bread and circuses, then the people would be content. And then Bourbollon, that indolent fool, would launch military expeditions to retake the other five planets. There would be full-scale nuclear war.'

'Sir.' Mann didn't respond to the nightmare scenario.

'Forgive me. You have the William Ashbless poetry. Shall we make another appointment?' Brown asked.

They arranged to meet at eleven o'clock the next evening.

Brown severed the phone link as Mann continued to thank him for his release from detention. He returned to his paperwork.

He thought of the threat from the military. Bourbollon was a fool. Another one trying to prevent the Federation descending into chaos; he would be no more successful than the Archon. In front of the Althosian system lay only eternal darkness.

Brown looked at a photograph of his wife on his desk. She had been so beautiful. This was how he remembered her, rather than as the cancer-pained rag doll he had nursed until her death. Her optimism, her joy of life in those last hours, had nourished the medical staff. He held her hand as she died. But it all meant nothing to him. We are merely animals, creatures that are brought kicking and screaming into this world and then die. There is no more. He slammed his clenched fist into the desk, and began to cry. Was there a supreme God, or was He powerless, subject to the machinations of a higher force in this universe?

The Doctor had walked into the fog. Blake stayed at a distance, following him along the Victorian streets. What was the stranger intending to do? The Doctor pulled the half-eaten apple out of his pocket and began to consume it. His walk was aimless; he kept changing direction. He was lost! He pulled out a coin from his pocket and flipped it into the air. He was obviously moving left or right depending on the fall of the coin.

The Doctor stopped in front of a warehouse alongside the Thames. A river barge was moored nearby, and a host of characters were busily unloading its contents, dairy products from the Kentish farms. The Doctor placed the remainder of the apple in his mouth and proceeded to eat the core, stalk and pips. It was time for Blake to re-acquaint himself with the stranger.

'Doctor,' Blake said, walking up to him.

'Hmnn. Oh, hello . . .' the Doctor replied, not able to tell who was bearing down on him in the fog.

'It's Blake,' he said.

'What? My good man, it's marvellous to see you.' The Doctor shook Blake's hand as if they were long lost friends. 'Now what can I do for you?'

Blake didn't know if he should hit the Doctor. 'Doctor, this is 1888. It is seventy years later than when I should have arrived.'

'Yes.' The Doctor was pensive. 'How long have you been here?'

'About five hours,' Blake replied.

'Yes, as I thought. I was seconds behind you, entering the hole, but I've only just arrived. This means that where we were doesn't exist in the space or time of this universe. How do I explain it to you?' He looked around and, seeing the cheeses, walked over to them. 'Imagine our universe is a huge cheese, and where we were is another cheese. Are you following it so far?'

Blake had initially wondered if the Doctor was being deliberately obtuse. He thought it more likely that the Doctor was an escaped madman, probably an entertainer from Bedlam, wandering around, attempting to persuade the world his madness was the truth of life.

'I'll carry on. These cheeses are situated together, and

135

it's possible to move from one cheese to another. These cheeses have their own identity, and nothing about one cheese changes the nature of the other cheeses. Do you see?'

'No.' Blake stared at the stranger.

The Doctor looked puzzled. 'My friend Isaac Newton managed to explain the concept of gravity by talking about an apple. I seem to have failed to describe parallel universes by using cheeses.'

'The next thing you will be telling me is that the moon is made of green cheese,' Blake snarled.

'No, young man.'

'Young man? I am fifty-four. You are but two-thirds of my age.'

'I'm over a thousand years old,' the Doctor replied.

Sometimes when the Doctor spoke he told the truth, equally often it seemed he spoke lies and evasions; he was a trickster.

The dockers unloading the barge were looking over. They were obviously concerned that he and the Doctor were planning to rob them of their livelihood. Blake indicated to the Doctor that it would be sensible to move on. The Doctor was preoccupied, thinking of old times.

'William,' he said, and then as an after-thought added: 'You don't mind if I call you that?'

'No. What's your name?'

'I don't remember.' An obvious lie, but the Doctor had not meant to offend. 'I left my own planet centuries ago. My people, the Time Lords, are a remarkably dull race. They sit around all day and ponder. The most technologically advanced race in the universe, and all they do is seek knowledge. They do nothing useful.'

The Doctor's conversation made little sense to Blake. He wanted to be returned to his own time.

'There's a vague memory in my mind.' Blake was about to agree, but the Doctor continued, 'I don't have a name for it. There's a blank. I thought it was a dream . . . eyes looking at me. But then, back there in the desert, It knew what was in the void. It knew and I didn't. The Time

Lords of Gallifrey . . .' The Doctor rapidly changed the subject. 'Do you play chess?'

'Yes. Not very well, but I play,' Blake replied.

'I feel that I'm playing a game with someone, and I don't know the rules or the stakes. Perhaps the Time Lords are right. Stay out; don't become involved. More and more often I don't see what good comes from my involvement.'

Blake directed the stranger away from the Thames towards the hustle and bustle of the East End. Children were playing and throwing a ball for each other to catch. The ball flew towards the travellers, and one of the street urchins collided with the Doctor. The traveller put out his hands and saved the child from falling on to the ground.

'Cheers, mate,' the child said, picking up the ball and running to his friends.

Thomas looked at the woman. She was beginning to stir. Her face creased with pain. The ball of fire had licked her body.

He wondered who she was. She had run from the exploding craft and collapsed. He had picked her up and carried her from the flames.

She was now feeling the ground underneath her back. She stopped moving and appeared to be listening. The only sound she'd be able to hear was the crackling of the fire. Slowly, she opened her eyes. She looked at the burnt-out hopper and the forest savaged by the cataclysmic explosion. The red weed bordered the site of the devastation. It was moving closer.

She moaned, 'This nightmare continues. Is there no escape?'

Her body was thin and underdeveloped. Short brunette hair exposing a dry and poor scalp. Her skin was covered in eczema. She might have been pretty once, but not any more. She looked undernourished and ill-kept, like most of the population of Nicaea. She looked at him. She had blue eyes.

'And who are you?' she asked.

'I'm Thomas. Second Lieutenant of the Fourth Tactical Wing of the Justice Police of Nicaea.'

'An android! You're not going to kill me are you?' she whimpered.

'No. What happened?'

'A bomb. I don't understand,' she said.

'Tell me, what are you doing on this forbidden world?'

Thomas had to consider whether this was one of the shapechangers. However, the shapechangers had not travelled to this planet in a space hopper. Although there had been no evidence on their computers of the shapechangers' craft being on the planet, it had been monitored heading towards this unwelcoming world. General Kopyion had ordered that the criminals should not be stopped in deep space due to the risks of the nuclear device being detonated.

Thomas felt that if this was one of the shapechangers then it would have transformed itself into a creature which would have been untouched by the explosion. He was not certain; he would not trust the woman until he knew more about her presence here.

She sighed, said, 'Don't ask,' then continued to tell him about her husband, his experiments, his painful and sudden death, and the bomb aboard the craft. She was tired, and her conversation wandered off into comments on the animal life, the river and her nightmares.

She asked what he was doing on the planet. He weighed up what he needed to tell her about the shapechangers and theft of the nuclear device. In the end, he said that he was the only survivor of a four man crew of Killer-type androids sent here to annihilate two criminals and return an object to his controllers.

'If you're a programmed Killer, why did you save my life?' she asked.

It was a weakness. She was right in that he should have either let her die or executed her. He could not let anyone stand in the way of the mission.

'I am retribution, created to carry out the task of destroying those that would threaten the security of the

Seven Planets. I'm a perfectly engineered Kill machine, which will carry out its orders until they've been implemented or I've been destroyed. If you get in my way then I'll destroy you. Until then, you have the right to be protected.'

Thomas was sure the other androids would have rescued her from the burning ship but, discovering she was not part of their mission, would then have executed her. He felt there were too many unknowns.

He was more concerned about the red weed, currently spreading over the surface of this world. He looked at the bomb site. The weed had taken hold of the space craft. The sound of the fire had ceased. And the flames had stopped. He could still see the red shape of burning flames, but they were frozen in time. It looked like a blaze photographed with a filter that transformed everything into shades of the same colour. He could see that the weed was moving towards them.

'We must go,' he said, pointing at the encroaching paralysis. As he started to walk away, she stood up.

'By the way, my name is Ell,' she shouted after him, and then to herself, 'and I need your help . . .'

The space station had plummeted from the sky thousands of years before, scattering debris over many kilometres. The impact had caused a massive explosion which had ravaged the planet. Hundreds of kilometres of forest and vegetation had been scorched. Now nothing grew on the plain. The huge, metallic object was basically intact. It was about five miles round and must have resembled a spinning top, floating above this anonymous planet. The symbol of a lost civilization which had walked this way when the cosmos was still young.

The khthons showed no interest in the ancient relic. Swarf shouted for them to speed up. Time was catching up with them.

Chopra had not told the shapechanger that his brother was dead. The shapechanger's body had been enveloped by the force suffocating the planet. Chopra felt it happen. There was no pain. It was the beginning of the end.

Chopra stared at the space station, trying to pick up the memories of a past age.

And then It sensed him. It knew he was there.

Chopra staggered, and slumped on to the floor.

He had looked into the other world, and he had been caught peering through. He looked up at the sky and saw two eyes staring at him. A yellow face, bloodshot eyes, and the feeling of incredible age.

It was close but far. It had waited. And now It knew him.

'No, no,' he whispered.

As he cowered on the ground, a small insect ran from the space station. Chopra saw it out of the corner of his eye. He watched it head towards him. It was the size of a beetle, but mechanical. Apart from its legs it resembled an old fashioned typewriter with a carriage and Qwerty keyboard. There was a piece of paper sticking up from its back. He bent closer to read it.

'Whom Gods destroy they first send Mad.'

The typewriter made a clicking sound and then ran towards the space station. Chopra watched it disappear.

The stars moved across the emptiness of space. Brown sat looking through an ancient telescope at the clockwork precision of the galaxy. His top-storey apartment had a glass dome which allowed him to sit watching the falling stars. Before an important meeting he usually sat for an hour staring deep into the void, reminding himself of man's place in the cosmos.

He tried to empty his mind of all thoughts, preparing for what only the most naive would fail to see as the last meeting of the Academy. He had taken a couple of tablets of synthesized dope. He couldn't relax, though. He had tried to contact General Bourbollon, but all vidphones were 'temporarily out of action'. He thought that either the military were arresting all the leading dissidents and had cut his communication links with the outside world, or the rebels had succeeded in crippling the vidphone network. Looking out of his window he could see the once beautiful Nicaean capital in flames. Every few seconds the sounds of shots and explosions broke the fragile silence.

The door alarm sounded. He had visitors. It was his turn. He wondered whether to stand and fight. An antique revolver on display in his bookcase had not been fired since he had purchased it. What good would it do? He flipped a switch and the front door opened. He hadn't checked how many had come to arrest him. A single set of footsteps echoed up the stairs. He wondered if there was something he should be doing.

'Brown?' A familiar voice.

'Kopyion,' he said, surprised.

'You were expecting someone else?' Kopyion replied.

'No. I didn't think . . .'

'I've come to escort you to the Academy,' Kopyion said. Brown still seemed uncertain. 'My troops are down-stairs.'

'I thought, with the vidphones not working . . .'

'Temporary power failure,' said Kopyion.

'Yes.'

'Have you got everything you need?'

Kopyion was dressed in skull cap and black cloak. He sounded more matter of fact and tired than he had during their last contact. He walked to the telescope and looked through the eye piece.

Brown looked at the old man. They had spent so much time together, but hardly knew each other.

'I like watching the stars,' said Kopyion.

'Have you ever read any of the old Earth literature, postulating what it would be like out in space and in the future. Would it be a time of wonder, or would it be the old conflicts continued? Would mankind enter a new phase of evolution? I suppose we have entered a new phase. We and the machines now rule the galaxy,' Brown continued. 'But when you walk the streets you still pass the prostitutes, the drug takers, the street scum and the unpleasant smell of poverty. What has our technology created?'

He had been thinking. What were the forces at the heart of human darkness?

He had sat and formulated his final speech to the Academy.

Soon it would be a different life.

Kopyion pulled a jar of dates from his pocket and with a wooden fork took one out and began to chew it.

'On medieval Earth they used to label maps with "Here Be Dragons". An old idea, that beyond a certain point you just find hideous monsters,' Kopyion said. 'I agree, technology hasn't liberated mankind. But nature isn't an intricately wrought machine. Machines are our tools. They're not our saviours. We all serve the great plan.'

'And what is the great plan?' Brown asked. 'The Book says we're all the children of Adam and Eve, tainted by the fruits of original sin. But I think there's a more powerful force in this universe than the Prime Mover. We're all children of the Serpent, the spawn of the Form Manipulator. That would explain why there is still war and death.'

Kopyion shook his head. 'Time . . .'

Brown picked up his papers. Kopyion stood in the corner of the room, away from the light.

'When I look around me I see the Maelstrom. I remember that the Form Manipulator will try and deceive. This is all appearance,' Kopyion said.

He walked towards the stairs.

'Kopyion,' Brown shouted after him. The old man turned. 'I'm sorry for burdening you.'

Kopyion sighed and walked down the stairs.

The major patrolled the outside of the Academy building. The Justice Police had sealed off the streets and were only allowing in members of parliament who agreed to be body-searched. Carlson had been ordered to prevent the civil war exploding in the parliament building.

Riots were increasing over the capital, and communications had been broken with the other two major cities of Nicaea. He'd heard rumours that the military were planning to declare martial law. Satellite reports confirmed that over three hundred armoured carriers were parked around the perimeter of the city; large sections of the capital were blacked out and quiet after hours of gunfire and arson attacks.

He watched the parliamentarians arrive, and then walked into the old building.

The Academy was a riot of colours, a babble of voices, and a host of opinions. It had once stood for all that was right and true in the Seven Planets. Debate had occurred, and democracy had appeared to govern in the interests of all. But the annexation of the other planets of the Althosian system had left Nicaea economically and morally bankrupt.

Although originally based on the Greek ideal of Philosopher Kings, the mixture of academics, priests and the military actually led to decision making designed only to protect sectional interests.

Carlson understood the feelings of the rebels; he thought it unlikely any of their issues would be dealt with here. He could see that all the interest groups were doing was shifting the balance of power, leaving some more powerful at the expense of others. He had once believed in the perfect system. Now he didn't believe any system was perfect.

There were reports about groups of ordinary people taking to the streets, holding hands, approaching armoured carriers and calling for peace. He didn't feel that there would be anyone here speaking for them.

Academician Brown arrived. He nodded to Carlson as he walked into the hall. Was the Academician laughing at him?

The murders might have a political motive. The major was aware that the main suspect had been freed on the orders of the opposition leader. He had checked on the computer but couldn't find any other link between the two men.

A group of people applauded as Brown entered.

The radio reported that the air transporter, carrying the Supreme Leader of the Nicaean Federation, had landed.

As the Archon entered, a silence descended over the gathered parliamentarians. He walked through the crowd and to his throne.

He requested that the people pray.

'May the Prime Mover protect us under his divine providence. And may peace and harmony return to a troubled people. I serve. Today we gather to make a decision about the future of our planet. Our future. We make a collective decision, together, for peace or for strife. We must bury our differences and work together. If we cannot then we shall all lose. My people, I do not feel powerless. None of us should feel powerless. We have the future in our hands. Let our children remember this day.'

The Archon sat down. It would be a formality for a representative of the Assembly to ask the Archon to propose the opening motion.

Brown stood and requested that he be allowed to speak. The Archon agreed.

'As a known representative of the people, I denounce this Assembly.' A wave of shock went through the hall. This was not the speech the Archon had been expecting. 'The people demand the formal dissolution of the Nicaean Federation, massive cutbacks in the military – who should only exist to defend our world against the encroachment of outside interests – and a redistribution of food and clothes to all peoples of this nation. Starvation and cold are the main agendas today.'

There was no applause.

The military sat silent. The major looked over their benches. General Bourbollon was missing. The old general was a traditionalist who believed in the rule of authority, and was well known for his right-wing views. If the military were to seize power under Bourbollon, the clampdown would be fierce.

The Archon rose to address the awaiting masses. However, a priest stood on the floor of the parliament and refused to yield before being allowed to speak. The power struggle went on for about a minute, then the Archon sat down. He was not expecting this display of outright defiance. The priest wore a cowl over his head. Although his voice failed to carry as far as those of the Academicians', there was no possibility of failing to recognize the message.

'It is Time. The beginning of the End, when the forces of Light battle the forces of Darkness. Those who do not stand with us and fight, align themselves with the Enemy and will be annihilated with the forces of Darkness. This is a holy war, and only the Prime Mover can decide who lives and who dies. The creatures of Darkness have declared this war. They have seized our children; they have attacked our villages. We have stood by and allowed them. The Hunters must be destroyed, and the liberals and voices who fail to support the Chosen Path must be annihilated. I call on you all to line up . . .'

The priest threw back his cowl. His head was shaved, and he had diagonal lines of green and red painted down his face. He held his arms in the air and crossed them above his head.

'War, war, war!' he shouted.

The other priests also stood and removed the cowls from over their heads. Male or female, all were shaved and painted. One by one, in unison, they began to chant:

'War, war, war . . .'

The major looked away. He felt sadness. Nicaea was in a state of civil war and there would be no turning back.

DAY FIVE
16:00–20:00

As daylight filtered through the sea mist, the hostile and uncertain London of Blake's future began to take the more reassuring form of a busy port. The night creatures which had drifted through the streets were no more, and the market stalls and poverty-stricken beggars took on the more comforting image of a capital apparently little changed since Blake's day. Cockneys, Irishmen, Poles, Jews, Chinamen; all milled around the streets. The familiar odours of onions and fat, roasted coffee and decaying fish drifted towards the Thames.

It had been less than two days since he had met the Doctor, and he had had little rest. The stranger was pacing around. He seemed burdened with melancholic thoughts and dark visions as he wrestled with his pursuing demons. He talked about the murder victim sprawled across the pavement, and then wandered off into a conversation about a comedian called Ken Dodd.

As they walked, Blake heard the Doctor talking to himself, counting numbers quickly as if trying to catch himself out. Blake asked him about Jack the Ripper. The Doctor explained that in the late nineteenth century there had been a series of unsolved murders committed in the East End of London. By one man, it had been said. He had become known as Jack the Ripper. The police initially reported that he had a knowledge of surgery and, due to a message scrawled on a wall over one of the victims, it was suggested that he belonged to a secret organization, the Freemasons. Over the years various suspects had been identified as the killer, including members of the Royal Family. Blake had no interest in this bloodthirsty subject; he wanted to return home.

'Where do we start unravelling a mystery?' the Doctor asked. Blake was understandably puzzled.

'The beginning,' he suggested.

'No. The answer is in the question. It's where the mystery unravels. It only becomes a mystery because we notice that there are too few facts to draw a conclusion. It's a mathematical shape. How do we solve a murder mystery – return to the scene of the crime or,' the Doctor stopped and pointed his umbrella to a nearby building, 'explore that . . .'

'Whorehouse?'

'Yes,' the Doctor said, smiling with an inane grin.

'We go back to the scene of the crime.'

'No,' the Doctor said. 'We enter that building.'

The Doctor marched towards a Georgian building which bore all the signs of being a sailors' brothel. Blake was not averse to entering such places, but could think of a number of things he'd prefer to do at this time.

'Why?' Blake shouted.

The Doctor didn't stop, but shouted at the top of his voice for all to hear:

'Because this is a game. And I don't want to play . . .'

The brothel resembled an old abandoned house with the scuttle of rats across the floorboards and the moth-eaten curtains.

A fat whore looked uninterested, and told the travellers to follow her. Blake muttered he'd rather not. The Doctor said 'Madam', cocking his hat with respect. There was a smell of lemon juice about the place, although the cleanliness of the establishment was in doubt. The whore sniffed and tried to walk with a ladylike gait; she seemed a little drunk and occasionally stopped to pause for breath. Her red dress had not been made to walk in and had seen better days.

She led them down a narrow corridor and into a comfortable lounge. Three young women sat around the edges of the room; they looked bored and a little cold in their scanty bodices. Another couple of girls, who looked about ten or eleven, were playing marbles; they saw the strangers enter, stopped their game, sidled over and forced tired and dead smiles.

'Excuse me. I want a little information,' said the Doctor.

'You what?' said the fat whore.

The Doctor went over to the marbles, found a jack and started to play a solitary game.

'Flocihilipilifaction,' the Doctor said, stressing all the syllables. One of the girls walked over to the time traveller and smiled a genuine welcoming grin.

'I once played this with Kublai Khan,' he said.

The girl knelt down and began to play a game of marbles with the Doctor. Blake looked at the other girl; her eyes were dead. Long ago she had retreated from all the suffering into her own world.

'What's all this about?' the whore asked. 'This 'ere ain't no doss house. We want money for your pleasure.'

Blake was embarrassed. The Doctor continued to play marbles, oblivious of the protestations of the woman.

'If you just want to look, then you can get lost. I'll get some men folk and they'll see to you.'

'I'm hungry,' said the girl.

The Doctor pulled money out of his pocket and handed it over. There was a handful of notes, of different denominations and a variety of origins. The whore went to take them from the child.

'Leave her alone,' the Doctor shouted in a dark and ominous tone. The whore backed off, cursing the travellers.

The women sitting around the room had begun to stir once they had seen the money.

'Sir, your pleasure,' a whore said to Blake.

The Doctor talked quietly to the child. '"When I was a child I spake as a child, I understood as a child, I thought as a child, but when I became a man, I put away childish things. For now we see through a glass, darkly: but then face to face: now I know in part; but then I shall know even as also I am known."'

'Corinthians, thirteen eleven' Blake said.

The Doctor nodded. 'A pastor I knew used it as the basis of his final sermon, before facing his greatest fear. We must never abandon the child in all of us.'

The Doctor stood and walked over to the women. He looked at them carefully.

'I'm looking for Jack the Ripper,' he said.

The women sniggered. The other girl who had been talking to Blake walked over to the Doctor. She told him crudely what services were on offer, and the cost of each. Her eyes never left his face. He was becoming more and more angry. He stared at her.

'Let's go,' he said to Blake.

The girl playing marbles didn't even look up as the travellers left. The other girl laughed. Blake needed to run to keep up with the indignant Doctor.

Outside, the poet turned to the Doctor and raged at him. Why had they gone into that building, asked a stupid question and then left? It didn't make sense.

The Doctor stopped and answered simply, 'I thought they'd help.'

He looked puzzled and uncertain. Blake told him that his actions made no sense, and that if he had been genuinely interested in uncovering the mass murderer his methodology would have to change. The Doctor muttered that he knew best and that life was rarely logical.

Outside the brothel a coach and horses was pulling up. The coach was a polished jet black with golden initials engraved on the side. Two thoroughbred stallions panted heavily as if driven at some pace. Although the passengers were concealed by drawn curtains, an unpleasant thug dressed in a coachman's uniform could be seen dismounting from behind the reins. The thug ignored the two travellers. His appearance was sufficiently unusual, together with the aristocratic coach, to stop Blake in his tracks. The coachman resembled a carnival strongman, with well-developed muscles, a bald head and an oriental moustache. The Doctor pushed Blake but the poet failed to move.

The near side curtain opened slightly. The sight made Blake look away. A pale face, a shock of white hair and pink staring eyes. An albino! As the travellers walked away the strongman carried the huddled figure into the brothel. A cloak concealed his body from prying eyes.

The Doctor showed little interest in the events. He was still smarting from his encounter with the child prostitute.

'Why?' he barked. 'I'm so powerless.'

They walked from the brothel through the streets and arrived at the Thames. They stood on the banks and looked across at the blanket of fog coming from the river. The Doctor bought some roast chestnuts and both nibbled at the snack. Blake sat on the ground while the Doctor hung over a wall, listening to the boats pass on their way to the sea.

'Doctor, tell me about Gallifrey,' Blake said.

The Doctor recited: 'According to legend, the people of Gallifrey had supernatural powers. We could read minds. We lived in a period of superstition and dread. And then a great scientist, Rassilon, led the people into the scientific age. He overthrew the Pythia, who with her ancestors had ruled for an eternity. She cursed Gallifrey; a deadly plague ravaged our planet.

'We discovered time travel, but my people just sit and watch the events of the universe without getting involved. We are scientific geniuses but we do nothing. Look around you. What the Time Lords could have achieved . . .'

The Doctor was wistful.

Blake repeated, 'According to legend?'

The Doctor said, 'There's a saying on my planet, which roughly translates as "never trust a Time Lord".'

'Even you?'

'Especially me.' The Doctor was becoming thoughtful again. 'I have lost my innocence.'

'We all grow older,' Blake said, 'but you are a sad man. Humanity is struggling . . .'

'Against what?'

'Its own nature, the fall from grace, the eating of the

fruit of the knowledge of good and evil? Whatever interpretation you put on it we are trying to maintain progress,' Blake continued.

The Doctor looked extremely confused. 'I remember Jo Grant. She was so young and fragile. She left me.' He looked at Blake and smiled his idiotic grin. 'She was a companion of mine four regenerations ago.' He started to look panicked. 'I wonder where Bernice is. We have to get back to that planet – she's in grave danger.'

The Doctor threw the remaining roast chestnuts, which he'd barely touched, into the river. He marched off into the heart of Whitechapel. Blake was becoming tired of the stranger's mood swings. Although he sometimes wondered if the Doctor was dangerous, he needed him to return to his own time.

Suddenly, the Doctor stopped, frantically searching his pockets. Blake was beckoned over to the stranger.

'My sonic screwdriver is missing,' the Doctor said.

'So?'

'It must have been the child who bumped into me. If such advanced technology were to get into the wrong hands, it could change the history of this planet.'

'It might not do,' Blake volunteered.

'We must get it back,' the Doctor barked.

Striding together the Doctor and Blake returned to the murder scene. Blake hoped that his companion was not still wanted as a suspect. The atmosphere of the East End was not as unpleasant as in the night hours, but there was an air of threat and intimidation. The Doctor talked about 'the police' as having little control, and 'as yet' not having a scientific methodology to investigate crimes.

Blake was the first to notice that they were being followed. He saw about a dozen street ruffians trailing them through the streets. They were unwashed and unkempt, with tattered shirts and holey knee-length culottes.

'Not Baker Street Irregulars,' the Doctor said cryptically. 'Is the boy who robbed us there?'

'I think so,' Blake said.

'Good. We'll buy the screwdriver back.'

'What?' Blake shouted, as the Doctor headed towards the criminals. He could see the small figure pulling bank-notes out of his pocket, trying to explain why he wanted his machinery returned. Why couldn't he walk off and leave the Doctor? Blake suspected that he was not the first person who had asked himself that question or had come to the same irrational conclusion. Blake walked over to his travelling companion, still arguing with the street gang.

'You can have the money, and if you return the piece of machinery I won't be angry.'

Suddenly the criminals launched an attack on the time traveller. Blake managed to stop the first punch reaching its mark, but soon realized that he was also a target and a dozen people lashing out at him and his companion were not good odds. He ducked and dived. A fist crashed into his mouth. A shadow. He looked up and saw a wooden stave falling towards his head. As he collapsed he saw the Doctor being pummelled by the mob. Blood was pouring from the side of the Doctor's face.

'Doctor,' Blake groaned and lost consciousness.

Ell had difficulties walking through the jungle. Although she was by no means fit, needing sporadic rests to catch her breath, the effects of the explosion were less than Thomas had expected. Apart from burn marks on her clothes and hair, the only noticeable effect of the explosion was a dried, strained voice and occasional coughing, due to breathing in the smoke. He felt the odds on anyone surviving such an explosion were extremely low.

He was more concerned about the red weed paralysing the planet. This whole world was being plunged into a dreadful silence. Even the birds which had swarmed across the sky had disappeared.

Ell continued to worry about why her husband had been sent by the Academy to the planet. Why had there been a bomb aboard their ship? None of this made sense. He had no answer and wished she would concentrate on the problems at hand. She apologized for slowing him down and twice advised him to leave her. Although Thomas felt her husband had been stupid to bring a woman like this to the planet, he did not intend to abandon her to the mercy of the hostile environment and the murderous shapechanger.

The jungle remained dark and uninviting. Even without the woman, progress would be slow. The jungle floor was covered in vines and growths which attacked the feet, impeding movement. He found his foot stuck in a branch and he bent to free himself. The ground rose underneath him.

Ell screamed.

A huge snake was unravelling from a tree, sliding along the forest floor. His left foot was trapped beneath the moving snake. The creature was dark green and about seven metres in length. It hissed and moved its head to within a few centimetres of the android. It appeared to be trying to hypnotize him. The body of the creature began to wind around him. Although Thomas didn't know whether it was poisonous, the creature surely had enough power to squeeze the life out of him.

Ell was shouting hysterically. He had to keep his arms free as he needed them to keep the snake from suffocating him.

Thomas plunged his arm deep into the creature's mouth and then forced his fist upwards through the larynx. The snake began to choke as it tried to swallow his arm and simultaneously dislodge the obstruction from its windpipe. Its body thrashed and collided with a tree. Thomas shut his eyes and hung on with all his might.

After a struggle the creature stopped breathing. Thomas pulled his arm out of the mouth. His arm was broken in a number of places. He stood breathing heavily and holding his arm; wounded but in no pain.

'What the . . .' Ell shouted, pointing at the snake. She looked shocked, but not about the dead body. She walked over and kicked the snake. It didn't move but Thomas could clearly see what she was pointing at. Over the ground lay circuits and microchips. Small pieces of electronic equipment had spilled out of the snake. It was mechanical.

They spent several minutes examining the artificial creature. Near the head was a small imprint, 'Mirage Enterprises'. Thomas looked at her. The corporation that manufactured the androids had also made the snake. This didn't make any sense.

'I was wondering why everything seemed so familiar. We're millions of miles from Earth, yet many of the animals and birds are slight variations of long extinct creatures from the home world.' Ell looked around. 'Is anything real?'

She walked over to the tree the creature had crashed into. There was a hole in the bark. Inside were wires.

'This whole planet is a fake. My husband was right that nothing could exist on this planet. Now, android,' she looked at him, 'why would the corporation create an artificial world and then ban anyone from visiting?'

He looked at her, opened his mouth to reply and wished that he had an answer.

Blake opened his eyes once more. The sooner he and the stranger parted company, the happier he would be. His head ached. He looked around. He and the Doctor were tied up. They appeared to be in a dungeon. The Doctor was shuffling and trying to untie the knots which fastened his arms behind his back.

'Don't worry,' the Doctor said. 'I trained with the great Harry Houdini, escape artist extraordinaire.'

Blake closed his eyes but kept being kicked by the Doctor, attempting to escape from his bonds.

The dungeon reeked of mould. It was poorly lit, with burning torches hanging from the walls, casting long shadows across the cold floor. Blake's eyes gradually focused on the indistinct objects positioned around the room. An altar stood in the centre of the room in the middle of a chalk circle. It was draped with a black cloth and embroidered with a gold pentagram. An ancient chalice and a ceremonial knife stood on the altar. In the corner of the room a hen was squawking in a wooden cage.

Blake realized that they were to be part of some evil black magic ceremony.

There was the sound of a gong in the distance. A door opened. Thirteen figures entered. Each wore a different animal mask; goats, pigs, horses, many unrecognizable but all hideous, grinning and mocking beasts. The figures wore dark robes and carried small incense burners.

The final entrance was that of a huddled figure who needed to be carried into the room. It wore a goat's mask, with a single horn growing from the forehead.

'Doctor,' Blake interrupted the stranger, who was still trying to escape from the rope. He apparently hadn't noticed the figures filing into the room. 'Can you get us out of here? Now?'

The Doctor looked up. 'The problem is that I learnt this trick whilst tied up and submerged in a barrel of water. This is a little harder.'

A tall, sculpted chair was brought into the room and placed before the altar. Shapes of naked half-men half-beasts writhing in some hideous dance were carved on to the mahogany chair.

The goat's mask figure was lowered on to the chair. It signalled for the visitors to be pulled to their feet. Neither of the travellers resisted. The figure removed its mask. It was the albino.

'I am interested in you,' the albino said.

Blake was drawn to the staring pink eyes.

The albino pulled out an object, barely visible in the dark. 'What is this?'

'Do we get a number of guesses? Animal, vegetable or mineral?' the Doctor replied.

He was forcefully kicked in his stomach, and bent over groaning with the pain.

'This object was taken from you by my servants. Do not try to deceive me.'

155

'It can be of no use to you. I demand it back,' shouted the Doctor, recognizing his sonic screwdriver.

'Tonight the Fellowship meet to celebrate the return,' continued the albino. 'We have already sacrificed one unbeliever today. As the time draws nearer more shall perish; their blood will – '

'Oh no,' the Doctor said.

The albino stopped talking.

'Do you know what he's talking about?' Blake asked.

'The usual tired cliches. Any moment now he's going to tell us that we're going to be sacrificed,' said the Doctor.

A couple of blows rained on the crouching Time Lord. Blood poured from his mouth.

' – mark the return of the true masters. More and more will die to celebrate their glory.'

'No!' the Doctor stood up, and shouted at the top of his voice.

'After all, why should our victims always be female?' the albino asked.

Blake and the Doctor were pulled into the centre of the circle.

The albino was handed a small ornate chest full of white powder. He placed a small amount of the substance in his hand and one by one the worshippers knelt down and licked it like hungry animals.

The followers danced around the room, chanting in Latin. Blake recognized the Lord's Prayer spoken backwards. They were in the middle of a hideous ritual, and they were the sacrificial victims. A time to die.

The albino began to recount a guttural and frenzied incantation. The Fellowship disrobed and stood naked. The hen was taken out of the cage, held up and its throat cut. Blood dripped into the chalice. The life fluid of the dead bird was drunk. The atmosphere was strange. Blake sought a word to describe this nightmare.

Blake thought the burning incense could have been a hallucinogenic drug which was altering his perception.

The people bounding around the room appeared to be

transforming, taking on the shape and form of the animal masks they were wearing.

The Fellowship wore medallions around their necks. Due to the speed of movement and poor visibility it was difficult to see exactly what was carved on the amulets – it looked like worms, curling around each other.

'Tell me, what is this? Is this a symbol of power?' the albino spoke quietly.

'You are all fools. What you're doing is celebrating the forces of Evil,' the Doctor shouted. 'You're inviting into your lives a negative force, welcoming that which tempts us all, but transforming that emptiness, that jealousy, that hatred into a living, breeding monstrosity. I know there are terrible things out there, but that isn't an excuse for giving up on that which sustains us in this life. Although there are things that thrive on chaos and misery, we don't have to. We can make a choice between struggling on or surrendering forever to the forces of death.'

'We do not agree with your slave morality,' the albino spoke to the time traveller.

Blake looked around. Animals appeared to be bounding and bellowing around the room. The dungeon had taken on the squalid smell of the cave back in hell. Strange couplings and odd noises were rising out of the performances in the dungeon. The chanting had taken on the form of animal howls and disgusting collections of words screamed out by the blood-frenzied mob.

In the corner of the room a weird mist seemed to be forming. Blake shook his head to make sure he wasn't falling asleep. He wasn't. The followers were calling up a half-glimpsed nightmare. Blake tried to look away. A vile-smelling monstrosity was beginning to take shape in their prison. It looked like a bird with slime-encrusted feathers, three or four foot tall, standing in a pool of blood drifting across the floor.

'Don't look,' shouted the Doctor. 'It's a hallucination – It can't come through here. Although we're near a hole in time there's no way it can escape into our universe. Yet. These are just fanatics who follow the path.'

'Are you sure?' Blake shouted.

'No,' the Doctor replied.

The Doctor ran from the centre of the room loosening his hands as he fled. He had remembered what the escapologist had taught him! He grabbed a flaming torch and wielded it in front of him. One of the Fellowship moved too close to the flames and a bull's mask went up in flames. Screams of pain and ecstasy rose from the wounded man. The man fell against the altar, trying to remove the mask from his face. His hands burnt. The fire caught and spread across the ceremonial cloth.

It was an almighty conflagration. The wooden beams and ceiling were crackling in the extreme heat. Another of the Fellowship slowly moved towards the battling Time Lord. It was the strong-armed man. Blake launched his fifty-four year old body at the lumbering figure. As the strong-armed man turned towards him Blake hit him in the stomach.

The Doctor shouted at him to get out. The fire was spreading. The robes left in the circle were the next casualties of the flames.

'Get out,' the Doctor shouted again.

He bounded over to the chest containing the strange white powder. He picked it up and threw it into the flames. He moved over to the dungeon door to prevent anyone from escaping.

'Doctor, you've got to let them out,' Blake shouted.

'No,' he replied.

Blake could hardly breathe and felt that he was going to faint.

'You go,' the Doctor said, opening the door.

The air rushed in, creating a fire ball. Blake was thrown down with the force of the implosion. Fire raged all around him. The heat was overpowering. He picked himself up and staggered down a corridor.

He glanced back. The fire was creeping along the corridor behind him.

He couldn't see anything in the room and couldn't hear

any shouts or screams. All he could see and hear was the fire.

All those in the room must have perished.

He carried on, eventually finding his way to the street. He collapsed outside an old warehouse. He saw that the building itself was on fire.

And so perishes the Doctor.

He was going to miss the funny little man. He bent his head to the ground, trying to catch his breath as he listened to the warning bells of the horse-drawn fire engines, heading to the inferno.

'Day 5, 18 hours, 36 minutes and counting . . .'

The Dragonslayer had been receiving signals from the unnamed planet. Unknown to the androids, it had the ability to monitor their life functions and activities. The signals indicated that one of the shapechangers had been terminated. The more serious threat of the expanding red weed had taken over as the immediate concern of the controllers. There were now only forty-eight hours left until the craft carried out its programmed instructions. Unless it received an abort message from Nicaea its self destruction would be like the force of a sun collapsing, wrenching this star system apart.

Time continued to tick away.

'Day 5, 18 hours 37 minutes and counting . . .'

Darkness was again falling. However, the London skyline was lit up with the huge warehouse fire. Blake felt people gathering around him and staring at the warehouse now transformed into a burning pyre. The police were trying to keep the crowd away from the fire.

However, as Blake was splashed with water he realized that many of the people had come to help put out the fire. He watched as buckets were passed from the river. Dockers and warehousemen were trying to drown the fire with what were effectively thimble-fulls of water. Hundreds of people were lined up. He didn't know if they would succeed, but it showed that, even here, there were people prepared to work together for the common good.

He felt something touch his leg. And again. He lashed out with his hand but to no effect. Another tap.

'Come on. We'd better move before too many questions are asked.'

The Doctor stood in front of him waving his umbrella. He had a serious expression on his face and there were no signs that he had just escaped a raging inferno. He smiled and held up his sonic screwdriver with childish glee.

'I reclaimed it.'

'How?' Blake asked.

'How what?' the Doctor asked.

'Your clothes are untouched. You don't look like a man who's just escaped from a fire.'

'I told you. I was trained by Harry Houdini.'

'But as I remember, you were submerged in a barrel of water.'

'Yes, but it was on fire at the time. Didn't I mention that? Anyway, we need to get back to the other world.'

Blake stood. Crowds of people were rushing the other way, towards the conflagration, to try to stem the fire before it spread to the other wooden buildings by the river.

The Doctor and Blake walked down an alleyway heading back to the entrance to hell. The Doctor appeared to have an innate sense of direction. The houses all looked alike. They were three storeys high, hardly six foot apart, with broken windows repaired with paper and rags.

Whitechapel reminded the poet of a scene from Dante's *Inferno*.

His body wasn't going to take much more. He desperately needed sleep and a decent meal. After about ten minutes the Doctor turned to Blake and said, 'Where do you think we go now?'

'You're lost?' Blake raged.

The Doctor smiled. 'Shall I toss a coin?'

'No,' Blake shouted, hobbling away from the Doctor.

Suddenly he heard something, and looked up. From the darkness in front of them Blake could see a black shape bounding towards them. Its movements were deliberately slow and mannered.

'A demon,' Blake shouted.

Initially he saw only one of the hideous creatures, but more of the demons appeared out of the darkness, loping into the alley. Blake couldn't say whether the creatures were pursuing them or had their own sinister reason for haunting this part of London.

'Come on,' said the Doctor. 'We need to follow them. They've come through the hole in time. They're Hunters, scavengers around holes in time. Don't worry, they're not demons I promise you . . .'

Although Blake didn't know whether to believe the Doctor, he walked with the Time Lord, following the hideous apparitions through the streets of Whitechapel. After about ten minutes, they found themselves back where they'd first arrived in Victorian London. Several of the demons disappeared through the hole. Others flew up the sides of houses. They latched on to walls and remained motionless.

Blake turned to the Doctor. 'We'll go through together this time.'

The Doctor nodded. They matched their stride and stepped into the hole together. Blake took a last look at Victorian London. An infernal machine.

The cold sweet smell of the British countryside swept over the poet. Blake looked around. The Doctor had fallen on to plush green grass. This was neither hell nor Cambridge, 1811. The recognizable form of the monolithic slabs of Stonehenge stood in front of them, guarded by futuristic troops. A light drizzle cast a threatening hue over the day.

'Stonehenge?' Blake asked.

The Doctor looked up. 'I don't know.'

The soldiers' battle garb was different from that of the armies in Blake's time. Here they were all in uniform and

161

all carried weapons. This army tried to outfit all its soldiers. Dark green jacket and trousers, and a hard hat.

The travellers were noticed. A soldier pointed out the strangers to his commanding officer. A four-wheeled vehicle was dispatched. Blake couldn't see any form of power and assumed this was a machine-driven contraption.

'What do you think?' Blake asked.

'I think we're probably where we shouldn't be.'

'Yes.' Blake had realized that the Doctor somehow always managed to find situations where his presence started events, causing ripple effects like a pebble thrown into a pool.

The machine stopped in front of them.

Three soldiers faced them. Blake didn't recognize the uniforms or the rifles. The soldiers' expressions were business like.

'Hello,' said the Doctor.

A gun was placed to his forehead.

'United Nations Intelligence Taskforce,' a soldier said. 'You are trespassing on government property.'

The Doctor raised his arms into the air. 'I surrender.'

DAY FIVE
20:00–24:00

On the vidscreen a priest was eulogizing about the next life. The staring eyes and wild appearance – with the shaved, painted head – drew the viewer's attention to the discordant painful message. The occasional broadcasts had been taken over by the priests with their simplistic message of all-out war with the Hunters and, the more disturbing subtext, of the people needing to repent and place their fate in the hands of the Prime Mover.

Academician Brown sat at his desk. The vidscreen image once again went blank. He wondered if this would be the last time. He looked across at General Kopyion. Their world had been taken over by an insanity.

The return journey from the Academy had been quiet. They had passed lone people wandering around, screaming at the moon. Mobs hunted in packs, smashing windows and looting goods. Kopyion had sat opposite him in the hovercar, contemplating the momentous events unravelling on the planet. Brown felt desperation. He had spoken to a world no longer able to listen.

He had seen a man being chased by two Riotsville hoodlums. They had cornered him in an alley. A light from the upstairs window of a nearby house had come on. It had shone on the thugs who had turned and run. Brown thought about how lucky that man had been.

The armoured carriers had started to move through the city, to 'restore calm'. There were no reports of any response to this show of force. However, at this time of night most people would be asleep, and a response would only be felt in the cold light of day.

Kopyion walked around the room. He picked up an old ornament: a serpent winding itself around a globe;

an appropriate image. Brown felt that Nicaea was now descending into the chaos he felt inside himself, that had torn him apart since his wife's death. He wanted to scream and shout, beat the wall and call down the forces of destruction. Why wouldn't these feelings go away? He looked at Kopyion, loitering as if he wanted to say something.

Brown spoke first. 'It's all over.'

'Why?' Kopyion asked.

Brown was puzzled by the enigmatic figure. He didn't know how to reply to the open-ended question. After a few moments' silence Kopyion shrugged his shoulders and walked off, down the stairs. His footsteps echoed as he left.

Brown was alone, again.

Carlson felt sick. The ride in the air transporter had been bumpy due to air missiles fired in their direction. The missiles were military equipment and confirmed that the army had descended into chaos.

As they flew over the capital, returning the Archon to the Imperial Palace, the sight below was of units of soldiers fighting hand to hand battles with other military units. General Bourbollon obviously could not count on the support of the entire military. Carlson was aware of conflicting reports: that Bourbollon had been assassinated earlier in the day; that he had committed suicide rather than face capture by freedom fighters. Neither report was confirmed. The streets were rife with rumour and fear. Armoured carriers had taken up positions in the east of the city but the western approaches seemed to be still subject to heavy fighting.

The Archon looked tired and drawn. He stared out of the craft and looked at the insect sized life forms below. He told the major he feared that in retiring to the palace he was imprisoning himself and would never be able to escape back to the real world.

The major wanted to return home, curl up with his wife, and lock the door.

The high-speed craft made quick progress to the safety of the Palace. Android security police guarded the area. They checked the two men as they left the air transporter. The major walked to the main door.

The Archon's young daughter stood waiting for her father.

'Daddy, daddy,' she shouted, throwing her arms around him. She was carrying a small doll. He held his daughter in his arms and kissed her. The major smiled.

'Daddy,' she asked, 'no-one will take my dolls away, will they?'

'No,' replied the Archon. 'We're safe here.'

The major watched them walking down the corridor, holding hands.

Bernice had tried to explain to her android companion about the man who had saved her from drowning in the quicksand. He gave no reply but hadn't believed her. *She* didn't believe it. A man, whose face she had been unable to see, had suddenly appeared, pulled her out of the shit, and then disappeared. In twentieth century slang, this planet was 'doing her head in'.

She kept close to Spike, making sure he didn't wander out of her sight. They were moving towards the space station. For over five kilometres they had seen debris and signs of an ancient fireball which had scorched the earth. The station resembled the early Earth Pioneer space stations which had been built outwards from the home planet to the stars. They had helped the refuelling and restocking of colonists' ships fleeing the overpopulation, radiation and ozone poisoning. However, this was ten times the size of the Terran designs and had been built centuries before man had even discovered fire.

She looked at Spike. He too was curious. She asked if they could explore the craft. He nodded in agreement. She knew that it wasn't desire for the acquisition of knowledge that drove him, but the programmed need to find the bomb. He must suspect that the bomb, or the other shapechanger, could be found within the station.

'You don't still think that I'm one of the shapechangers do you?' Bernice asked.

'I don't know what to believe,' he replied.

'You fool.' Bernice went to slap him on the back. He responded with lightning reflexes, turning to grab her hand. She stopped, and he completely missed grabbing hold of her.

He hadn't much longer before he ceased to function. She felt angry. She didn't know what about. Perhaps the sight of his body visibly aging in front of her. We all have to die, she thought. But this seems so purposeless.

'I'm sorry,' she said.

'No, I am sorry,' Spike said, with a vague embarrassment. 'I did not know . . .'

She walked towards the craft. She didn't look back at him.

The klaxons were sounding. Bells were ringing and lights were flashing. The major ran through the front door of the Palace, heading for the throne room. The air carrier had returned him as quickly as possible. At the entrance, androids saluted him. He replied falteringly with the customary, 'I serve'.

He passed the little girl. She was in her nightdress, bare legs and large slippers. She didn't have her dolly. She was standing in the corridor, crying and alone. She was saying repeatedly, 'Daddy'. He wanted to stop and hold her, but carried on. The corridors of the Palace were otherwise empty.

He entered the throne room. Various androids guarded the door. The room was hectic. Flashlights indicated the taking of photographs. Some security police were measuring distances; others were looking for clues. They seemed faintly absurd. Initially, he couldn't see the body, and then he noticed the tell-tale blanket draped over a shape on the floor. He walked over and pulled the blanket off the body.

The Archon was dead. He had been crucified on to the floor and, like the last victim, had been alive when this had occurred. There was a terrible look of horror on his face. Carlson replaced the blanket over the dead man.

This had been the supreme ruler of the Althosian system. The major was sweating. He thought it was because of the heat. He looked around. People were milling. They had investigated many murders before, but this was not a murder; this was the destruction of the entire planetary system of government. There was no natural successor to the Archon. It would have been down to the Academy to appoint the next ruler of the Seven Planets. The Academy was defunct. There was no hope. The room radiated a complete emptiness.

Suddenly, the major noticed General Kopyion sitting in a corner of the room, watching him. In a daze, Carlson walked through the crowd and up to his senior officer.

'I . . .' he began to say, then stopped, unaware of who exactly it was he was now pledging allegiance to. 'How long have you been here?'

Kopyion didn't answer. His eyes stared into the room.

'Sir, what happens now?'

Kopyion turned to look at him. 'Get the alarms turned off. I'm getting a headache.'

'Sir.' Carlson stood facing Kopyion. He didn't know what to say. He just wanted to go, find his wife and return home. 'Who's done this?'

'I gave you an order, major.'

'Sir,' he replied, wandering off to find the alarm controls.

The weather was deteriorating. Salisbury Plain had changed little since Blake's day. Open green pastures and the distinctive monoliths gathered together in a circle.

Blake had stopped off in Salisbury one fierce night, some two hundred years before, and had wondered about the purpose of the stone circle then. Some argued that it was a druidical sacrificial place of worship; others that it was a gigantic cosmic clock. Blake was not surprised to be told by the Doctor that its origin and purpose remained unknown.

The fresh air made a welcome change from the polluted Victorian London atmosphere. But the skies were darkening and the rain was pouring down over the fields.

The Doctor and Blake had been escorted to a small workman's shed. They were not locked in, but a guard was posted outside to make sure they didn't escape.

The Doctor explained to the colonel apparently in charge of the troops that he was the scientific advisor for UNIT. He suggested that the military man could contact either a Brigadier Lethbridge-Stewart or a Brigadier Bambera for clarification of his position. He added that it had been some years since he had been back in England. The colonel had gone off to contact Geneva. The travellers were not told why the military had cordoned off part of Salisbury Plain and were arresting anyone who strayed into the exclusion zone.

Blake found being a passenger in the mechanical 'land-rovers', with their noise and billowing fumes, frightening. The pace of life seemed much quicker. People were running around, bellowing orders, and there was a constant chattering of 'radios' and military equipment.

'I'm worried,' said the Doctor.

'You told the truth?' Blake asked.

'Yes. But this is my favourite place in the universe. From all my travels, and my journeys across the galaxies, I always return to this country, in this time zone. And now it's under threat.'

'It is so peaceful here.' Blake wondered why a man who could choose anywhere and anytime in creation would pick twentieth century England.

'There have been invasions before on this "insignificant" little planet. But this is something terrible.' The Doctor stared into an inner space.

'You're beginning to regain your memory?' Blake asked.

'No. It's because of the void in my mind that I'm worried.' He changed the subject. 'Do you ever have the feeling that we're being watched?'

'No,' Blake lied.

'We all need our own security. Somewhere safe.' The Doctor had again been taken over by his thoughts. Blake felt it was like the muse which inspired him, and dictated from a hidden recess that he must write and what he had to write.

The colonel returned. He was in his late forties, dash of red hair, full moustache, six foot four and Highland accent. He had contacted UNIT HQ and had confirmed that for a period in the 1970s and 1980s there had been a scientific advisor to Brigadier Lethbridge-Stewart. A wanderer, an iconoclast, whose mind had only been matched by his eccentricity. The colonel said that he had received extraordinary instructions. It did not matter what the man looked like, but he should be listened to. If the Doctor was present it meant there was an extreme danger to this planet.

Blake was amazed at the discussion and how these men could talk about a whole planet in one conversation; in his day it was not unusual for a conversation to centre solely on one part of London, and only in times of war was England ever considered as a single entity under threat.

The Doctor had explained that in 1969 a man had walked on the moon; that unmanned space flights to other stars had been sent out in the 1970s and towards the end of the twentieth century manned space flights had visited other planets in the solar system.

The Doctor and his companion were led across a field to an archaeological dig. Colonel Philips explained that they had thought initially that they had discovered a danger similar to that which had caused the Hob's Lane disaster.

A group of men and women in multi-coloured coats had dug a hole in the ground, which the military had then sealed off. Blake couldn't understand what they were doing. The explanation that they were looking for bones and relics of ancient races puzzled the poet. Who cared? The colonel explained that the reason for the exclusion zone would become clear once they saw what had been found in the excavation.

The Doctor whistled a short, sharp sound in disbelief. The excavation was over a mile round and about twenty foot under the surrounding land level.

'What the hell is it?' Blake asked.

Inside the excavation were the bones of some huge creature. It looked like a dragon, or some type of crocodile. It appeared to have had wings, and a number of spikes sticking out of its back. If this was one creature, it had stood over half a mile high.

'Is this a dinosaur?' Blake remembered the much smaller pterodactyls which had attacked them in hell.

'No.' They were joined by the chief archaeologist, Professor Roberts. He was a small stubby man with glasses and a trimmed dark beard. He was smoking a lethal smelling cigarette. The colonel introduced him to the Doctor.

'And your name, sir?' the colonel asked.

'William Blake.'

'No relation to the poet?' the archaeologist asked.

'What poet?' Blake replied, not familiar with any other poet with his name.

The archaeologist explained that the skeleton's place in the soil strata and its size meant that it was not a dinosaur.

'A long time ago . . .' muttered the Doctor quietly to himself. 'Colonel, you must destroy this now. Destroy the skeleton, pulverize the bones. Now!' He had begun to shout.

'But Doctor, this is an extraterrestrial life-form, many thousands of years old. Look around the remains. There are clearly the signs of a huge fire. This creature crash-landed on our planet many thousands of years ago.' The archaeologist was excitedly describing his theories.

'If this thing flew through space, is millennia old, is many miles in size, then you can have no idea of its power. You can't even know if it *is* dead.'

'What?' the colonel replied. 'I can *see* it's dead.'

'No, you can see it's lying dormant. There are a number

of species in the universe which don't suffer death as you understand the concept. You must destroy it,' shouted the Doctor, 'before it's too late.'

Colonel Philips shook his head. 'No, Doctor. My orders are for this skeleton to be taken to the Natural History Museum in London, where scientific tests will reveal more about its true nature. I'm very surprised your attitude is that we should cover it up and hide it away rather than try and elucidate its value for science. You are a scientist.'

The book lay on the table in front of them. Brown was too excited to pick it up. He had ordered the William Ashbless poetry over a month ago, and now it had finally arrived. He had made some artificial coffee, with added caffeine, and treated the antique dealer to a rare cup of the banned drink.

Members of the Academy turned a blind eye to the black marketeers, because the Seven Planets needed food and supplies and the corporations wouldn't trade with independent worlds. The black marketeers also smuggled in cultural items, originating in the much-desired late twentieth century, for the rich collectors who invariably held positions of power on the planet.

Mann was tired, and still thanking the Academician for managing to free him from the security police. He had travelled across the city from the suburbs to the apartments of the ruling elite.

He told Brown that he had seen some soldiers breaking into a shop, stealing worthless electrical equipment and shooting the protesting store owner. Looting had become a serious problem and there were no food shops which had any stocks left; most were burnt out and vandalized. He had also caught a glimpse of a gang of young kids from Riotsville moving through the streets, looking for some action. He avoided them and carried on. Near the residential apartments he had seen an exploded armoured carrier, and more dead soldiers. Explosions and gunfire from the east side of the city suggested an attempt to

171

retake the civilian centres was underway. However, the military were not having much success so far.

Brown was happy. The book was all he had been waiting for, and all was going according to plan. The book of poetry had been produced from real trees and the pages had a feel of genuine paper. The cover was made of leather and went back to the days when mankind used animals for food and clothing. He smelt the book.

'The value of this book is beyond money,' said Brown. 'The book is so rare.'

'It would be unheard of to damage such a priceless antique.' Brown smiled.

'The police didn't touch it. They left it in the shop.'

'You've done well,' Brown said to Mann.

He tore the cover off the book. Inside were three narrow bags full of a white powder.

He picked up a letter opener from his table and slipped the blade into one of the bags. Some of the white substance fell on to the floor. He sniffed and tasted the substance.

'Are you going to join me?' he asked, going to a drawer to collect a pipe.

Mann nodded. The pipe was filled with water, heated over a blue flame and a small quantity of the substance placed in.

They took it in turns to breathe in the smoke, as the substance sizzled with a malicious delight. Mann sat back on his chair, closed his eyes and began to dream. Brown started to giggle to himself, put his feet up on the sofa and waited for the images and feelings to take possession of him.

Out in space, through the sea of darkness, a rainbow of colours was exploding. Unimaginable shapes were swirling and lapping the shores of distant worlds. And then a bright light pulling forwards, hurtling through fiery reds and burning yellows; shadows of violet cast over undiscovered star streams. The speed was intense, but it was a feeling of being every shape and object within view; of being all of creation at once.

Brown knew that the universe was his own imagination, and that he just had to send thoughts and entire galaxies and peoples would no longer exist. He shouted out, in a low deep voice, that he was the Lord of Creation. He could see the sounds turn into dancing musical notes. He would have his vengeance on this meaningless universe, and in the banality of his imagination he would wipe out humanity. He would exorcise the anger from within himself, and destroy.

His vision was starting to cloud over, and take on a red tinge. No, this is not the way it should be! He wanted to be happy. But the anger and the fear were taking possession of him.

'Aaaarghh . . .' he screamed out. He was not alone in his dreams. Where was he? Who was he? The red death had taken over all in front of him but there were shapes moving towards him.

There were teeth all around him, snapping and gnawing. Intense close-ups of hideous faces; eyes staring, hundreds of eyes; sometimes they resembled dragons, other times worms. They had a putrid smell and faces of beasts.

Brown sat up off the sofa. He was soaked in sweat and shivering. He felt the things were still there, in the room. He was frightened, more frightened than ever before. A shape moved on the other side of the room. It was a shadow cast by the single lamp in the room. The curtain was swaying; the breeze of the open window. Mann lay still on the chair. Brown stood up and went over to see how the antique dealer was feeling. He was completely still.

'Mann,' he said quietly. There was no reply. He repeated his words and touched the body. Mann's head rolled to the side. Brown pushed him again. There was a wet feel to the body. Brown's hand was covered in something. He looked closer. Blood was pouring from the antique dealer's chest. Brown felt the forehead and opened the eyelids. Mann was dead. Brown examined the dead man's chest. He had been shot.

And then he heard a rustling sound. He stared into the dark recesses of the room. There was a figure standing in the corner by an open window. The sound of a gun being cocked; whoever it was had got hold of his antique gun.

'Listen, whoever you are – ' He was interrupted as the gun was fired three times. He felt the first bullet tear into his chest and was thrown against the wall.

DAY SIX
00:00–04:00

The major walked around the room. There had been two
more murders. The victims lay dead in the apartment.
Although many people were being killed daily, in the civil
war, this was an unusual crime. One of the victims was
the opposition leader. The other victim was the main
suspect in the ritualistic murders. Apart from the identity
of the second victim there seemed to be no connection
with his investigation. Last night's murders had not been
bizarre slayings. Both victims had been shot a number of
times by an antique revolver known to have belonged to
one of the victims. The gun was missing.

After his speech the night before in the Academy,
Brown had become an extremely unpopular figure
amongst the ruling elite. His assassination was predictable, although how the murderer passed by the android
security guards had yet to be explained. Carlson could
think of no reason why Bulbir Singh Mann should be the
target of assassins; presumably he had been in the way.

Although Carlson felt there was some connection with
the chaos and anarchy erupting over the Althosian system
he was sure none of the Freedom Party supporters would
have devised such a ruthless method for annihilating the
elite. He wondered if Brown had been murdered by the
military.

Carlson looked over the Academician's desk. An
almost finished game of snakes and ladders was laid out
amongst top secret briefing papers. One of the counters
had fallen down a snake to the bottom of the pit.

Kopyion looked at the sprawled body of the Academician.

'Cover it up,' he ordered one of the androids.

175

Carlson had been wondering for some time what was actually going on. Kopyion had expressed a great deal of interest in these killings but had not passed on all the information available to him. Even now, with Nicaea descending into a maelstrom of violence and recrimination, the head of the Justice Police was concentrating his energies on a series of grizzly murders. General Kopyion showed little interest in the events of the civil war, even with confirmed reports of a hovertrain being hijacked and two female Academicians having their homes broken into and being raped by soldiers.

Carlson wondered if Kopyion knew which side he was on, and was trying to remain neutral in the conflict.

The major pointed to a white substance on the floor.

'What do you think it is?' He bent over to scrape some of the substance off the floor.

'Don't touch it,' warned Kopyion.

'Whatever it was, it came from this book. See, the cover has been forcibly removed.' Carlson showed his superior a torn book which had been thrown into the waste disposal.

'It's drugs,' said Kopyion. 'Mann is a black market dealer who it's believed has been smuggling drugs into Nicaea.'

'What? You didn't mention this before.' Carlson was increasingly irritated with his superior officer.

'You aren't the only member of the Justice Police,' Kopyion replied in a cold, dry manner as if rehearsing a speech. 'We've been investigating this drug ring for some months. Annalisa Sellen was one of the undercover officers responsible for the operation. It was believed someone from the Academy was helping Mann with the finance and distribution of the drugs. We've discovered who that was. I suggest the investigation is now closed.'

Kopyion walked off. He stopped to let the body of his friend Brown be taken past him. As the stretcher passed by he pulled back the blanket. He uttered something under his breath, let the blanket drop, and hobbled down the steps.

176

Carlson watched him. There were many questions which the general had failed to answer in his summary of these crimes. Who had killed Brown? Where were the drugs now and what was the purpose of the ritualistic murders?

The investigation was far from over.

Torrential rain was drowning the countryside. The Doctor and Blake sat on the side of a hill watching the bones being carried from the archaeological dig to a large mechanical transporter. Due to their weight and size the ancient fossils were handled with military precision as they were placed inside the monstrous fire-breathing cart. Blake was very wary of the snorting machine which his travelling companion described as a 'juggernaut'. The machines made their own bilious sound which drowned the natural noise of the Earth. The Doctor stood up, taking in the distant sights of the great plain.

Blake recited the two lines of his poem, 'Milton'.

'And did those feet in Ancient times,
Walk upon England's mountains green?'

Rain ran down his face. He had not imagined, when he'd written the poem four years before, that he would ever be standing here, thinking of the Fall of Man.

The archaeologist was directing the loading of the bones. The Doctor walked over to him. The rain made the lifting slippery and dangerous.

'Why did you start digging here?' the Doctor asked.

Roberts looked nervous but kept a fixed smile.

'You were looking for the creature,' the Doctor realized. 'You knew it was here.' Roberts walked away. 'How? How could you have known where it was?'

The UNIT soldiers continued to load the bones. The task took some considerable time as each bone was labelled according to a blueprint held by the archaeologist. The Doctor paced around the excavation measuring the depth and imprint of the relics. He seemed to be looking for something. Blake suspected that it was a strand of memory.

'This is all wrong,' he shouted out, as the doors of the juggernaut were sealed.

Bernice had never been down so many corridors before she met the Doctor. It appeared to be an occupational hazard, walking down dark and dingy – or even brightly lit – corridors, waiting for strange creatures to pounce out at unexpected moments.

She was actually becoming quite blasé about the dangers lurking on their travels. She walked through the space station shouting, 'Yoohoo, we're here', and opening long-forgotten cupboards and going 'Boo'. Spike looked at her as if she was a complete idiot.

The space station was dead. It was a broken hulk, millennia of dust particles covering the displays and floors. A complex lighting system had once worked, but now the only illumination was from the gaps in the roof which allowed streams of sunlight to pour through into the empty, lifeless environment. There appeared to be miles of corridors intersecting, criss-crossing and going nowhere.

Certain parts of the station seemed to have been attacked and ripped apart. Most of the handles and doors had been removed, and mounds of bones seemed to be in their place. Spike said that it looked like Hunters had attacked the craft.

'What are Hunters?' Bernice asked.

'They are a hostile race of parasites, which raid unprotected interplanetary craft, attack lone colonists, abduct small children and animals,' Spike said. 'The Justice Police's main task is to protect the colony worlds from these creatures.'

'You've met these creatures?' Bernice asked.

'Yes. Many times. I once had to have a leg replaced when a couple of Hunters tore mine off. I once defended a small village on Trieste from over a hundred of these things. There were twenty people, including children, in

178

this new colony, and they were all slaughtered. When we first arrived the Hunters existed in far greater numbers, and were suicidal in their assaults on some of our military attack ships; they were controlled, though.'

Bernice didn't like the sound of this. 'Controlled?'

'Bacteriological weapons. They wiped out the majority of them. Within a couple of years only a few hundred of them survived. Unfortunately, they have continued to breed.'

Bernice looked again at the bones. 'What are they like?'

'Big, hairy, wings and lots of teeth. In hand to hand combat it would take two, perhaps three, androids to subdue just one of them. And I say subdue. I am like a David to their Goliath. We need advanced weaponry to destroy them.'

'Friendly creatures, then?' Bernice asked.

'It is said they can smell blood many kilometres away.'

Spike sounded terribly bitter in his description of the Hunters, as if he had a personal stake in their destruction.

'Out here on the frontiers of space there are many dangers.' Spike carried on walking down the faceless, uniform corridor.

The initial radio message had beggared belief. An aeroplane, carrying over five hundred passengers, had reported that they were under attack. On the slow descent to Bristol airport a creature had attached itself to one of the wings. Two more of the creatures hovered around the craft, walking over the wings and flashing their teeth at the hysterical passengers. They then began to play a game which involved tearing pieces off the aircraft and hurtling them at each other. Passengers were screaming and shouting. Blake could hear the pilot demanding advice and assistance, knowing that it would never come.

UNIT had been routinely monitoring the signals in the area and had picked up the SOS messages from the passenger aircraft. The ground control asked the crew to describe the creatures – bat-like, horrible – and then the

179

sound went dead. The plane had gone into a steep descent and an explosion ripped the air.

Blake and the Doctor travelled with the UNIT personnel, in two landrovers, towards the crash site. The juggernaut followed behind at a more respectable pace, through the waterlogged Wiltshire countryside. The torrential rain made driving hazardous. They had been heading back towards London when the strange conflict in the sky had been picked up by UNIT.

Blake knew that the creatures were the spawn of hell. It was the voices coming from the little boxes, and the concept of man flying between America and England in a few hours, that he found difficult to grasp. The Doctor's vague descriptions of bits of wire conducting sound waves through the air, and speed allowing gravity to be defeated, only succeeded in confusing the poet. He knew the Doctor was trying to be helpful, but it was all too unbelievable.

The landrover ride made him feel nauseous. Travelling at a speed of a hundred miles an hour made him worry that he would leave the safety of God's Earth. He closed his eyes, and thought of the nature of the world, the past and the future. The world of the twentieth century was more alien to him than the more recognizable vision of hell.

The journey finished at the fallen aircraft. Although parts were scattered over the surrounding fields, the main body of the plane had landed in one piece. The Doctor said it was a miracle that the pilot had managed to steer the plane down at all.

In a field in the middle of the countryside, ambulances and fire engines, with droning sirens and flashing blue lights, watched helplessly as the demons continued to attack the half-destroyed plane. Passengers screamed, but the Hunters, now increased in numbers to twenty or thirty, flew down and sank their claws and teeth into the injured and dying.

The colonel ordered his men to line up and commence 'rapid fire', but the twentieth century weaponry failed to combat the creatures. They treated it as a game.

As the creatures soared up and down, their laughter began to take on an eerie and mournful tone.

The juggernaut arrived. The soldiers escorting it used their weapons to help destroy the creatures.

Men and women from the ambulances risked their lives to rescue tormented souls. Some were immediately picked up by the demons, whilst others managed again and again to risk their lives before falling to the persistent attacks of the creatures from hell. Blake wanted to go and help, but was stopped by the Doctor.

'We have to go,' the Doctor said, pointing to the juggernaut.

Blake looked at the traveller with surprise. The Doctor had no intention of intervening to prevent further loss of life.

'There's no more we can do,' the Doctor hinted at an apology. 'We must return those bones to the otherworld.'

The traveller strolled off towards the juggernaut. The soldiers had moved closer to the aeroplane, desperately trying to fight the flying demons.

'Can you drive one of these?' the Doctor asked.

'No,' replied Blake.

'Never mind, I've always wanted to have a go.'

The Doctor's response gave the poet no confidence, but choice was limited; he either went along with the Doctor or he remained behind. It was the lesser of two evils.

'Going somewhere?'

The archaeologist appeared from the back of the juggernaut. He was smiling, but holding a gun out in front of him. His eyes seemed glazed over and the smile was stretched and impenetrable.

'There's no point in me explaining what you've actually got there, is there?' the Doctor asked.

The archaeologist shook his head. 'No.'

'And you're going to do all in your power to prevent us taking the remains of this creature,' the Doctor continued.

The archaeologist nodded. As he did, the Doctor moved forward, and with a lightning speed knocked the gun out of the archaeologist's hand with his umbrella. The Doctor leapt forward and became entangled with the archaeologist. As they fought, the archaeologist's shirt was torn, revealing a medallion hanging around his chest. It was a similar medallion to those worn by the Fellowship in Victorian London. A worm curled around the globe.

The gun had landed within a few inches of Blake. The poet picked it up and handed it over to the Time Lord.

'Come on,' said the Doctor. Blake climbed into the cab, followed by the Doctor. The archaeologist didn't move.

'There is no escape,' the archaeologist barked.

The juggernaut started with a cough and splutter, was thrown into gear and began to move off down the narrow road. The archaeologist ran in front of them and stood in the middle of the road. He wasn't going to move.

The Doctor threw the juggernaut into second gear and advanced.

Still no move.

The archaeologist had no intention of moving. As the truck was about to hit him, the Doctor turned the steering wheel sharply and drove along the hedge, avoiding the cursing figure.

Blake took a last look at the soldiers using high-powered explosives against the demons. It was a blood-bath, with few of the passengers still alive, and the forces of order and reason badly outnumbered. Soon all the passengers and soldiers would be dead.

The archaeologist stood watching them with that fixed grin, staring into their souls.

'Don't worry,' said the Doctor.

The juggernaut was building up speed and, looking down, it was easier to see where the road was clear and safe to travel.

The juggernaut passed uneventfully down the country lanes back to the hole in space and time. Blake felt tired and sick. He found it difficult to see what progress had been made since his time.

What was the future of the human race?

182

He looked at the Doctor, concentrating on trying to steer the mechanical transporter. He looked like he was enjoying it, although he kept making mistakes, forcing the juggernaut to shudder and shake to a standstill.

'What is going to happen, Doctor?' Blake asked.

'About what?'

'The demons.'

'They'll return back to their own world once they've had their fun. No-one will ever acknowledge what's happened today. The Earth has been visited many times in its history, but it's all been covered up. The bodies of the victims will be burnt or lost,' the Doctor said in a matter of fact manner.

'And us?'

'Just have hope . . .'

The juggernaut thundered through the countryside, returning to Salisbury Plain. The Doctor found the porthole to the otherworld almost instinctively. He slowed the lorry down and ground to a halt. 'You don't have to come,' he said.

Blake nodded, knowing there was no choice.

'What's there?' he had to ask.

'My past . . .' said the Doctor, putting the juggernaut into gear and driving into the hole.

The journey was almost at an end. The dark castle lay within an hour's walk. Although Swarf indicated all was going according to plan, Chopra knew this was not true. He sensed the deadness paralysing the planet, could feel the chaos and destruction unfolding on the distant worlds of the Althosian system.

He could not tell if there was any connection between the events on this minor planet and those on the outer worlds. However, he knew of the sacred prophecies.

The Dark Times were again descending over the universe. He didn't need to throw the stones. The message was the same, again and again. The collapse.

Swarf stood over him. The dwarf wanted to move on.

'I see beyond the veil of illusion,' Chopra said.

'No,' Swarf replied.

'You do not believe in the supernatural?'

'No.'

'Then what do you think is the purpose of life?'

Swarf changed the subject. 'Tell me of my brother.'

'He is . . .' Chopra could think of nothing more to say.

'Dead?' Swarf roared.

'I am sorry . . .'

'Then he failed and I wasn't told.'

Swarf struck him across the face and grabbed the stones. He clenched his fist and crushed them. He threw the pulverized contents into the air.

Chopra stared. His stones, destroyed. How would he survive without them? The shapechanger grabbed Chopra's hair and pulled him off the ground.

'I feel an emptiness,' Chopra said. 'You must beware. It is a paralysis spreading across this world.'

Swarf ignored him. 'Where are the androids and the women?'

'They are close by,' Chopra spluttered. 'I can feel one of the women and an android within a kilometre of our position. They are walking through the space station. I can see through her eyes. But they are not the enemy.'

The shapechanger dropped him on to the ground. He screamed, and his body was ripped open and transformed into a jet black bird.

'I will join you at the castle. I have some unfinished business. Nothing must stop us now.' The bird squawked and launched itself skywards.

Chopra watched the bird fly up to the heavens.

Bernice still had a feeling of being watched. She was jumpy and had at one point been startled by her own shadow. She had the feeling that someone or something was watching her every movement.

She remembered when she was younger and had received religious indoctrination at school. There was always this idea that people lived on in some form after death, looking after you. She had liked that idea, and thought somehow that her mother kept a watchful eye on her.

'Hello, again,' said a voice.

She looked up. She had wandered off again.

Her mysterious saviour had returned. She felt close to him, although she couldn't quite see his features or his choice of clothes.

'What are you doing here?' he asked.

'I don't know.' She hadn't thought of a reason for her being here. She had followed the android hoping that the Doctor would reappear and save them. 'I'm looking for the Doctor.'

'The Time Lord?'

'Yes. Did I tell you that?'

The figure didn't reply.

'What are *you* doing here?' she asked.

'I'm protecting you,' he replied.

'From what?'

'The shapechanger.'

She was puzzled. This wasn't the type of conversation she particularly enjoyed. 'What are you talking about?'

'Tell me about your journeys,' the figure said.

'Look, I'd rather not. Spike!' she shouted out. 'Listen, it's not that I don't trust you, but . . . Spike!'

'He can't respond.'

'Oh my God!' Bernice shouted, as it dawned on her what was going on.

She ran down the corridor. And another corridor. Why do all these corridors look alike? 'Spike, Spike!' she shouted.

And then she heard a noise. It sounded like a body being thrown against the wall.

'Spike, I'm coming,' she shouted.

She turned the next corner.

She ran.

Spike lay propped against a wall. A green liquid was pouring from his broken and battered body. He had been terminated.

Standing over him was a lizard-like creature, dark

185

green, two legs, tyrannosaurus-featured head, and a huge tail which had inflicted most of the damage. The tail swung again and banged the android's head against the wall. Spike's head fell forwards and hit the floor.

'What do I smell?' the shapechanger said, turning towards her.

'You bastard,' she shouted.

It looked at her. She was now the prey. Its body began to shuffle up the corridor towards her.

She ran.

She opened the first door off the corridor. Another door lay on the other side of the room. She ran over and pulled the door. It was locked and not budging. She pulled as hard as she could. Damn. She'd have to go back. She turned. It was there in the doorway, sprouting tentacles from its tree-like chest. It stepped through the door and the tentacles started to slide along the walls towards her.

She glanced around the room. It was empty apart from a few chairs and a couple of tables. She had to defend herself somehow. She picked up one of the chairs. The tentacles were sliding closer to her.

She wielded the chair in front of her, trying to parry the approaching menace. As the creature moved within five metres of her, she held on to the chair with both hands and ran straight at the creature's unprotected stomach area. However, instead of driving the chair into the lumbering reptile, which would stop her impetus, she sidestepped, jumped past the creature and carried on running to the door.

Back in the corridor she ran to Spike. He was dead. Well, you're on your own now girl, she thought. She looked down at the body and felt sadness.

'Woman,' the thing shouted.

She ran. Turning the next corner she saw a hole in the roof, where the sunlight was streaming in. Hearing the slithering sound behind her she jumped up and pulled herself through the roof. It was a tight squeeze and she tore her jacket. She lay on the roof looking through the artificial skylight.

The creature was coming closer. As it moved beneath the hole it stopped. And then she saw a strip of her jacket stuck on the jagged edge of the hole. The creature was right below her, and if it looked up . . . She would have to lean over. It's now or never. She stretched over and pulled the material off the torn metal.

It turned towards the roof. She stared at it and held her breath. It wasn't moving. One of the tentacles began to move up and pushed through the hole.

And then there was a sound from somewhere else in the space station.

It hadn't seen her. The tentacle retracted quickly. The creature slithered away down the corridor.

She saw the creature disappear and she breathed again.

After a few moments she climbed down to the space station and ran off in the opposite direction to the shape-changer.

'Check to you, but it's not mate. Not yet anyway,' Bernice said to herself.

Part Three

DAY SIX
04:00–08:00

The red weed was taking possession of the surface of the planet. As Thomas watched, he saw the raging torrent of the river turn into a glacier of red ice, frozen in time. The trees and shrubs wavering in the wind had stilled and now resembled a child's Plasticine world.

It reminded him of when he had guarded a colonial nursery, after an unexpected attack by Hunters had resulted in the abduction of two small infants. The class had seen their friends carried off to a certain death. He had looked at the children's modelling and their puzzling drawings of oversized objects – single, primary colours and minute figures dwarfed by the chaotic world around them. The children didn't talk about the kidnapping, but kept glancing out of the windows and stopped trusting the adults who looked after them.

The weed was only a few metres from where Ell had slept. It was now creeping over to the edge of the escarpment. Thomas looked over the marshlands which showed no sign of impending doom. He was sure it was only a matter of time.

On the final part of their walk they had passed by numerous strange and wondrous animals which had been frozen as they ate, slept or strolled. There was no pain or suffering, just the overwhelming image of the red death. They had also seen migratory birds in the sky directly above the paralysis, suddenly stop and remain suspended in the air. This fate could well await them.

Military training provided androids with a range of survival skills including the basic knowledge of how to make a shelter and a parachute. As many of the battles with the Hunters were either fought on inhospitable and barren asteroids or in the upper atmospheres of colonial planets, both pieces of knowledge were essential for survival.

He had adapted the parachute design to produce a homemade hang-glider. Gliders were regularly used by androids in battles with Hunters. However, the gliders were usually fitted with a range of Kill weapons to give the android the extra edge. This glider looked sturdy enough, but he couldn't be certain that it would return to the ground safely.

He had prised apart various parts of the forest around them to build the glider. The artificial trees were constructed from metal and hard plastic; with his superhuman strength he had bent the materials into the necessary shape. To produce a sail he had ripped apart his military uniform.

Ell looked with horror at the makeshift glider. She didn't like flying. Thomas said that he was going and if she wished to remain behind, then that was up to her.

'You're all I've got,' she said, resigning herself to her fate.

The glider wasn't built for two. He strapped Ell in. He would cling on to the craft and try to steer it.

He ran off the cliff and leapt into the air. The weight of the glider and the woman slowed him down, but he could feel the warm air currents. The glider rose up into the atmosphere.

Ell screamed.

The skies around them were dark and oppressive. He closed his mind for a silent prayer, but his thoughts kept returning to the danger that he and the woman now faced.

He looked again at the woman. She was clinging desperately to the hang-glider. The glider circled the escarpment and was carried with the warm air currents into the upper atmosphere.

Ell was in the wrong place and he felt sorry for her.

His mind was still trying to work out the puzzle she had set him. She had asked him about the planet. Why were some of the objects around them fake? Some of the trees, the vegetation and the animals were mechanical creations of Mirage Enterprises.

He could sense the Form Manipulator working to disguise the real world around him. He must place his trust in the Prime Mover.

This was not the time for prayer. He could not concentrate. He nudged Ell. She opened her eyes and cursed him for disturbing her silent thoughts. He was in pursuit of the shapechanger. As the only android left the success of the mission was down to him.

Ell looked from the glider to the escarpment. 'I'm not sure I can manage this.'

He didn't need to see the look on her face. Her body was trembling with fear. After the death of her husband, and surviving the destruction of her only means home, the woman had difficulties keeping up with him. If they had climbed down the side of the escarpment he had no doubt that she would not have made it.

Sometimes she seemed a little too useless.

She screamed again. She had seen something. Thomas had thought at first that it was a shadow. But now he was certain – there was a Hunter in the skies with them. He could hear the wings cracking, like whips beating the air. He couldn't turn round.

'Look,' he shouted to her. 'The entire escarpment is covered with the red weed.'

As she looked down he felt a tug at the upper sail, and saw a flash of a wing.

It had come in for the attack. A face suddenly lunged at him, its teeth bared.

He heard a loud tear. The sail had been bitten in two. The Hunter's razor sharp teeth now turned their attention to him. He felt the incisors sink into his arm.

He pulled on the simple steering mechanism and the glider turned in the air. The Hunter had been left behind. The flapping remained in the distance. They had escaped!

Suddenly the air currents grabbed the craft. With the torn sail he was powerless to regain control of the glider. He felt the glider pulled towards the plain. They were tossed and turned upside down. The earth rushed towards them. He pulled the controls to direct the glider back into the atmosphere. His strength could do nothing against the tempest throwing them out of the heavens. Ell was screaming again. The ground loomed and certain death faced them in a matter of seconds.

The dark castle was forbidding, standing alone and mysterious on the marshy plain. The smell of damp and the whisper of cobwebs combined to create an eerie, haunted feeling. Small fires burnt in torches hung along the walls, adding the smell of acrid smoke, and flickering shadows to the already inhospitable atmosphere of the alien edifice. Black slabs of indeterminate material had been used to construct the ancient castle. A castle of memories.

Chopra had felt ill at ease since entering the strange domain. The journey across the marshland had seen three khthons swallowed in the quicksand. There were now only seven alive.

Chopra's visions still continued to trouble him.

The khthons had finished the journey on their own. Swarf had gone to finish the murderous task his brother had failed to accomplish. However, Chopra had felt nothing.

He could still sense the young woman close by, and felt no change in the plan mapped out in the cosmic game of life.

He had no understanding of the purpose of life. He accepted the grand design and his insignificant part. It was enough that he should receive food and shelter most nights; many of his family had not been so lucky.

The huge doors of the castle had been open. The shape-changers had left the planet only a few days before, having prepared the castle for their return.

At the exact centre of the castle lay a vast, bare courtyard. Pillars ran around the circular enclosure, and the myriad corridors all seemed to disappear off to an elaborate pattern. The centrepiece of the courtyard was a deep well. Directly above this the courtyard roof had a large pentagonal opening through which could be seen the stars, hanging above them in the heavens.

Around the well was an incongruous array of advanced mining machinery and laboratory equipment to analyse and synthesize drugs. The most advanced electronic equipment of the age.

The khthons laboured and connected 'Pandora's Box' to the machinery. Chopra supervised the dismantling of the missile and the removal of the unstable core.

The energy force throbbed.

The mining equipment was lined up over the shaft. The drill would be lowered downwards. Chopra still did not know what was being excavated, or why they had stolen the most powerful thermonuclear device ever created.

He knew that he didn't want to explore the castle. He was trying desperately to keep memories at bay.

His thoughts were interrupted. The shapechanger was approaching; he was hot and bothered and, for the first time, Chopra had access to his mind. The shapechanger sensed him and cloaked his thoughts. Chopra had felt pain; the pain of mere existence. He had also seen into the mind.

The dwarf entered. Chopra contemplated what he had seen: a series of disconnected limbs squirming and fighting in what appeared to be a pool of mud. The image meant nothing to him, but appeared to have great significance for the shapechanger.

The khthons bowed their faces to the floor and moved out of the shapechanger's way. The dwarf revelled in their timidity and dread. He picked on one, demanding the results of the current analysis. The khthon stumbled over the response; Swarf just laughed.

'One per cent,' Chopra repeated, trying to divert attention from his friend.

'Excellent,' replied the shapechanger. 'Soon now . . .'

He could feel no pain, but his frame was broken and useless. Spike knew that he was within a few moments of termination. His memory was failing him. He remembered the attack by the shapechanger, his body tossed against the wall of the space station. The woman's face staring at him, her footsteps as she ran off and the stench of the multi-tentacled creature were all a blur as he lapsed in and out of consciousness.

His vision was impaired, with his sight deteriorating to monochrome, out of focus images and then a series of dots and hiss. He wondered if he could hear any more.

His last moments.

He retched, and bile from his stomach poured from his open mouth. He couldn't close his eyes.

But it didn't matter anymore.

And then he sensed someone or something standing next to him. He felt a warmth. He could turn his head, and he could see!

It looked like a white light. But there was a figure standing there. It was the Prime Mover. He smiled . . . and everything faded away.

The ground had rushed up before them but they had survived. Thomas groaned. He had taken the full force of the fall but had managed to control the descent well enough to make a controlled crash landing. He felt proud of himself. The only damage was a sprained leg. He had managed to fight on with worse injuries. Ell had scraped her shins and there was a nasty wound dispensing blood over the marsh.

There was a smell of methane, and his sensory equipment indicated an over abundance of hydrogen and nitrous monoxide. The air was breathable for his travelling companion, but would cause problems if it was necessary to run.

Marshland swept towards the horizon for kilometres, interrupted by the castle in the distance and, a little closer, the remains of a space station. The brown muddy plain had sparse vegetation, most of which appeared to have been burnt away in a centuries old holocaust which had dried out and cracked most of the mud. Thomas suspected this was caused by the fuel rods from the space station exploding on impact with the surface.

Ell was quiet. She found the marching pace tiring and her clothes would not be recommended for military training, but she rarely complained.

Night would be falling soon on the planet.

He looked at Ell and her muddy face. He smiled. But his thoughts were elsewhere, as he still couldn't understand why the Academy would send anyone down to this class D planet. Why was Ell's husband authorized to come to this place to carry out tests on the atmosphere and water? More puzzling was why the Justice Police had not been informed.

They continued their journey. There would be answers soon.

The major was shocked. He had been escorted to the market area of the capital. The air force had launched an attack with chemical weapons. The sight was appalling. Dead bodies lay on the streets. Men, women and children desperate for food had been systematically annihilated by the burning toxins. A cursory count established the initial death toll to be about seventy. So far, another two hundred and thirty had been taken to the nearest hospital, although few were expected to survive the next twenty-four hours.

Screams and desperate cries for help filled the streets. The crawling and wriggling carcasses had been the innocent victims of the chaos taking possession of their world.

He stood powerless. He couldn't do anything to help them. He had come to find out more about the antique dealer. But there were no shops any more. They had been looted and torched. Fires were burning over a third of the city.

He couldn't find the answer to the girl's death. He realized that he didn't know her name. She wasn't a person. Just a victim, a statistic. He felt the pain of her parents.

The Form Manipulator was at work. Trying to conceal

and sow the seeds of discontent. Carlson remembered the passage in the Book which talked about the Form Manipulator trying to break down the power of love. 'Evil cannot exist where there is love,' said the Book. 'And this universe is the battleground.'

Who knows why certain people are called up to join the Prime Mover? It must be part of a plan. People don't just die. The Book tells of a purpose. But one unknowable to ordinary people. Perhaps the Form Manipulator was trying to influence all those around the victims to give up their faith. Despair. The void.

He tried to ignore the pain.

'John,' a voice called out.

He turned to smile. It was involuntary. He could hear his wife.

'I love you,' she said.

He couldn't see her. Around him the volunteer nurses and doctors were tending the sick and the dying. But he couldn't see her.

'Melanie,' he shouted.

He walked over to one of the nurses. Had she seen Melanie Carlson? The woman shook her head. She'd been out with an earlier crew. She hadn't come out with them.

She was wrong. He'd heard her talk to him.

He carried on walking through the bodies, looking at the nurses. She wasn't there. He must be hearing things.

'John.' He heard it again. But louder, clearer.

'Melanie,' he shouted back.

' . . . love you . . .' said the voice.

'I know, I know,' he shouted.

And then he saw her.

She lay on the floor where she'd fallen in the gas attack. Her face and hands were blistered. She wasn't moving. He was glad about that. She wouldn't have suffered too much.

He knelt down and held her hand.

'Don't do that, you'll burn yourself,' barked a nurse.

'Go away! Go away!' he shouted back. The nurse shuffled away.

He put his arms around his wife and held her face to his.

'I love you,' he said.

DAY SIX
08:00–12:00

Carlson returned to the Justice Police Headquarters. The patrols around the perimeter seemed more nervous and aggressive. He'd received a number of reports suggesting that the secret police were losing troops as, fearing the end was at hand, they were leaving their posts and returning to their families and homes. This would soon leave only the androids protecting the security state apparatus.

And him. He'd nowhere to go.

The building was quiet. It seemed to be abandoned. He'd planned to storm up to General Kopyion and demand to be told what the Justice Police were doing to prevent further bloodshed. But Kopyion was not in his office. The vidscreen monitor on his desk was alive and chattering with images. He took a quick look. It appeared to be an old two-dimensional film presentation; an old fashioned oil-driven military vehicle was speeding across a verdant green field. Is this how the head of the security police was passing his time?

An amulet, featuring a worm curled around a globe, was also on the general's desk. He picked it up. It seemed an odd thing for the general to possess.

His thoughts went back to his wife. He couldn't forget. The body thrown on to the ambulance. He clasped her hand. His skin had burnt, and he said goodbye.

He didn't know why he had returned to Police Headquarters. Things didn't seem to matter anymore. He thought about the words in the Book. Just words. He wanted his loved one.

The mother of the first victim had slapped his face.

He felt alone.

He left the general's office and proceeded to the vaults, full of the secrets of the Seven Planets.

There were no android security guards to stop him. The door was locked. His staser would burn the lock out. A bolt of high energy ripped a hole in the door. He went into the room and walked past the rows of documentation too secret to be placed on computer disc. He didn't know what he was looking for.

He had to blame someone. But who?

This place had all the answers.

He walked around picking up files, looking at them and then throwing them on to the floor. He grabbed hold of one case of files and pushed it over.

'Halt!' a voice ordered.

The major turned. Two androids stood at the door, pointing their weapons in his direction.

How had they known he was here?

He looked at them. And then at the chaos of the vault. The room looked as if it had been torn apart. Had he done this?

And then he heard the automatic alarms. The warning alert must have been sounding since he had broken into the room.

What had he done?

'Throw down your weapons or I shoot,' shouted one of the androids.

He put his hands into the air.

Kopyion sat at his desk looking at the major. The androids had pulled the shaking and distraught officer from the wreck of the room and taken him directly to their controller. Kopyion looked faintly bemused. He dismissed the androids and turned to face Carlson.

'I don't know why I did it,' Carlson said. And he didn't.

Kopyion poured him a drink of wine and offered him a date.

'No, I don't want them,' he replied abruptly.

Kopyion chewed a date and filled his glass of wine with mineral water.

'Why don't you do something! Why can't you stop it!' Carlson realized he was shouting.

'Make it go away?' the general asked.

'Yes.' Carlson tried to steady himself.

'How?'

'I don't know. Have you been out there? They're slaughtering each other. I've come from the market.' He paused. He didn't know how much to say. 'There are bodies stacked up where the airforce, for some godforsaken reason, launched an attack with chemical weapons on a civilian crowd . . .'

'They called it "a mob",' Kopyion reported.

'What's going on?' the major asked. Why is there death? Why did she have to die? 'I've checked all the recent reports from our agents, and do you know what I found out?'

'Nothing,' Kopyion said. 'You found out only what you already knew. We're keeping an eye on gangsters, black marketeers and revolutionaries. You found out that we're monitoring the ranks of the military, Academicians and priests. We have produced thousands of pages of reports. All of which say absolutely nothing.'

'Yes.' The major stared at his superior officer.

'It's just madness out there,' said Kopyion.

'Stop it then!'

Please stop it! Make it go away!

'I can't.' Kopyion fell silent.

'I want to re-open the investigation into the ritualistic murders. You said there were drugs involved. Someone must have killed Brown and the antique dealer . . .'

'These murders again . . .'

'Yes. I think there's a connection with what's happening on Nicaea.'

'Such as?' Kopyion asked.

There is an answer. There must be an answer.

'There's a plot, a highly organized attempt to overthrow the government, by a select group of the elite,' said Carlson.

'The investigations so far have shown no evidence of

such an elaborate organization,' Kopyion seemed to answer before he'd finished. But the commander was not dismissing his views. His eyes seemed to be trying to assess how much he knew.

Perhaps Carlson was becoming paranoid. A lot had happened.

'The reports are bland and could have been doctored.'

'A conspiracy theory,' said Kopyion.

'No. More than that,' Carlson replied.

'What are you suggesting, then?' Kopyion asked.

'That these events are all linked. The priests are saying this is the predicted last battle across the face of the universe, when every man must choose,' the major looked intently at Kopyion, 'between good and evil.'

'I do believe there is a great design, and that Good and Evil are inextricably linked in a metaphysical battle across space and time. I also believe that people are capable of bad, sick and harmful actions.'

'Then what do you see as causing the chaos on this planet?'

'What do *you* see?' Kopyion asked, picking up the amulet. He ran the chain through his hand.

'Armageddon is the only explanation,' Carlson shouted.

He didn't know if he meant it. But there had to be a word, an explanation. He had lost everything he had loved. He couldn't be powerless. He had to do something for her. Anything.

'Let me re-open the murder inquiry,' the major begged.

'No.'

The major left the room, punching the wall. He was angry. His fist was bruised but he punched the wall again. He could feel a knot in his stomach twisting, creating a painful stabbing feeling in his guts. He found it so difficult to concentrate. He had to do something. The murders were the key to unravelling the chaos on the planet. Why couldn't the general appreciate that? It was so simple.

He was going to wait in the corridor until Kopyion

came out, and he would confront him. Until then he would just blend in with the walls.

Bernice continued to walk through the endless corridors. The space station was an empty hulk. Most of the craft had been cannibalized and ripped apart. There were no clues to its original purpose. The remains of the machinery indicated a technology far in advance of Earth. What had happened to the once mighty race which had built this superior piece of engineering?

Her thoughts drifted back to Spike, the metal man, who had been killed less than an hour ago. She felt ashamed that she had left him and made her own escape.

She had enjoyed travelling down the river with him. She remembered her parents, lost long ago. All she had were her memories.

And then she stopped. She heard a sound. A door being pulled open. Whispers. Two people talking. Damn! The other androids! She had forgotten about them, but they were still after her.

She couldn't identify the direction of the sounds. The sounds echoed around the station but the other life-forms could be anywhere in the myriad corridors.

She stood still. Where was she going to go? Even if she left the station there was nowhere to go to. The shapechangers were not going to offer her any protection.

She was so tired. She desperately needed sleep. They would never find her if she crawled into a cupboard and hid away. She could sleep for a thousand years.

As she looked for a hiding place she could hear the voices increasing in volume. She caught a few words: marsh, explosion, death. Nothing that enlightened her. She had to escape from here. They were too close.

She tried to walk faster. She was too tired. Her muscles ached. She realized that she wasn't walking in a straight line and was unsteady on her feet. She began to run and fell over.

'Come on, come on,' she said to herself. 'Bernice, this isn't a good idea, you've got to move.'

The voices were close behind her. She had to move. Just a little further. With all her strength, she forced herself to stand and threw herself around the corner.

She ran headlong into a woman. The woman fell over and Bernice collapsed on top of the struggling body. An android stood over her. If this was death then she would stare it in the face. Although she had run out of steam and no longer cared whether she lived or died, there was no way she was going to give up. With all her energy she clenched her fists and drove them between the android's legs. It hurt her arms but had no effect on the android. He picked her up and threw her a few metres down the corridor.

'It's just me and you,' she said to herself. The android was ignoring her, talking to the woman. He was asking if the woman was all right. He then turned his attention to her, lumbering over. He was about two and a half metres tall; naked muscular chest and short dark hair. He was dragging a damaged left leg.

'Hey, I'm not a shapechanger. I'm not . . .' she shouted. Perhaps the louder she shouted the more he would believe her. He stopped.

'Kill me, but I'm not who you're looking for.'

'This banned world is crowded with unwelcome visitors,' he said. The android appeared to accept that she wasn't his target.

Bernice told him that she and her friend, the Doctor, had crash-landed on the planet. The Doctor had disappeared. She and Spike journeyed down the river until they arrived at the space station. Spike had been killed in an attack by one of the shapechangers.

'Spike survived?' the android asked.

'Until the attack,' she replied.

'Now I know I am alone,' he continued.

She discovered Thomas was one of the androids who had tried to kill her earlier, and the woman was the wife of a scientist sent to the planet to analyse the water. She listened to their stories of a red paralysis slowly expanding over the planet. The weed seemed to stop time within its

205

boundaries. She was also told that some of the creatures and vegetation on the planet were not real, but the product of a Nicaean corporation.

The woman didn't seem interested in meeting her. She seemed a little jealous. Bernice could understand that. She had felt possessive of Spike's help and company. Ell wasn't unfriendly to Bernice. Ell talked to her and offered her support, but with it there was a feeling of coldness.

Thomas and Ell seemed to make a good couple. Both of them rarely talked. She wanted to go back home and he wanted to fulfil his mission and destroy the shapechangers. He was similar to Spike in build and single-mindedness.

Bernice was tired. She wanted a rest, and some hot food. Thomas needed to catch up with the shapechanger. There was no time for respite from the task at hand.

She followed the android outside. Ell was talking about life on Nicaea: the vidscreen soaps, her simple typing job and her small apartment. Bernice looked her over; a pale-looking creature. Although Bernice could understand her wish for peace and quiet, Ell must be joking saying that she would prefer to be back home.

Thomas was eager to continue to the castle where the one remaining shapechanger could be found, and his mission completed. Bernice's escape from the planet was looking less likely. She looked again across the plain. A red glow was rising from the marsh.

Night had also started to fall.

She thought about the TARDIS. Would the red weed affect the time machine? Even if it didn't, how would she get back to the ship?

'I need to find the Doctor,' Bernice said. She had been thinking more about her companion since the death of Spike.

'It looks so beautiful,' said Ell.

'But that beauty is death,' replied Thomas. They all looked at the spreading crystal world.

Suddenly Thomas pointed up to the sky. 'We've got visitors.'

206

Bernice saw creatures flying in the sky about two kilo-metres away. They seemed to be dropping hundreds of metres, unfolding their wings, then rising with the air currents into the upper atmosphere. They made a sound like hysterical laughter as they played their games. Ten of them had landed on the burnt-out branches of the witch trees and were silhouetted against the fiery red death. They looked like demons from mediaeval Earth folklore.

'What are they?' Bernice asked.

'Hunters . . .' Ell replied.

'Right,' Bernice said, remembering what Spike had told her about them.

'We've got to get out of here,' Thomas said firmly. He began to move off towards the castle.

Bernice could see thirty or forty of the Hunters hover-ing in the skies. They seemed to be amassing in the heavens.

'Yes.' She turned to find her companions had already begun the final march to the castle. She ran after them. 'Hold on.'

The major followed Kopyion into the radio communi-cations room. As the major entered, a lone police officer stood to attention. Carlson felt it unnecessary to return the customary military salute. He was trying to grasp the events going on around him.

Kopyion, appearing not to notice him, continued col-lecting messages, reading through them quickly and then shredding them.

The major felt there was too much going on in his head. The images of the dead bodies in the streets kept taking over his mind and seeping into his everyday thoughts. He didn't feel like eating, and even breathing had become a painful labour. He found his body shaking again. He had considered that he was having a heart attack; that would explain the pains in his side and the hot and cold sweats tormenting him.

The chatter of the machines was increasing. The sounds were becoming uncomfortable.

'Sir,' he said to the general.

Kopyion stared at him.

'I think you should go home,' said Kopyion.

'What's happening?' He felt so powerless.

'The priests have ordered all their followers to pray for the Prime Mover's eternal mercy. A couple of Hunters were captured and torn apart by the hysterical mob. Many people were killed. In a frenzy, followers ran along the streets screaming, shouting, attacking anyone. These are the final days . . .'

'I didn't think you believed,' Carlson said. He slumped on to the floor, curling into a ball.

Kopyion stepped around him. 'It is time . . .'

'What are you going to do?' Carlson asked.

'A long time ago I lost this arm,' Kopyion ran his hand against his left shoulder, 'on the unnamed planet. Now I must return there. That's where the secret to all of this lies.'

'I don't understand,' said Carlson.

'No,' Kopyion replied, returning to his office.

The castle was bathed in a flickering light. The core of the missile had been strapped into place. The mining equipment had powered up and was descending into the depths of the shaft.

'Sixty three per cent,' Chopra said, reading out the machine dials.

Swarf looked pleased and hobbled around the courtyard, laughing to himself. His plan was obviously to process enough drugs to flood all human-occupied space. But where was the source of the substances?

Chopra thought of his training in the occult world. How his powers had been used by slave traders, who had murdered the rest of his family, and then by the T'Ka drug cartel.

He had smoked simple compound narcotics, to accept the veil of illusion, but had never experimented with the more complex chemical compounds. They did things to the mind. You felt you had entered new worlds and discovered all that it was necessary to know about life. It was all a deception by the Form Manipulator.

The reality of things was hidden from ordinary folk like him. They were just pawns in the grand design. Swarf thought he knew, but he too was being controlled. The images of the bodies wrapped around each other in mud had stuck with the shapechanger all his life. Chopra had glimpsed into the mind and understood; an understanding which had only recently come to him, as his body aged and his life-force drained away.

It was Time. The one dimension that could not be controlled. The endless drift from the past to the future. The shapechangers had sought to control their lives with their willpower, able to transform their bodies into any form, but they were still prisoners of this mortal, finite universe.

And then he could hear Them calling again . . .

Chopra had to keep his mind in order. There were too many things trying to break into his thoughts.

The place was haunted. Chopra could sense ghosts drifting around the castle.

Voices and wispy figures haunted this place. He could hear them in the rooms above. And the noises! Why had he to suffer them?

They had waited. Not for him. For the other.

The other.

The hovercar sped through the capital. Most of the city was aflame, and bitter fighting had taken over the downtown suburbs. The major looked out of the car. Riots and looting had destroyed most of the retail and industrial areas. Although there were occasional shots in the direction of the bulletproof car, the crowds ignored the Justice Police commander. Carlson was glad that he couldn't hear the sounds of the chaos. The images of the victims of the chemical attack stuck in his mind. How could people do that to one another?

209

To his wife.

Melanie.

General Kopyion was quiet.

It had taken Carlson some time but he believed that he had finally worked out who was responsible for the ritualistic murders on the planet. The answer had been staring him in the face. It was Kopyion, his commander-in-chief, who had killed or ordered the deaths. This would explain why Kopyion was not making any efforts to control the anarchy let loose across Nicaea. He was making an attempt to become the Archon. Kopyion was going to leave the planet and return with 'Pandora's Box', the ultimate weapon. He would order the androids to suppress all dissent and extinguish all opposition, and then return to become supreme ruler of the Althosian system.

The major had thought about it. He could throw his lot in with the Lord General, and perhaps become a governor of one of the colony worlds. Or he could stop him.

He had to stop him. The images of the dead came to his mind and he knew that he had to stop Kopyion. Democracy, for all its faults, should continue. That was the reason for the declaration of independence from the Earth corporation. That was the reason he'd come out here.

He held her hand.

Goodbye.

Carlson felt more reassured as they arrived at the hoverport. Androids saluted the car. They had taken the area from the rebels and were defending it on the orders of General Kopyion.

Kopyion left the car and walked towards the space hoppers. Carlson said to the driver and the security guards that Kopyion wished to be left alone.

He walked on his own to his final destination. Kopyion had tried to persuade him that he did not need to come to the hoverport. But Carlson was insistent. He had a job to do.

He had no doubts that the androids would kill him once

his crime had been discovered. He felt a tear in his eye. What had happened to his beloved world? What would happen to it in the future?

He was the only one who could stop Kopyion now. Perhaps he would be remembered for that. It didn't matter. He remembered his oath, that he would 'serve'.

The hopper was apart from the others. There was something about it that seemed different, but he couldn't tell what it was. Kopyion was kneeling as if in prayer.

Kopyion turned. He seemed calm, almost as if he had been expecting his deputy's treachery.

'I asked you not to come,' Kopyion said.

'General . . .' the major said. 'It was you. You committed the murders.'

Kopyion looked at the staser pointed at him and stood to face the major.

'It's been staring me in the face,' Carlson continued.

'You're ill, put the weapon down,' Kopyion replied.

'Don't come any closer,' the major shouted. Kopyion continued to approach him. 'I mean it. Stop!'

As Kopyion walked towards him, Carlson ordered him to stop, aimed his weapon and fired it at the general's shoulder. The general flew backwards with a look of shock on his face. He held his shoulder.

'You killed all those people. Why?' Carlson asked.

Kopyion bounded forward and slammed his arm against Carlson's chest.

The staser fell.

Kopyion punched Carlson in the face and then in the stomach. The major was winded. The old man had more power than the major expected. The experience of war had not left him.

Kopyion dodged a fist and threw another punch at his solar plexus.

The major fell on to the ground.

Kopyion pulled out the old revolver stolen from the Academician's apartment and moved over the fallen figure.

The major saw a coldness in the old man's face.

211

He saw Kopyion stand over him, pull back the safety mechanism of the revolver and put the barrel directly over his forehead.

'I'm sorry,' said Kopyion. He pulled the trigger.

DAY SIX
12:00–16:00

The otherworld lay in front of them. The harsh desert was exposed and yellow, but there was no heat or sign of any change in the climate. Diamonds and rare jewels were strewn across the floor as if they had been there for millennia. The juggernaut continued on its journey. The travellers had been driving for six hours, and as the meter in the cab had been showing a steady sixty miles an hour, they must have covered over three hundred and fifty miles. But there was no sign of any sentient life or activity. The smoke poured up towards the horizon and they were no closer to arriving at their destination, wherever and whatever that might be.

They drove past an elephant wandering around lost, looking confused and desperate for food. At one point they also passed a beached whale squirming in the desert.

The Doctor did not appear surprised, and the journey continued, wordless. Blake found the continuous stark colours and the bare, uninhabited world disturbing in a way he could not identify. There was a feel to the world unlike anything he had come across back in England. The Doctor had talked about a drug being in the atmosphere which created a feeling of unnatural well-being, but there was something else here.

'You know something more than you are telling me,' Blake said to his companion.

'This is all an illusion. This machine should have run out of petrol many hours ago,' said the Doctor, sounding as if he did not want to be interrupted. He wanted to be left to himself.

Blake decided that his thoughts were not welcomed by the time traveller. He sat back in the motor vehicle as

213

the Doctor noticeably increased the speed of the journey. The juggernaut bucked and the poet held on to the side to prevent himself being thrown around. He momentarily closed his eyes.

It was difficult to tell the passage of time, but when Blake opened his eyes they appeared to be within reach of the rising smoke. He must have been asleep for hours. He looked behind and saw the desert stretched out.

'How long have I been asleep?' Blake asked.

'What is time?' the Doctor replied enigmatically.

The juggernaut was approaching the origin of the smoke. Thousands of slaves, naked and in pain, were breaking rocks and moving the rubble in long columns towards the burning embers of a huge pyre. Slave masters strode through the crowds of men and women whipping them if they slowed down or showed any interest in the travellers.

'Cuj ach,' one of the slaves begged, breaking free and looking towards the travellers. Although his chains still held him tight, the slavers grabbed him and burnt him with searing irons. He screamed and then was silent.

'Ach n'kai,' the Doctor muttered to himself.

Closer to the smoking fire, Blake could see that the colours of the flames varied with the different amounts of crushed rocks thrown on to the pyre.

'Chemicals?' Blake asked.

The Doctor nodded.

The slaves continued to pound away. They seemed demoralized and miserable, operating an endless mechanical process.

As the travellers continued their journey, they passed a number of open mines. At each one slaves carried out rocks and deposited them in piles. The rocks were also found lying on the ground.

'Doctor,' Blake interrupted his travelling companion's silent thoughts. The Doctor did not acknowledge him. 'I have made a study of the Fall, how men challenged the Gods in their search for knowledge and were banished

214

from Eden. I believe the story in the Bible – and other holy books – is a myth, but based on a simple truth.'

The Doctor did not reply immediately. There seemed to be a tear in his eye. 'As I've travelled the universe, I've come across the myths of many planets. They all share certain elements in common. One of those elements is the story of an all-powerful race who tried to conquer and destroy Creation. A race banished from this universe. The myths of Gallifrey talk about nameless horrors infesting our universe which were only defeated through the might of the Time Lords.

'I didn't think it was real. But then on my travels I met a vampire which had escaped a great war with the Time Lords of Gallifrey.

'The High Council had kept it a secret. I didn't know why. I still don't know why.'

Blake listened as the Doctor tried to explain the confusion in his head.

'What is happening here?' Blake asked.

'I think that It is once again preparing an attack on our universe. Not just the crazed fanatics who follow It, but It and Its legions,' the Doctor replied.

'Vampires?'

'Hideous, half-glimpsed nightmare creatures.'

'Does It have a name?' Blake asked.

The Doctor pondered. 'Yssgaroth . . .'

Blake repeated, 'Yees-gar-oth?'

'A word used by frightened children to describe nameless, formless horrors which await you in the fog, or around the next corner.'

The travellers were heading out into the empty desert. The Doctor stopped the juggernaut. He said that he wanted to inspect the rocks on the ground. He left the vehicle and moved over to the rocks. He kicked one, and it disintegrated into a white powder. He rubbed some of the powder in his hands, sniffed it and threw it back on to the ground. Blake went to pick up a handful of the substance, but the Doctor kicked it out of his grasp.

'You must leave it alone. Don't touch it.'

'What is it?' Blake asked.

'It's an addictive, hallucinogenic drug. Throughout the universe it's known as "Dream B". Its followers used the drug in their hideous rituals in Victorian London. I didn't think it was known on Earth, not yet . . . I've visited future worlds which have been devastated by the drug, where the young people have been completely wiped out by this substance.'

Suddenly, as they talked, arrows started to rain down on them, landing uncomfortably close to the two travellers. The Doctor ran for cover, grabbing the poet's sleeve and pulling him to the side. The attack was aimed at the motor vehicle.

As Blake lay on the floor, he watched the arrows soaring into the air, about a hundred yards away, and then falling towards their target. Whispers of smoke were visible on the arrows. Twenty flaming arrows hit the juggernaut. The cab caught fire.

'Down,' the Doctor shouted, pushing the poet's head into the sand. As Blake wriggled, he heard the sound of an explosion and felt a rush of cold air.

Blake looked up. The juggernaut was in flames. They were not going to escape from hell in the twentieth century craft. A dozen figures stood up, cheering. Their faces were painted to look like skulls. They ran over to the two prostrate travellers, and danced insanely around them. They were armed with bows and arrows, were all male and had shaved heads. They jumped up and down, signalling wildly. Occasionally they would beat on their chests, sit on the ground and then stand up. Their eyes darted excitedly around.

The Doctor was nodding, as if in agreement.

'What are they saying?' Blake asked his companion.

'I've no idea. It sounds like gibberish to me,' the Doctor said.

The figures moved around them, waving their arms in a coordinated movement towards each other. And then Blake heard music. It sounded like a mouth organ. The

216

figures were dancing. He thought that this was extra-ordinary. He turned to the Doctor.

The Doctor was holding a harmonica, tapping his feet and playing a piece of music he called 'Jimmy Crack Corn'. The traveller's music captured a feel of adventure yet sorrow.

'It's called the Blues,' the Doctor shouted, taking a pause for breath. Blake looked on astonished. He thought they should be trying to escape, not entertaining the enemy. The musical interlude went on for ten minutes and finished with the mad figures collapsing on the ground. The Doctor smiled cheerfully, waved and walked off.

'Come on,' the Doctor said under his breath. 'And smile.'

Blake followed.

'Be be be,' one of the figures said, standing up.

'No, we've finished,' said the Doctor.

'Be be be.' Another figure stood, looking far from friendly. He walked over to the Doctor, waving a knife at the traveller's throat.

'Well, if you insist,' the Doctor said.

'Be be be.' The figure put the knife at the Doctor's throat. The skull figures grabbed hold of the travellers.

'A most unappreciative audience,' the Doctor said.

They walked for about an hour before arriving at their destination. However, the Doctor was happy as they were brought directly to the industrial centre of the world. Blake didn't know how much longer he would survive. The journey was unbearable; marching along with the chattering fools, and the Doctor more interested in the past of his people.

They arrived at a huge dome. The structure appeared to have been built into the air, with scaffolding and support systems running up towards the sky. Thousands of slaves marched in step. The slave masters ran around, punishing anyone who slowed down or became disobedient. Drums beat to mark the rhythm of the work. However, within fifteen minutes of their arrival, the speed increased twice.

A number of silos were positioned about a mile from the structure. They appeared to contain tons of Dream B. Bapputchin delivered further supplies.

Blake noticed the demons flying overhead.

'What is the building?' Blake asked.

'A bridgehead,' the Doctor replied.

The Cun wandered round, trying to buy bodies. They continued their bloodthirsty chatter, as they identified the weak and the injured and went over to negotiate a purchase price.

'Death will be very welcome,' Blake said.

He was tired and, seeing all the pain, felt a quick death would be more inviting a proposition than a hot bath. The Doctor turned to him.

'You don't understand. There's no death here. These slaves have been here thousands of years. They've been digging for the chemicals, been tortured and crucified, again and again. There is no welcome release here. There's just pain, and more pain.'

'Why don't they revolt?' Blake asked.

'Where is there to go? They're trapped here.'

A Cun walked over to take a closer look at the two travellers. It hissed and spat in their faces. It wiped the spittle, trying to clean off the dirt. It shook its head and walked away. After much discussion, the Cun traded a bag of raw meat in exchange for the travellers.

The Cun sniffed around them. One particularly gross creature walked alongside them with its stomach rumbling. Blake said to his companion that he should take a last look at the hole in time, and their escape. The Doctor pointed elsewhere. One of the Cun seemed to be in an argument with a jackal-creature which the Doctor said was a 'Galk'.

Four Galks stood listening to the conversation. They were twice the size of dogs and stood erect on their hind feet. The Cun appeared to be reticent about arguing with them. Eventually a Cun bowed and indicated for his brethren to follow him; the others snarled at the Galks and walked away. Blake began to follow them, but the main Galk stood in his way.

As the Galks led them into the desert, the travellers could see the Cun arguing with the skull people, trying to reclaim their raw meat.

The Galks moved with a slow, pronounced movement.

'Hello. I'm the Doctor and this is William Blake. The poet, you know,' the Doctor said, trying his simpleton act. It didn't work. The Galks ignored him.

'Any chance of some food?' the Doctor asked.

After about fifteen minutes they arrived at their destination. A throne stood in the middle of the desert. The throne was made of gold, and sparkled with a multitude of jewels. The Galks untied the travellers, bowed to the throne and retreated.

The poet and the time traveller stood alone in the desert.

'I think we're about to meet our hosts,' the Doctor said.

Blake stared at the empty throne. There seemed to be something happening; his vision was misting over. And then in front of them appeared a small lamb. He smiled. The lamb bounded on to the seat of the throne and turned to face them.

'I hope you are all right, gentlemen,' it said, in a high, squeaky voice.

'Thank you,' said the poet. The Doctor remained silent.

'I want to help you escape from this terrible place,' said the lamb. Blake felt comfortable because the lamb offered to return them home.

'I don't believe you,' the Doctor shouted. Blake looked at him. What was he talking about? Why was he being so rude?

'Doctor, he is trying to help,' Blake explained.

'No. You might be able to influence my friend, but I won't believe you and I will stand up to you. There's nothing you can do,' the Doctor continued.

A long tongue came out of the lamb's mouth as it licked its lips. It laughed to itself.

'Doctor, you fail to go along with my charade. That upsets me. Don't you realize that I can inflict billions of years of exquisite suffering and pain on you,' the lamb said.

The Doctor started to scream. He held his head as if his brain was exploding.

'Don't you realize, Time Lord. We are returning to your paltry universe. And nothing can stop us now! Abandon all hope . . .'

The Time Lord fell on to the floor and the pain ceased. The lamb bounded around laughing and then disappeared. The throne was empty.

And then Blake felt the ground tremble. It was like an earthquake. The desert was shaking around them. The sands started to rise up like a cloud of dust.

'What is it?' Blake started to ask, and then he saw. From around the throne, something was unravelling its body. It was hundreds of feet long, initially resembling a huge snake uncoiling itself. The skin was covered with a wet, dripping substance. He could also see bits of horns or wings down the side. Could this thing fly?

Blake couldn't believe that this was one creature. It seemed many of these things were squirming around together. And then there was the smell of rotting flesh. He felt he was going to . . . And then he vomited. The stench was overpowering.

'Doctor, what's your plan?' Blake asked.

'After much consideration, and examining all the options, I suggest we – run. Now!' the Doctor shouted.

Blake agreed with his companion, and beat a hasty retreat back to the hole in time. It never occurred to him that he was too tired or ill. He had to run for his life.

'Don't look back, just run,' shouted the Doctor.

The travellers' flight took them across the desert.

'We must destroy the hole and prevent them returning to our universe,' the Doctor said.

'Isn't that what the Time Lords tried to do and failed,'

Blake replied. 'And anyway, there are many of these holes from which the monsters could escape into our universe.'

'We can't give up,' the Doctor said. Blake needed to rest. He turned around and slowed down, seeing no sign of the monsters. The Doctor didn't seem tired and continued to run. 'Don't stop,' he shouted, running on ahead.

Blake sighed, and ran to catch up with his travelling companion. He had lost his watch back in Victorian London and so had no clear idea of time; it may have taken minutes or hours to get back to the hole in time.

There were thousands more slaves now, working to finish the bridgehead. They marched in columns, ten slaves wide. Thousands moving as one together. As one slave put his left foot forward, so did several hundred others.

Hunters were gathering over the dome. Hundreds of the creatures hovered in the air, swooping down in mock delight. The air was full of their squawking. Blake looked around.

'How are we going to get out of here?'

'We're not,' said the Doctor. 'We have to stop them.'

'There are two of us, and hundreds of thousands of them,' Blake said.

'I admit the odds aren't in our favour.' The Doctor smiled. 'But we must do something.'

He moved up to a slave. The slave didn't even glance at him. The slave looked fifty, with pale battered skin, hopeless eyes and an emaciated, run-down body. Thousands of similar slaves worked all around them.

The Doctor tried to communicate with the slave in English, but received no response.

'A'sleek, m'jn ta omo,' the Doctor said.

Hearing the ancient Gallifreyan language, the slave slowed down in his work. He looked at the Doctor and spat in his face. He moved off, continuing his heavy work. The Doctor looked sad and tired.

Blake shivered. As the Doctor continued his efforts to communicate with the slaves, Blake noticed the Galks

221

talking to the Cun. A Galk hit a Cun across the face and then tore into it with savage teeth. The Galks left the injured Cun and began to walk amongst the slaves searching for the travellers.

The demons noticed the injured body and began to fly over the struggling figure.

'The Harpies of destruction,' Blake said.

'Time is running out,' said the Doctor.

'What?' Blake asked.

'I didn't want to come back here. Somehow, I knew what existed here went back to the ancient history of my people. To a time when all seemed ideal.' The Doctor smiled again. 'I wanted to run away, to hide, but I had to return to this lonely, meaningless place.'

The Doctor joined a slow moving column of slaves, carrying concrete slabs over to the dome. He moved down the column. He smiled, said 'hello' and then unexpectedly stuck out his foot and tripped up one of the slaves. As the slave stumbled, so did another, and then another. The whole column proceeded to fall on to the ground.

The Doctor darted over to a pile of broken rocks. He pulled out his sonic screwdriver. The screwdriver emitted a loud, incessant scream. Blake shook with the pain. Smoke started to pour out of the mounds, and the crackling of small fireworks sounded from inside the stocks of Dream B. The Doctor filled his pockets with the rocks.

The Galks saw the time traveller, lowered themselves on to all fours, and bounded across the desert.

The Doctor ignored them, climbing up the scaffolding to the roof of the dome. Blake followed the Doctor.

'What are we doing, Doctor?' Blake asked.

'Sabotage. We'll set fire to the rocks up here and create a huge explosion. It will stop the Yssgaroth for a few hours . . .'

'And kill us in the meantime.'

'I'm sorry, I can't think of anything else,' the Doctor replied.

Blake had a good view of the world from the roof of the dome. From where they stood, everything seemed to be smaller. He could see people and creatures on the ground below, and in the distance shapes moved under the desert sands. The Yssgaroth were sliding underneath the surface of the earth towards them.

The Doctor had filled his pockets with Dream B. He pulled out the rocks and placed them in small piles.

'What's the purpose of the dome?' Blake asked.

'To transport It and Its forces into our universe,' the Doctor said.

'We've moved through the hole in time. So have the Hunters. Can't the monsters too?' Blake asked.

'Obviously not,' the Doctor replied, trying to prevent the rocks slipping down the roof of the dome. His footing was precarious.

'Doctor, what are you going to do? The powder isn't going to have any effect on the dome.'

The Doctor replied in a drifting Scottish accent. 'I know, but we have to do something. We have to . . .'

As he spoke, he lost his balance and he fell.

He tumbled through the air and stopped.

He started floating to the hole.

Blake was astonished, and found himself moving towards the Doctor. Blake felt that he was standing on something. He stretched out his arms but had no room to manoeuvre. He was in a cage. An invisible cage. Blake struggled, but to no avail. The cage moved away from the dome and towards the hole.

'No, I need to stay,' the Doctor shouted, desperately.

They were powerless to resist. The invisible cage removed them from the otherworld.

DAY SIX
16:00–20:00

A red glow radiated from the depths of the shaft. They were up to 78 per cent full power. The breakthrough would occur in eight hours. The khthons were waiting and praying. Chopra moved between them, calming their fractious nerves. He could sense an immense power enveloping the planet, and knew his death was only hours away. The visions continued to haunt him. He had tried to sleep, but the horrific apparitions surfaced out of the recesses of his unconscious and frightened him.

The shapechanger was inspecting the operation. Although he was pleased that they had managed to set everything up on time, he continued to mutter about the remaining android being alive, threatening them from somewhere on the planet.

Chopra sensed the two women were together and within a kilometre of the castle. There was something else with them. He suspected that this was the artificial man. Although he told Swarf about the visitors, the shapechanger refused to listen to his worries about the red death.

'It is the Empire that never Ended,' Chopra said.

'You're still preaching death and destruction. Your people are so morbid. If the exploration of the galaxy had been left to the khthons, we'd all still be living in caves,' Swarf said.

'And so we should,' Chopra replied. That had been their perfect existence before the empire builders had come in their tall ships. The universe was about to be plunged again into eternal darkness. The khthons had known that the Earth colonists would one day re-awaken the Elder Gods; they would come to this planet and open the gates of their imprisonment.

224

Many khthons were butchered when the imperialists first arrived. As a race, they had prayed for death before the return of the Monsters. The myths of their people told how the Elder Gods had broken through and laid waste to the cosmos. Only through the sacrifice of a distant people had the Old Ones been vanquished, and order been returned to the universe. The khthons had known that it was not over and they waited, sheltering in their cave world, for the storm to return.

This was all a veil of illusion. Chopra wished he didn't possess the sight. The imperialists carried on their day-to-day life, and he felt sorry for them. They did not understand, but theirs was a simpler existence.

The pain hit him. All the way down his left side. He slipped on to the cold floor. He tried to breathe steadily, but the noises from upstairs disturbed him. Ghosts walked the castle and screamed out in panic.

White figures glided overhead. They were trapped, screaming for help and mercy.

He could see them in chains, walking in bloodied battle armour through the ancient corridors. And then the torture instruments – used by the Servants of the Old Ones – tore off flesh, inflicted pain and maimed their captives. Chopra wanted it to stop. But there was no escape from the strange visions haunting this place. The weird feasts, insane dancing and animals copulating in the dirt . . .

. . . and the Monsters.

He let out a scream.

The invisible cage imprisoned them. The Doctor had railed against the unseen forces which had abducted them, but to no avail. The travellers had been transported through the hole in time to their place of capture. They could see only darkness from the invisible bars of their prison. They were obviously in a dark room, but where in space or time was unknown.

Blake lay on the floor of their cell. This provided a welcome relief from the constant travelling of the last three days. The Doctor was less impressed. He was seeth-

225

ing with anger. Blake tried to persuade him that there was little he could have done anyway, but the time traveller would not agree. He would have found some means of stopping the Yssgaroth.

The poet suspected that the Doctor was trying to deal with his confused thoughts about the past. The Doctor would pace around, shaking his head, trying to say something that was stuck in his throat.

'Why?' the Doctor exploded.

There was no response.

The sunlight was deteriorating. It would be nightfall soon. Bernice shivered. She had been looking at the castle for the last hour. Perhaps it was here that ogres and giants used to lure their victims.

As they approached the castle they realized that the advance of the red weed was increasing in speed. Most of the surrounding marshland had fallen to the crippling infection. Thousands of the Hunters flew in a hysterical dance over the ascending chaos. Behind her, there was just the stillness. She felt a coldness inside her and did her best to remember the happy times of her childhood. She again remembered the fishing and the picnic. The events of her childhood that she could really call happy.

She recognized the coldness inside her as also present inside the Doctor. The funny man who had found her on a distant planet and had treated her as a human being. He hadn't tried to get her drunk or rape her. He wandered the universe, searching for something. He called it truth and justice. In a rare moment of self-disclosure, he had talked about wanting to go up to God and ask 'why?' He hadn't explained whether he actually believed in the existence of God, or what he was going to seek the reason for in his meeting with the almighty. She laughed to herself.

Why was she on this distant planet, trying to discover how the Althosian civilization was destroyed? The Doctor had offered her a journey to see some of the beautiful sights of the universe. She thought that someday she would settle down. There had to be an escape. Although Bernice had been dealt a few rough cards in her life, she still thought that there could be something better. She had coped so far.

They were now a kilometre from the castle. They were trying to sneak up and gain entry without being seen by the shapechanger. Thomas had a mission, to destroy the missile and prevent the shapechanger from carrying out his criminal activities.

Bernice saw a little creature run in front of them. It looked like a typewriter. But that was stupid. They continued to walk on, through dried mud and stinging grasses. And then she saw the creature again. It appeared behind a clump of dead plants, ran over and stopped five metres from them. Another smaller one appeared and shot past the stationary one, chattering madly to itself. Suddenly it saw them and also stopped. It retreated slowly.

'What are they?' Bernice asked.

'I don't know,' Ell replied.

Bernice moved over to the creatures. She held an arm out, saying she meant no harm. The creatures backed off. She stopped, waited, and continued towards them. The little one made a shrill noise and ran back into the desiccated bush. It tried to hide itself. Bernice approached the larger of the two. It *was* a typewriter, and had a piece of paper sticking out of its back. The paper had writing on.

'Bernice. This is the Doctor. Do not believe anything you see. You are in great danger. Remember the Alamo.'

She had been joined by her two travelling companions. She looked at them.

'I thought he was dead,' Thomas said.

'Perhaps he is,' said Ell.

'No, he's very much alive,' said Bernice. This made her a lot happier. Somewhere the Doctor was alive, and watching out for her.

She giggled and walked over to the other machine. The Doctor would have some answer to all of this. She peered at the smaller typewriter's message:

227

'The other printer is not telling the truth. They are trying to deceive you but you are safe at the moment. The Doctor.'

'Useful information,' said Ell.

Thomas picked up the larger typewriter. He stood on the smaller machine. It smashed, and machinery scattered over the ground. As the larger machine struggled the android pulled it apart. Its legs continued to move even when the body was removed.

Thomas grunted that they had wasted enough time and must continue on their journey. He walked off.

They were less than a quarter of a kilometre from the castle. The slope up to the castle was winding and steep, and where they now stood was cast in shadows. Suddenly, Thomas put his finger to his mouth, beckoning the others to be quiet. He had heard something. There was a slight movement close to their position.

Small, wizened men with parched skin and hairless bodies appeared around them. There were six of them. All carried small hand weapons. Thomas lunged at two of the enemy. Even with his injuries he managed to connect with his targets. Both creatures collapsed with broken necks. Bernice threw herself at another of the creatures. The creature's weapon fired but missed her. She threw a punch and hit the creature in the mouth.

'What are they?' Bernice shouted.

'Khthons,' Thomas replied. 'They're the native life form of the planet Trieste.'

'We've got a fight on our hands,' said Bernice.

Ell didn't move. She shouted at her companions, pointing towards the marshland.

Bernice looked. Although there was a clear path from the space station to the castle, the red death was within metres of their position. It had enveloped the marshland.

A creature lunged forward. Thomas moved, knocking it into the red weed. The creature staggered for a few seconds and turned to scream. There was no sound and no more movement. It had petrified and been frozen in space and time.

228

The other creatures screeched nervously, but they weren't running away.

Above them, Hunters swarmed in increasing numbers. They seemed to be laughing and mocking the battle going on below.

'Give up, just give up,' Ell shouted. 'We've got to get inside the castle. We don't have time to stand and fight. Bernice, please!'

Thomas stood still. He was controlling his body and was ready to explode and attack the khthons. Bernice looked at him, and shook her head. Ell was right. She moved over to the android and touched his arm.

'We don't have a choice,' she said. She walked towards the khthons putting her arms up. Ell followed. The khthons were in control and waved their guns as if they had captured the travellers.

Thomas shouted, 'No!' However, there was no point, and he raised his arms in surrender, following his companions.

They entered the castle. The dank corridors led to a courtyard. The four khthons pushed them as if hurrying to return to safety behind the walls of the castle. The captives' hands were bound with thick metallic rope. Bernice could see Thomas trying to prise his hands apart, but his broken arm proved to be a burden.

The shapechanger was waiting in the centre of the castle. A huge drill had been lowered into a shaft in the ground. The drill was screaming and an intense heat was rising from deep inside the shaft. Khthons ran around, checking the operation and the equipment.

The dwarf sat on the floor, guiding the operation. Swarf turned to face Bernice. He was snarling.

'We meet again. And you are now here to witness my greatest triumph.'

Bernice looked around the mediaeval castle. Hideous gargoyles stared down from the corners of the room, and a clammy dampness seemed to cover the black walls.

Swarf hobbled over. His body squelched as he moved.

The khthons held on to their prisoners.

The shapechanger smiled. He spat as he talked.

'Chopra, tell me what is in their minds.'

Another khthon came forward. His gait was unsteady and he seemed to have difficulty focusing on them. He moved over and stared into Bernice's eyes. She could feel a strange tugging, almost like an itch inside her head. The khthon was trying to explore her thoughts. He moved along, apparently looking into her companions' minds. He coughed.

'The darkness is taking over,' Chopra said. 'I read their minds. There is something terrible out there. The red weed. The paralysis that has crept over the planet. I sense it is within a kilometre of the castle. They surrendered because they were more frightened of what is out there than in here.'

The shapechanger walked over to Bernice and stood in front of her. His breath stank. 'Put them in the dungeon.'

Thomas struggled.

Chopra added, 'This one will kill you. He is programmed to retrieve the missile and annihilate you.'

Swarf laughed. 'It is already too late. The missile has been dismantled. Take them away.'

The khthon looked strangely at Ell. Bernice wondered why. But she had other worries.

The khthon said, 'But what about the red weed?'

'We'll seal off the castle. We'll be safe in here.'

Bernice looked at the khthon. He didn't believe the shapechanger. He nodded politely, but his whole body language indicated that he didn't agree. At that moment Bernice was very afraid. It meant that the criminals were not in control. She had thought the shapechanger was in control of what was occurring on the planet. But it wasn't true. He thought that they could simply close the doors and everything would be all right.

They were manhandled towards the mighty front door. The khthons had been ordered to seal off the castle from the unknown forces. The door stood over ten metres high and was made of a silvery metal. Three khthons pushed the door shut. The sound of the door being closed reverberated around the silent corridors of the castle. Bernice looked at her captors. They were frightened.

And they were all trapped.

Part Four

DAY SIX
20:00–24:00

Darkness had fallen. The lights flickered. The three khthons shivered with uncertainty. Further into the depths of the castle, Bernice saw the walls were draped with ancient standards, crumbling into dust. She stopped for a moment.

Ell looked at her. 'What is it?'

Bernice stared at a faded yellow cloth, hanging from the ceiling. A gold pattern was woven into the material. She thought she recognized the design.

'I don't know,' Bernice replied.

One of the khthons pushed her. She turned to hurl abuse at the creature.

'You . . .' She stopped herself.

It was frightened. Not of her, but of the castle. It was on edge. Eerie sounds echoed around the passageways.

Thomas said nothing. His attempts to break free had failed.

The corridor ended. A narrow stairwell wound like a corkscrew into the dungeons of the castle. The steps were well worn. The torches flickered and occasionally blew out, plunging the descent into a shadowy darkness. The old stones reeked of damp. Bernice felt nauseous. The khthons were chattering nervously. Suddenly they stopped.

A long groan drifted up the steps. A deep, mournful sound.

She looked in front of them and couldn't see anything. The khthons stirred and continued into the darkness.

His memory had failed. He couldn't remember how he came to be here. His body felt that it had been in a terrible accident. His mind scanned his body functions. His legs and back were broken in numerous places. Three of the fingers on his right hand were undamaged, but both arms had been crushed. Whatever had done this to him had great strength. His brain was half destroyed. His thinking was not logical. Random images were pouring into his mind.

The figure standing over him.

And the shapechanger! He remembered the battle aboard the space station. He had tried to prevent the creature from finding his woman companion. He didn't know if he had succeeded or failed. His body had been thrown against the walls. His life-force had drained away. What was he doing here? He should have been terminated. His internal clock indicated that his energy levels were at zero. However, that part of his brain may have been damaged and unable to give an accurate reading.

He tried to open his eyes. His face was paralysed. His external sensors seemed to be partially operable. He had no sense of taste or smell, but his hearing was working.

What was he going to do now?

He had to retrieve 'Pandora's Box'. His programming offered no alternative but to continue his mission. Perhaps it was this that kept him alive. His over-riding sense of purpose. Even with his body almost destroyed he had to continue until his life-functions were terminated or his mission was carried out.

Silently he prayed. The Prime Mover must be able to offer him some hope.

He had no sense of time. His body lay broken and discarded. And then he heard a sound he recognized. A sound he knew too well. The flapping of wings. He could not tell how many of them there were. But Spike knew that he was surrounded by Hunters.

He tried to open his eyes again. Slowly, the left eyelid opened. It was worse than he had imagined. Three of the Hunters were prodding his legs. They had obviously discovered some scrap to take with them, and it was him.

'Please kill me, please,' he begged. But no words came

from his mouth. His eye was the only part of his body that he could move. One of the Hunters looked over the android's body; its demonic face staring down at the android's features. It stared at the good eye moving frantically in its socket. It moved forward, stretching out a scaly finger towards the android's eye. It hissed, and one of its fellow creatures also came closer to have a look. The other Hunter hissed.

The first Hunter then lunged forward and grabbed hold of Spike's chest. With its powerful arms it threw the android over its shoulder. Spike lay over the Hunter's back, facing the ground. The Hunters moved with a distorted slow-motion gait through the corridors of the abandoned station, occasionally taking off and flying a few metres.

And then they were outside. But it was an atmosphere vastly different to when the android had entered the space station. His sensors must have been more badly damaged than he had originally thought. A timeless red glow seemed to radiate all around.

A stygian gloom had fallen over the world. The colour reminded him of the paintings of hell by the mediaeval painter, Ferdinand Breughel. His mind was not working. Perhaps he was dead.

The Hunter's wings began to strike the air, and the creature levitated off the ground. The other creatures also began to fly, and soon they were all airborne. There were hundreds of the Hunters, darting and soaring through the air.

Spike closed his eye and again lost consciousness.

Blake opened his eyes. His slumber had not been at all restful. The Doctor had been pacing around the invisible prison, punching at the walls and muttering to himself. Blake had tried to advise him to relax, and when that hadn't worked had shouted at the Time Lord. The Doctor sat at the other side of the cell, sulking.

The poet wondered how much longer this would go on. He missed the simple luxuries of life, from soap to a regular meal. His dreams had all been about home. If he'd had a paper and a pencil he might have continued his epic composition, or drawn sketches, but he had had no opportunity in this strange land. He had picked up on his travels that the future history of Earth was not the progressive revolution which he and many others had imagined. He felt a vague disappointment which he couldn't put into words.

'Doctor,' Blake said. His companion ignored him. 'What are we going to do now?'

The Doctor stood and walked over.

'I don't like computers,' ranted the Doctor.

'What?' said Blake.

'We're imprisoned at the moment by a computer defence programme.'

'I don't understand,' Blake said.

'A computer is like a mechanical human brain which carries out various specific operations. This whole planet is controlled by a vast defence system. This is what stopped the TARDIS in mid-flight . . .'

'Defending what?' Blake asked.

'The entrance to the hole? My memories? I don't know.' The Doctor took the sonic screwdriver out of his pocket. 'I've been trying to unlock the doors of the cell using this device. I've escaped from many places with this . . .' Blake looked at the exasperated face of the Doctor, ' . . . but this computer can predict what I'm going to do. Everything I try to do it counters with more tortuous and convoluted traps.'

Blake nodded. 'Then we have to wait.'

The Doctor turned around without acknowledging the poet's statement. 'I'm not a children's plaything to be toyed with,' he shouted. 'Do you hear me, whoever you are . . .'

There was no reply.

'It's quite interesting, Doctor,' said Blake. 'Do you know that in the mythology of Earth the concept of freedom only came into existence after male and female ate of the Tree of the Knowledge of Good and Evil. They were then cast out of the Garden – '

'I haven't come here for a history lesson,' said the Doctor.

'Did you also eat of that tree? Did you rebel?'

'I was loyal to the Time Lords. To my people. But they prognosticated. They pondered. They observed. Do you know the literal translation of the word "Gallifrey" is "they that walk in the shadows". That's their problem. They know everything and yet they know nothing. I left Gallifrey because I was bored, and because of something that happened, a long time ago . . .'

Blake listened as the Doctor's tones became quieter and more restrained. For the first time since he had met him, Blake felt compassion for the old Time Lord.

'The myths of Gallifrey tell of the Dark Times. They tell of an army of warriors who fought a terrible war. Against a race of Monsters. Hideous creatures from another universe. A legendary figure, Liall a Mahajetsu, led an army of warriors for millennia, in distant battles across the cosmos. At the end of the apocalyptic conflict there were no survivors. All the warriors were dead.

'There are no records. It's a story now told only to children.

'The repository of knowledge, the Matrix, doesn't even refer to the war. Even memories are lost in the mists of time.'

'And the Time Lords don't have a record of these Monsters?'

'The Yssgaroth are a story to frighten children.' The Doctor was thoughtful.

'The Time Lords seem to have a secret. A secret which they have tried to hide. Is that possible?'

'Yes, I'm afraid it is.' The Doctor looked intensely at the poet. 'Do you ever feel alone? Very alone . . .'

The dungeon stank. Bernice sat in the corner of the room writing in her diary. The khthons had untied them and left a torch before locking the dungeon door. She tried to ignore the stench but found her thoughts continually returning to her physical situation. Although she knew no amount of imagination would take her away from this prison, for fleeting moments she did manage to escape into her book.

Thomas was silent.

Ell looked uninterested but not scared. Bernice was trying to describe the Nicaean woman to her diary. It must be odd, she thought, for a stranger to be suddenly caught up in these life or death struggles. It was part of Bernice's life. As she was about to tell herself that she enjoyed this lifestyle, she realized this was not true.

The sound of footsteps echoed down the stairs and along the passageway. The door was unlocked. A khthon bent down and slid a tray across the floor. The door was closed.

On the tray were a jug of tepid water, a plate of raw bloody meat and two mouldy lemons. Bernice couldn't face eating any of the uncooked or rotten food. However, Ell moved quickly over and picked up the raw meat. She crammed the meat into her mouth and a glob of blood trickled down the side of her face. Bernice thought the woman's eating habits were repulsive, and turned away.

And then she heard it again. The sound of scratching behind the wall! It was as if something was trying to break into the room. Perhaps it was rats. She thought about moving from the corner. But outside the moaning had started again. Although they had decided that it was a drill motor, Bernice's imagination turned it into all sorts of monsters.

Ell had finished eating. She sat looking bored and didn't seem perturbed about the noises around them. No imagination, Bernice decided.

'Come on you two, we've got to do something,' Bernice said.

'What?' Thomas asked.

'We're in the lion's den. We've got to make our move,' Bernice tried to explain to him. Thomas moved to the door and slammed his arms into it. The door wasn't even dented.

'This dungeon has been built to hold mightier things than us.' Thomas shook his head.

'Maybe. But we have our intelligence.'

Thomas looked blankly at her.

'You can't give up,' Bernice continued.

'I'm a machine, constructed for one purpose – to serve my masters. I've been programmed with memories and tactics for use in various conflicts . . .'

'So what?' Bernice asked.

'I don't have the knowledge to escape,' said Thomas.

'Don't be stupid,' Bernice retorted.

'I'm a machine.' Thomas turned away.

Suddenly, all the sounds were drowned out by the whining and screaming of the huge drill. It was like the sound of fingernails being dragged down a blackboard.

'It sounds like the drill's made contact,' Ell shouted. 'It may be only a matter of minutes before they break through.'

'What?' Bernice screamed, over the sound of the machinery.

DAY SEVEN
00:00–04:00

Swarf did not look concerned. Chopra had told him about the changes transforming the planet, but the shapechanger just smiled knowingly. Even the order to shut the main castle doors was more of a sop to the khthons than an acknowledgement that things had gone terribly wrong.

Chopra felt frightened as they walked up the narrow stairway to the battlements. He had been sensing the red death for many days. It had spread over the jungle and then had devoured the marshland. He felt that the emptiness was trying to possess him. The monsters were stirring, like babies in the womb, waiting to be reborn.

Swarf stood on the battlement. He surveyed the new world sprawled in front of him. He couldn't understand what had happened. There was an expression of shock on the shapechanger's face.

The planet had faded into a deep gloom. Above, storm clouds veiled the heavens, blocking the sunlight, and below the red stillness covered the surface of the planet. Their world was petrified, and only fifty metres separated their sanctuary from the sea of red death. The silence was overpowering.

Hunters played their incessant games in the skies overhead. There were thousands of the creatures flying above them and ominously silhouetted on the witch trees at the edge of the plain. They seemed to be able to move through the red death without being frozen in time. This was the largest collection of these creatures Chopra had come across; normally, they hunted alone or in small packs. This looked like an army.

This was also the shapechanger's perception.

'They seem to be watching us,' Swarf said.

'They're waiting,' replied Chopra.

Swarf looked up. One Hunter was hovering just above the castle. They could hear the hissing of one, maybe two others, close by. Chopra leant over the battlements.

He moved back, startled.

Attached to the wall of the castle were forty of the creatures, hanging upside down and gently hissing at each other. Their claws were holding tightly on to the nooks and crannies of the walls.

Swarf looked.

'What are they waiting for?' he asked.

Chopra shook his head. He didn't know.

'Bring some of your men up here. Watch the skies.'

'Apart from me, there are only four khthons,' Chopra said.

'If they attack we must be prepared to defend ourselves.' Swarf swallowed nervously and descended back into the castle.

Chopra looked out into the night sky. He wished it didn't have to end this way.

The Doctor's pacing around the cage had stopped. He sat opposite Blake. His eyes were closed and his mind was elsewhere. In the few days that Blake had known the Doctor, he had never seen him fall asleep. He seemed perpetually on edge. Now, in the cage, he mumbled and turned, his brain trying to sort out answers even when his body slept.

It had been almost three days since they had first met in hell, in the arena where the mysterious traveller had fought his deadly foe. Blake felt sad for the Time Lord. He seemed a man without either a past or a future. Something in him kept him going. To call it hope would limit it. The Doctor stirred up numerous feelings in the poet. Even knowing he would die, and that the revolutions stirring over the planet would not create the Earthly paradise he so desired, Blake felt he could trust the stranger.

Perhaps the knowledge that he would one day die actually gave the poet comfort. The prospect of eternity did not appeal to him.

As he looked over at the stranger he suddenly became aware of someone else in the room. Just outside the cage, there seemed to be a figure standing and watching them. The faint light radiating from the cage threw out enough illumination to identify a motionless, shadowy form about six foot from their prison. It seemed to be draped in black, its face hidden.

'Hello,' shouted Blake.

The figure stepped backwards into the darkness. There had been a definite movement. It wasn't his imagination. There was somebody there. The Doctor sat up.

'What is it?' he asked.

'There's somebody watching us,' Blake said.

'Where?' the Doctor asked, peering out of the cage.

'It's gone from sight. It's there, ten foot from the cage.'

The Doctor strained his eyes, but there was nothing to see. The darkness had swallowed up the watcher.

'What did it look like?' the Doctor asked.

'It wasn't a demon. I don't know. I couldn't see very well.' Blake was unsure. 'I don't know what I saw.'

'How long have you been watching me?' the Doctor shouted.

'Khatori, m'y,' a voice echoed from out of the darkness. It was deep and flowing, offering a reassurance from the unknown.

'Saved me! How dare you! Who says I wanted saving? I was on the point of destroying any chance the Monsters had of breaking into this universe.'

'You were on the point of dying,' the voice continued. 'I could not have allowed that.'

'You could not have allowed!' The Doctor's accent had deteriorated into an almost unrecognizable Scottish drawl. 'Who do you think you are?'

The figure stirred and moved out of the shadows towards them. It was draped in a black cloak, with a cowl covering the face. As it walked forward Blake saw a hand illuminated by the pale lights. The mysterious disguise hid the identity of the figure, but could not conceal that it only had one arm. The hood was thrown back and the cloak slid away from the old man's body. A further dark robe hid the damaged frame from view, but the face had a pull, like magnetism. A small beard grew around the mouth and a pony tail weaved down his back.

Blake turned to look at the Doctor. He had sunk to his knees and was bowing his head.

'You ask me who I am,' the figure's voice became louder. 'I am Kopyion . . .'

'Forgive me,' the Doctor whispered, falling prone to the floor.

' . . . Liall a Mahajetsu, the Lord Defender of the Faith of the Peoples of Gallifrey.'

The old man moved painfully, closer to the cage. His body had been damaged by some long distant war. However, his eyes shone with the brightness and power of a great intellect.

Blake stood back, overpowered by the sight of this man. The man was a mythical figure from the Doctor's past. A man who, according to the time traveller, had died thousands of years ago. Yet here he was, standing in front of them on this distant planet.

The figure pressed a switch on the wall and the bars of the cage disappeared. Blake could now see that they were in a large white room, part of a much larger edifice.

The figure stood over the prostrate Doctor.

'You may rise,' said the figure.

The Doctor raised his head and pulled himself to his feet.

'Liall Kopyion, I thank you,' the Doctor said, holding his arm out beseechingly. The figure moved out of reach and appeared to sneer.

'You got in my way,' Kopyion stated in a cold, humourless manner, 'and I am afraid the consequences will be grave.'

'I didn't want to interfere,' said the Doctor.

'No,' Kopyion replied. He started to walk away. The Doctor waved to the poet that they should follow him.

245

'Where are we?' the Doctor asked.

'This is a deep space monitoring station. It slipped out of orbit many centuries ago,' Kopyion said.

'I'm worried about my companion, Bernice Summerfield. Do you know anything of her?' the Doctor asked. Kopyion looked him over.

'You are tiresome. The woman is still alive. She is a prisoner of the shapechanger. I have far larger tasks than to worry over her petty life,' Kopyion said.

Blake followed the two men down a corridor.

A door opened automatically and they entered a huge control room. Screens were erected on the walls. Dials and switches flashed on and off. The screens had images from many different worlds, including Mediaeval Christendom, an airless barren world with a red moon, a futuristic city where men were shooting each other with guns firing burning light, Victorian London, and hell.

A large yellow flag acted as the centrepiece of the room. The crest bore a distinctive design of overlapping circles, resembling an over-elaborate number eight. A warrior's uniform hung up next to the standards. The items appeared to be centuries old.

'What are they?' Blake asked.

'They're relics of the early Time Lords,' the Doctor replied.

'They are not,' said Kopyion. 'These predate the Time Lords by thousands of years . . .'

Somehow that triggered the Doctor, and he interrupted the old man.

'We fought a war, didn't we? Against the Monsters. Why was it kept a secret?'

'We made a terrible mistake when the Time Lords set themselves up as guardians of all space and time,' Kopyion replied.

'That isn't an answer,' said the Doctor.

Kopyion began to laugh. 'It is the answer.'

The Doctor looked furious, as if the old man was laughing at him. Kopyion walked over to the screens. He looked intently at the pictures conjured up before him.

'Please,' said the Doctor. 'I need to know. We've both seen much suffering and horror . . .' The Doctor grasped the old man's sleeve. ' . . . sometimes I think the light flickers.'

The Doctor stared at Kopyion's face. The old man grabbed hold of the Time Lord's hand and removed it from him.

'What light?' Kopyion replied. 'I am doomed for all eternity.'

Kopyion pointed at one of the screens. Blake leant closer. It seemed to be a moving picture of an ancient courtyard. Flames were pouring out of a well. Figures were running around in chaos.

Kopyion tapped the screen. 'Soon . . .'

The machinery was rocking. The power building up in the shaft was starting to have an effect on the castle. The old stone pillars were shaking as if they were being brought back to life. The screams of the drill drowned out all other sounds. Shadows moved all around them as if coming to life.

Chopra stood unsteadily on his feet. The shapechanger bounded around with excitement.

Chopra could tell something had happened. Whatever had walked the corridors of the castle had started to stir again. It was no longer the voices he could hear, but movement. The Monsters themselves . . .

He could hear the wailing. Like the cry of a banshee, the sounds of the Elder Gods re-awakening from their slumber bore only the prophecy of death.

A long, blood-curdling howl . . .

'The ancients believed that they could create immortality,' said the shapechanger. 'Now we are so close to achieving their ends. We will import into this universe huge amounts of Dream B. People can then enter into their own worlds, where they can live forever as Gods.'

Chopra looked at him. This man was not mad. He really did not care about the effect of his actions. As long as he became rich, it didn't matter. His brother had died, but it didn't matter.

Chopra could feel no malice. After all, they were all pawns in a game. A game played out for millennia. Their lives were all mapped out. There was no free will.

Somewhere, hands were moving chess pieces across a board.

Bernice didn't like the sounds. She could hear howling. Thomas told her that it was the Hunters. He had heard the voices before. He told his fellow prisoners of an attack on a colonial settlement where the creatures had made the same noises just before they raided and massacred the colonists. Bernice didn't feel like writing any more in her diary.

Ell had smartened herself up and started to harangue the android about his apparent surrender to fate. She told him that they couldn't possibly stay down here, and that he had to make some effort to escape. It was his mission and he had to fulfil it, she said.

Bernice wondered if there had been anything in the cold meat the woman had eaten. She seemed to have gone through a character change. Perhaps it was panic setting in. The three of them seemed to have been inexorably drawn together with each step they had taken. They were boxed in. There was now only a slim chance of escape. Bernice didn't like this woman. She couldn't understand why the woman's husband had brought her on to this hazardous planet. But then, she had survived and he hadn't.

'They're barbarians. You must do something,' Ell said to the android.

Suddenly, Bernice heard something move in the corner of the room. She turned quickly, expecting to see a rat staring at her. However, it was one of the typewriter creatures that had managed to dig its way into the cell. It scuttled over to her. A message was being typed out.

Bernice looked at it.

'Bernice. This is the Doctor. There is cosmic evil on this planet. Beware . . .'

As Bernice tried to read the next line, Ell moved forward and stamped on the creature. It was crushed, its parts scattered across the room. Bernice turned to rage at the woman.

'I hate those things,' Ell said, smiling.

I cannot cope with the pain, Spike thought. If only he could make a sound or move his body. He was being tortured by the Hunters, and there was nothing he could do to stop it.

They had flown into the atmosphere and had carried his broken body to the other side of the castle. They seemed to have landed away from the red paralysis, but as he looked around he could see the castle being encroached upon from all directions by the strange weed. He was laid down on brittle pampas grass and then man-handled by the creatures. He couldn't tell whether there was a steady stream of them, or whether it was the same five or six Hunters who were torturing him. He was reminded of the behaviour of domestic felines – how they would kidnap smaller creatures from the garden, take them into the house and then taunt them, keeping them alive until they starved or the cats became bored with the game.

He wondered whether prayer would do any good. The last time he had prayed he appeared to have been granted a few more minutes before termination. But for what purpose? He decided that although the Prime Mover had granted his wish, it was up to him how he used that time; but with his badly broken body there was little he could do. Spike couldn't rant against the Prime Mover. His wish had been granted, but he had only been given more time to experience cruel and unabated pain. Some philosophers argued that the Prime Mover did not exist, or was a weak and feeble deity who was impotent to intervene in the machinations of the universe: Spike could not believe that.

The lead Hunter appeared to have a mane around its neck. This was the creature which had picked him up and flown with him. Spike's one eye tried to focus on the movements occurring in front of him. He couldn't close his eyelid. That part of his mechanism had seized up. The leader stood back and watched as two, perhaps three, Hunters covered his body in a gold paste. Spike watched them spit the stuff out of their mouths and then spread it over his skin with their claws. And it hurt! It was like acid, and made his whole body scream with pain.

'Stop, stop,' he wanted to shout out. But there was only silence. He was powerless to stop this terrible torture.

Every synapse and electronic membrane of his machine body burnt with the intensity of a thousand deaths. He stared out of his bodily prison and cursed them. A Hunter rubbed the cold, clammy substance over his face, making sure that it covered his one remaining eye. His vision misted over and he could no longer see.

It hurts!

Why could they not let him die?

The gel covered his body, and Spike's mind struggled to cope with the signals from every neuron in his artificial frame.

He started to realize that he was experiencing sensations from parts of his body which he had thought had ceased to function. This did not make sense. Perhaps the substance also had effects on the mind. He was aware of strange thoughts and sensations swimming through his mind, but he could not cope with the pain. He heard himself whisper the word, 'Help . . .' and then he lost consciousness.

When he awoke he could not tell if he had fainted or had been asleep for hours or even days. The pain was gone. His body felt pleasant and warm. He felt his hair being stroked and opened both eyes. He still had difficulties focusing, but could tell clearly enough what was happening in front of him. The lead Hunter knelt to the side of his face and was gently running its claws through the android's hair. It was purring, like a pet cat.

The heat in the throne room was building up. Steam was pouring out of the mine shaft. A watery mist drifted along the corridors of the castle. The mist took on the form of tentacles seeping from the otherworld and manoeuvring a gossamer-like web around them. Chopra could sense they were merely minutes away from the opening of the gateway.

One of the three khthons began to hum a sorrowful melody. Although it was wordless, Chopra recognized the tune and the homesick sentiments inspiring the ancient lullaby. The khthon was rocking his head to and fro. Chopra began to join in. His voice echoed his fellow khthon's morose singing. The song was one sung by all khthons as Death approached. Stories were told of whole communities sitting down and wailing the old tune whilst waiting for the slave masters to arrive and incarcerate their bodies and souls.

Swarf turned, screaming for them to stop. This was his triumph. He would soon be rich. Chopra could see into his mind. The shapechanger could not face up to his failure; with only five khthons left there would be no mass production of the drug. Swarf thought he could come to this world, steal the treasures of another race and escape with immortality and immeasurable riches. There was no escape.

'Stop it!' shouted Swarf. The khthons didn't listen. The third khthon was also swaying and chanting a welcome to death.

The shapechanger's mind was confused. Swarf was panicking. He had lost control, and didn't know what to do. Suddenly Swarf lunged forward, grabbed one of the khthons and strangled him.

Swarf smiled in triumph, letting the body fall on to the ground.

The singing stopped.

'No,' Chopra shouted. 'It is over for us all. Let us make our peace before we die.'

'You can see the signs, but you can't read them,' said

Swarf. 'I promised you riches beyond the avarice of man. And you shall have them.'

Bernice decided that Ell had been watching too many films. She had suggested that one of them should pretend to be ill, shout for help and then, when one of their captors responded, the others should attack him. Ell had once seen a vidfilm where that had been used for an escape bid. Bernice had seen a number of films where that had succeeded, and more importantly thought it likely that everybody had seen at least one film where that less than daring idea had been tried. Thomas was apathetic, and said he would go along with whatever plans everybody else had.

'We're not arranging a night out, you know,' Bernice said.

Bernice agreed to lie on the ground and moan. Thomas stood behind the door. The three of them shouted. And eventually a khthon approached the cell. It looked through the small door window, asked what was going on, and then told them all to stand back. It entered and Thomas struck it.

Ell smiled.

'I don't believe it,' Bernice said, coming to the conclusion that the khthons didn't have many cinemas.

The khthon had been killed instantly. Bernice felt sorry, but thought many more would die before they escaped from the castle. They had decided that they should not walk up the staircase to the throne room but find another route to approach their captors. They took the torch with them.

One of the typewriter creatures was following them. It seemed to be watching them.

As they walked through the dungeons, Bernice saw blood-splattered walls and rusty instruments of pain. She was frightened.

There were weird sounds and feelings brewing in the castle. The winds brushing through the tunnels and stairwells had an unnatural quality to them. There were

252

also other things moving around and making their presence felt.

Suddenly, all three of them froze as one of the inner walls appeared to vibrate and move. The stone walls seemed to buckle. The prisoners didn't wait to identify the cause of the disturbance but quickly carried on.

Ell pointed to scratch marks on the wall which she said had just appeared. Thomas said that the two women were very suggestible, that it was just the wind and that the claw marks were certainly many centuries old.

Bernice saw something which she didn't point out to her companions. It was a crest. She had first seen it on one of the standards fluttering in the throne room. It was also carved on to a number of the walls, as if to ward off Evil. She had finally recognized it. She didn't know what it meant but had seen it in some of the old books in the Doctor's TARDIS. It was the mark of the Time Lords of Gallifrey.

It was called the Seal of Rassilon.

'That was lucky,' Blake said, as they watched the three prisoners escape from the dungeon.

'There is no blind chance,' Kopyion said.

The screen flickered. They had seen the argument between the khthons and the shapechanger. Now the Doctor's companion, the woman and the android were walking through the dark corridors of the castle, trying to find some means of escape.

Blake couldn't understand what was happening in front of him. The moving pictures on the wall seemed to be of events occurring elsewhere on the planet, or in the universe, across the ages. But the events were all going on now.

'I created this whole planet, using Gallifreyan technology,' said Kopyion. 'Its purpose is to monitor the Yssgaroth. I knew they would return; perhaps tomorrow, in a year or in a million years, but they would be back. I have stood guard across the centuries.'

Blake looked at the old man. Kopyion sat on a chair,

staring out of half-blind eyes at the screens and eating dates from a little box on his lap. Kopyion's body seemed decayed, only able to move due to sheer strength of will.

'But why have the Time Lords kept this Great War a secret?' the Doctor asked.

He had seemed to be sulking. He was sitting on the floor with his legs crossed, and had said nothing for over an hour. Kopyion's refusal to answer any of his previous questions had irritated the Time Lord.

'I am sorry, Doctor. Do you want the truth?'

'Yes.' The Doctor looked suspiciously at him.

'It is a history lesson, but one that you will never have heard before.

'Gallifrey was an advanced civilization. Across the sentient worlds of the galaxy we were treated as gods. Our people were happy. We created works of art that could not even be imagined by lesser races; we pushed our bodies even further and devised whole new theories and systems to improve our way of life.

'We believed in God. We were a spiritual race. We prayed. And then it started. Philosophers argued about the existence of God. And then the scientists stated that we were alone in the universe, that we made our own destiny. There were many ideas, debates and arguments about our place in the cosmos.

'And one of our greatest scientists, Rassilon, announced that he had discovered the principles of time travel. All we had to do was harness the power of a black hole.' Kopyion shook his head. 'And the fools tried it. They exploded the most powerful device ever created, inside a black hole. Do you know what they did?'

'According to our history, they discovered the power to drive the experiments in time,' the Doctor replied.

'No. That was much later. The initial experiment went horribly wrong. They pierced the fabric of our universe; like a gunshot that ripped open the whole of space and time. They created holes throughout the cosmos, from our universe to the other side of the black hole. The other side . . .

'And then they came. Monsters. Hideous monsters, in their hordes. Star systems were destroyed. Billions died. The war went on for over a thousand years. And we were responsible . . .'

'This isn't true,' the Doctor said.

'And then, after the war, the newly formed High Council set themselves up as the Time Lords.'

'But Gallifreyan history isn't like that.'

'Your history is a lie. When I returned from the War, I wished I was dead. I saw a people half destroyed by plague. The virus had annihilated all those who knew of Rassilon's great mistake. A sole warrior survived the Eternal War. But he soon died. Most of the great men died.

'Rassilon had become the first President of the Time Lords of Gallifrey.

'He talked of science and reason. The rule of law. I argued. It was Evil which we had fought, dark desperate evil. I had seen things which no-one should ever see. But they were not interested, Rassilon and the scientists. They talked of the end of superstition and dread. The truth did not suit them. They re-wrote history. They were technologically advanced. They sat in their ivory towers.

'But the Time Lords were immoral.

'I could tell you so much. How in another experiment a scientist was sent into a black hole and was supposedly killed by the force of the explosion. He wasn't. He was sealed in there to prevent him ever telling of Rassilon's great mistake.

'I escaped. To keep a lone guard against an ancient and bitter enemy.'

The Doctor had stood up and was pacing around the room. He didn't seem able to agree with this version of his people's history. Blake didn't know what to think. He didn't agree with Kopyion. He saw scientists and thinkers as exploring the unknown, pushing forward their place in the universe. They had eaten of the forbidden fruit of knowledge and had been cast out of paradise. He didn't think there was a God. He had seen no signs of His existence in his journey with the Doctor.

'I don't understand how you knew they would come back here, to this time, at this place in the universe. I can see it's happening, but why here and now?' Blake asked.

'It's very simple. The Monsters want my body and soul. They want vengeance.'

'I see,' said Blake.

'I doubt whether you could understand how it feels to know for all eternity that the creations of hell are pursuing you,' Kopyion said.

'Can we get into the castle?' the Doctor asked. He was clearly concerned about his companion. 'I've heard what you've said. I don't know whether I believe you, but I feel powerless standing here.'

'There is a path, but it would be playing our hand too early. We would not be able to tell what the enemy's intentions are this time,' Kopyion replied. He offered Blake and the Doctor a date. Both declined.

'But Bernice might die,' the Doctor said, exasperated.

'Yes, she might,' said Kopyion.

Bernice stopped. She couldn't go any further forward. She pointed to the wall in front of them. Thomas couldn't see and bent forwards.

'Don't,' she said.

'Why not?' Thomas asked. And then he saw it as well.

In the centre of the wall was a crack. It was only a narrow mark on the wall, but all around seeped the red death. The paralysis bubbled and oozed through the small hole. This was worse than they had thought. The castle was not sealed off, and their lives were in utmost danger.

'Get back,' said Thomas.

'No,' Ell said. 'We've got to carry on.'

He looked at her.

'We only have a short time,' Ell said. Before Bernice could reply, Ell had walked past the red paralysis and had started to run down the corridor. She seemed to have lost interest in her companions.

'After you,' Bernice said to the android. He smiled a thank you. They shuffled past the paralysis.

'What's she running for?' Bernice asked.

'Perhaps she's scared,' suggested Thomas.

'I doubt it. Come on, we'd better keep an eye on her.'

They continued to walk along the corridors of the dungeons, until they came to another stairway. Bernice turned and faced the typewriter creature that was following them.

'I hope we're doing the right thing, Doctor,' she said.

She smiled, and then began to climb the stairs to the ground level and the shapechanger.

As she did, a cold shiver ran down her back.

DAY SEVEN
04:00–08:00

Spike closed his eyes again. He needed all his concentration to run the self-test on his level of functioning. He did not want the Hunters to be aware of his renewed strength. Although he did not have the strength, even when fully functioning, to defeat one Hunter in unarmed combat, he had the skill and training to give him an advantage. And he aimed to surprise them. He would go down fighting. The memory chips in his electronic brain were still badly damaged. However, he had 15 per cent arm and leg functioning. The self-tests also indicated that his battery pack had only twenty minutes of power before termination. It had to be enough.

The Hunters were moving around him. He could feel the beating of their wings. The creatures by his side and much further away were howling into the night sky. He knew that this indicated they planned to attack.

He couldn't feel any of the creatures pawing at his body. He listened carefully. There was the slight sound of undulating breath. He estimated that there was just one Hunter. Trying to sense where the noise was coming from, he concluded that the creature was a metre north north west of his head. It had to be crouched down, about a metre and a half off the ground. He couldn't open his eyes again. If it saw him do this it would be alarmed and prepared. He would have one chance only.

He silently prayed to the Prime Mover. As he came to the 'Amen', he tightened his body, and then uncoiled like a spring, throwing his arms backwards into what he hoped was the creature's face. His fists slammed into flesh. He turned his head, opening his eyes as he twisted his body into a kneeling position. He raised his arms above his head and brought them down with the full force he could muster on to the Hunter's face. It was the lead Hunter. It seemed to have a surprised, almost shocked expression on its face.

His plan had worked. As the Hunter lay on the ground he drove his fingers into the eyeballs. Blinded, the creature squirmed and tried to escape. But there would be no escape. Spike carried on the upward movement into the brain, and the creature shuddered and died.

The android commander looked around. The Hunters were attacking the castle. Hundreds of them were flying overhead, screeching and trying to land on the lone tower. Around him, the red weed had proceeded even further and was now only ten metres from his position. Whatever had happened to this world? The paralysis had covered the plain, and cast a dark shadow across the castle. This world did not have long to go before it was totally extinguished by the alien weed.

He fell on to all fours and crawled over to the castle. It wasn't easy, moving through muddy grass on his stomach for thirty metres. But he had to make sure that he wasn't seen.

He arrived at the base of the tower. Only fifteen minutes left. He checked his holster. The laser pistol remained in place. He hadn't had time to use it when attacked by the shapechanger, and the Hunters had shown no interest in it. He hoped it hadn't been damaged by the water. He looked up. The Hunters were flying and attacking the ramparts. He couldn't see what was happening in the castle. There might be hundreds of defenders protecting 'Pandora's Box'. He pulled himself parallel to the wall, stretched out his arm and grabbed for a handhold. Putting his left foot on the wall, he began to climb the steep tower.

The Hunters seemed not to notice him. When they flew close by, he would stop moving and only re-start when they had disappeared from view. Above him, it sounded as if a bloody and violent battle was going on for the possession of the battlements. Even if he could make it, he might be cut down by whoever won the fight.

But that was a future problem. First he had to climb to the top of the tower and survive the attention of the savages.

Seven minutes left before termination.

They had caught up with Ell. She was watching the final moments of the mining operation. She stood in the centre of a doorway to the courtyard, immobile and staring. She didn't seem to be concerned that she wasn't hidden from the shapechanger's sight.

Lightning bolts were descending from the upper atmosphere and striking the top of the mining equipment. The machinery roared. Sparks were flying everywhere. The room was bathed in a fiery glow. Thomas grabbed hold of Ell's shoulders.

'Come on, we've got to get her out of here,' Thomas said.

'Where to?' Bernice asked.

Swarf was running around. He was shouting orders at the lead khthon. The khthon was cowering, and seemed to be afraid of the bright lights.

Suddenly, all noise stopped.

The vapour started to rise up towards the hole in the roof and a hissing sound echoed around the chamber.

Swarf turned in triumph. 'Within moments, we will have broken through the fabric of another universe.'

The room started to shake. It felt as if the castle was sitting on top of a rocket about to explode. In the mist, Bernice could see glimpses of something. It was difficult to distinguish exactly what she was seeing. But she had never seen its like before. The mist swirled.

If it was one creature, it was a gargantuan Beast.

Its body resembled a huge serpent, with spikes and billowing dragon-like wings. Its reptilian head was lean, with dozens of eyes square in the forehead, savage teeth, long, languid tongue and small horns bulging from the crown.

As she stared, the Beast seemed to take on many forms. Glimpses. Was it one Monster, or a myriad? She thought she could see painted wings, like a death's-head moth, claws, wet feathers. Perhaps there were smaller creatures clinging to the main body, or maybe flying things hovering around the Beast. Whatever the Beast was, it rose up above the machinery, through the hole in the roof, and hundreds of metres into the heavens.

'What is it?' Swarf was staring up. He obviously hadn't been expecting this.

'You have opened up a gateway to the Abyss,' shouted the khthon.

'Aaaaarghh . . .' a scream seemed to come from a passageway. Isolated shouts, and cries of terror.

This castle is empty, Bernice told herself.

She shivered. Her breath condensed in the cold air.

Ell started to walk forward.

Swarf turned to her, surprised. What was she doing here? This woman had been locked in the dungeons. It didn't make sense.

She stood in front of the shapechanger. She had no fear.

'We have broken through,' Swarf said, trying to understand what was going on.

'I disagreed when my husband employed you. Why did the Followers need street scum like you to do our work? We suspected that you would try to double cross us. So we tempted you with Dream B. But it's not the drugs we want.' Ell smiled. 'The Time Lords were fools, all those centuries ago, to think that my Masters would simply rest and die.'

'What do you want?' Swarf struggled to ask the question.

'You have opened up the well of souls,' Ell said. 'We shall release the Masters from their imprisonment. Soon, darkness will fall over the whole of creation.'

'No,' Swarf shouted.

Kopyion stood. The typewriter creature had been watching the events unfolding in the throne room.

'It is time,' Kopyion said, walking over to the ceremonial robes. 'The enemy has revealed itself. We must move.'

Kopyion knelt down in front of the garments, spoke several words to himself, and stood. An ancient cloak was slung over his shoulders, a pointed skullcap covered his head and an impressive bejewelled sword was slipped into a sheath at the front of his body.

He picked up an amulet and placed it over his head. The amulet showed a worm curling around a globe. It was similar to that worn by the Fellowship in Victorian London.

'Doctor.' Blake pointed out the design to the Time Lord.

'It is a charm,' Kopyion stated. 'The ancients believed that you could use Evil to ward off Evil.'

He walked over to the yellow flag. With great effort, he picked it up and held it above his head. He looked across at the Doctor and nodded.

Kopyion began to walk down the corridor towards the unknown.

Bernice watched the unfolding drama with fascination. A young wife talking to a shapechanger. He appeared nervous and confused, continually glancing up at the Beast forming in the smoke above him. The lone khthon lay on the floor, praying. It seemed uninterested, appearing to be deaf to the cries for help. The shapechanger had been calling out for the other khthons, but there had been no reply. Bernice presumed that they were all dead.

Her head was spinning. Ghost-like apparitions drifted through her mind: creatures which were neither fish, flesh nor fowl but amorphous mutations and diseased imaginings.

'Back on Nicaea, the Followers have been conducting

sacrifices to celebrate the return of the ancient ones,' Ell said.

The shapechanger was swinging his arms desperately, as if fighting off invisible hordes. Bernice could see nothing near him, but he was screaming and shouting.

'They will leave this planet and once more expand across the universe,' Ell continued, ignoring what was going on around her.

Bernice felt a light tap on her shoulder. She turned.

'I know what to do,' Thomas said.

Bernice didn't know how to respond. The android was trying to communicate something to her.

'I – ' he started to say.

The castle shuddered again, sending the people sprawling. Ell stumbled. Thomas took a long look at Bernice, then ran towards the shapechanger. Ell seemed to be expecting the attack. She deftly stepped out of his way.

The android attacked. Two punches hit their target. The dwarf looked surprised. He tried to crawl across the floor, away from the android. Thomas slammed his arm down on the shapechanger's back. The dwarf seemed winded. Thomas fell on his knees and began to strangle the squirming figure.

But it didn't matter how hard the android squeezed, it had no effect on the neck muscles of the shapechanger. He turned his head unnaturally to face the android. Just a little further than was normally possible.

'If this is the gateway to hell . . .' he started to say. The body began to transform. The android couldn't hold it any more, and fell on to the floor.

A huge dog, the size of a horse, stood in the room. It had three heads. All barking and dripping saliva.

'No,' Thomas shouted. He struck out with his arm, blinding one of the heads. But the ferocity of the creature was too much.

The hell-hound plunged its savage teeth into the android's body. The chest and neck were torn away.

The android stopped moving.

Bernice looked away. The rabid attack was over in seconds.

'Oh android, what was your life but a hollow shell?' Ell asked. 'But the lives of mortal creatures are no different than those of metal men. There is no purpose.'

The dog continued to growl as the mist drifted around it. It snarled, barking at the barely visible Monsters.

'Leave me alone,' it shouted, transforming back into the dwarf. The wispy creatures continued to torment him. He waved his arms over his head.

Behind the shapechanger, Bernice could see a more ominous sight.

The red weed had broken through the wall. It covered an area of about three square metres and was advancing rapidly. An eerie stillness had taken hold of that end of the throne room.

The khthon was huddled on the floor. He was hiding his face. Ell walked over and knelt in front of him.

'Chopra, can you hear the voices?' Ell asked. His hearing was obviously better than that of Bernice. She couldn't hear anything, but the khthon's face tightened and showed him to be listening to some barely audible sounds.

'They're coming,' Ell said, 'and they're calling your name.' She held her arms wide and looked like she was about to cuddle him.

'Who are you?' Chopra asked.

'I am known by many names, but you know me as the "Empire that Never Ended" . . .' She paused, held the khthon's head and suddenly twisted it. There was a click, and his inert body fell to the floor. ' . . . I am Death.'

Ell turned away from the dead body of the khthon. She looked up at the monstrous form rising above her.

Kopyion walked, as if taking part in a ceremonial state occasion. Each step was taken, like part of a dance, to some long-lost plan. Kopyion held the flag, bearing the ancient heritage of Gallifrey. He walked along the corridors and out of the space station.

He was silent, his mind elsewhere.

264

Blake looked around. Darkness had fallen. However, the planet was stained deep red as if a bloody wound had opened and poured forth over the length and breadth of the land. There was a stillness, dreadful and intense, which appeared to have taken possession of the alien world.

'What is it?' Blake asked.

'It is contamination seeping through the hole,' Kopyion replied. 'In the seven days since the shapechangers started their experiments, it has spread rapidly and now become a deluge. They have been used . . .'

'Could this be the fate of the universe?' the Doctor asked.

'Yes,' Kopyion said.

'How are we going to walk through the weed?' Blake asked.

'You don't have to fear. I have been expecting this moment. This path has been created for centuries to allow a safe passage through the red death.'

'Gallifreyan technology?' the Doctor asked.

'And prayer,' Kopyion replied.

They walked along a symmetrical path, stretching from the Gallifreyan space station to the age-old castle. Kopyion told them not to try and touch the red weed. It would destroy their souls.

In the stygian gloom hundreds, if not thousands, of Hunters flew overhead screeching and crying out. However, Blake's eyes were drawn to an image growing in size and intensity, apparently reaching out to the heavens. He couldn't tell if it was one of the creatures that had attacked them in the otherworld, but he could sense an ancient evil thriving and pulsating as it looked out across the planets, stars and galaxies.

The eyes seemed to stare at him. Blake felt a coldness. The Doctor pushed him.

'You must keep moving,' the Doctor said.

There were only seconds left. Spike was confused. His mind and body were no longer coordinated. He had stumbled over the wall on to the parapet of the castle. Two khthons lay dead, their insides gouged out. They had stood no chance against the Hunters. The flying creatures now seemed more interested in the shape forming in the sky. Spike's energy level was so low that he could barely walk down the long stairway. He had to succeed. The pain was intense. If he just gave up and lay down then he would have eternal rest. He was aware of the thoughts, but he continued to struggle.

He found a doorway and tried to point his dying body in that direction. His feet didn't answer to his commands and he felt his body collapse on to the floor.

There was still energy left in his arms. He crawled along the stone floor and managed to go through the doorway. Although his strength was rapidly deteriorating, he continued, dragging himself along a corridor.

He found himself on a balcony above the throne room. Down below he could see one of the shapechangers and a woman he could not identify. And there was also Bernice! She had survived. He felt sorrow.

He could see machinery. A dark mist was rising out of a hole in the roof of the castle. He wondered if it was the strange shape which was so attracting the Hunters? He didn't know and didn't care. He had seen the missile. It was powering the machinery.

Nine seconds and he would be terminated. He pulled himself up and aimed the gun. He staggered around, dizzy.

Suddenly, a scream shattered his final moments. He looked down. The woman's mouth was pulled open in a shriek. Her eyes protruded and her right arm pointed accusingly at him.

'No,' she screamed.

He looked back at the missile and pulled the trigger. The gun discharged a high-energy bolt. But he couldn't see or hear. His body crumpled on to the floor and as he fell he sensed a tremendous blast of heat burn his skin.

He smiled.

A fiery light radiated out like an exploding sun. The castle exploded. Stone and rubble were blasted into the sky and the tower was ripped off and collapsed on to the ground. The three travellers were thrown off their feet and pushed backwards by the sheer force of the shockwave. The Doctor told Blake to cover his head and wait until the disturbance settled down. The very earth seemed to be shaking, as if roaring out in protest.

The air was scorching, and Blake found it difficult to breathe. It soon became bitingly cold as the air was sucked into the inferno which had been the dark castle.

And then everything seemed still.

Blake looked around him. Smoke was rising from the ashes of the ruin. The shape that had been forming in their universe was no more. The red weed had turned an insipid chalk colour and was withering all around them. Blake picked up some rubble from the castle and threw it at the weed. The stone landed, and the weed crumbled into dust. The parasite was no longer a threat to their safety.

Kopyion stood. He looked puzzled.

'What happened?' the Doctor asked.

Kopyion shrugged.

Blake, pointing around them, asked: 'Is it over?'

Kopyion shook his head.

DAY SEVEN
08:00–12:00

Bernice stirred. Her body ached, and she felt a weight across her chest and limbs. She opened her eyes. She was covered in a thin layer of dust. Her clothes had been burnt, and only rags covered her body. She remembered seeing Spike, realizing that he was still alive and then, as it dawned on her that he planned to destroy the missile, Ell saw him too and started to shriek. His aim had been accurate. However, Bernice was confused. Why had the most powerful weapon ever created not done more damage?

The roof of the courtyard had fallen in. Ell was crushed underneath the rubble. She was moving, but couldn't lift the slabs that had crashed down on her. The shapechanger was sitting on the floor, staring into the air. He seemed to be in shock.

Above them the night sky seemed to be showing the first signs of a new morning. The apparition had disappeared, and there seemed a much calmer atmosphere. It reminded Bernice of walking through the countryside on Earth after a thunderstorm; there was an electric charge in the air as if the land's natural batteries had been recharged. She thought of her childhood: she had been frightened of thunderstorms and one night, as one tore across the countryside, possessing her with unimaginable terror, her mother had held on to her tightly and taken her outside to watch a multicoloured, incandescent light show. Her mother had held her. The spirit of wonder she'd always found in her father's stories was transformed into a sense of beauty to be found in the natural world. She'd had an unpleasant childhood, but there were good times she would always remember.

Why should she remember that now? She felt a tear in her eye. Probably a speck of dust, she told herself.

The Hunters hovered two or three kilometres over the castle. An occasional Hunter overcame the instincts of the pack and descended to the ruins. The explosion had frightened them, but they seemed to be working up their courage.

As she stood, dusting down her body, she heard whistling. Someone was walking down the corridors of the castle. Was it not over yet? And then, as she listened, she recognized the discordant whistle.

'Row na row, row na row, row na row, dee dee da dee dee, dee dee da dee dee dee . . .'

It was a rough approximation of the sound of the engines of the TARDIS, travelling across time and space. The Doctor often whistled the sound when his mind was embroiled in thought, or when playing chess and trying to distract her.

He entered the room and his eyes caught hers immediately.

'I don't fancy the cleaning bill,' he said to her.

'Doctor,' Bernice shouted over to him.

He walked to her.

'We survived,' he said, lightly tapping her on the head. She would have liked him to put his arm around her. She needed a hug. Someone to hold on to her and say it would be all right. It wouldn't come from the Doctor, though.

She heard the sound of a voice, following the Doctor down the corridor.

'I just want to go home,' it said.

Two men entered the room. The first was dressed in Georgian clothes. He was filthy, and the expression on his face looked as if he had seen enough to last a lifetime. The other man seemed incredibly old, dressed in robes and skullcap and carrying a copy of the yellow standard which had been hanging up in the throne room. He looked around the room. He was searching for something.

'What happened here?' the Doctor asked her.

'Spike . . .'

'Spike?' he repeated.

'One of the androids. I thought the shapechanger had destroyed him. He was up there with a gun and he shot at the missile. There was an explosion. I don't know why we all weren't killed.' She had started to ramble. 'Doctor, what is all this about?'

As she spoke, the elderly man struggled across the room. He walked with a pronounced limp. He stood over Ell.

'Help me, will you?' she said, trying to shift the weight off her body. 'I can't move, I think I've broken a few bones. I can't feel my legs.'

The old man placed the standard on the floor.

The expression on his face didn't change. He pulled the sword out of its sheath. It was a heavy, machete-type weapon which he held with great difficulty in one hand.

'I have never met you personally, but I met your Masters a long time ago. Evil is so ostentatious. I monitored your associates, and observed the murders. Your compatriots, the murderers Mann and Brown, are dead. I don't know if I killed all of "the Followers", but it is over.'

'No, you are too late. The shapechanger has opened the well of souls . . .' She coughed, spluttered and then was still.

'No, the hole has closed again. The power source and the machinery have been destroyed,' the old man continued.

Ell stared at him and didn't move.

Bernice could see that she was dead. But this didn't stop the old man. He raised the sword above his head.

'I k'n Kopyion, Liall a Mahajetsu, Prenta goa mij t'ra vijtrak – '

'Stop!' the Doctor shouted, realizing what was about to happen.

' – s'lai yssgaroth.'

The sword plunged down into the dead woman's neck. Three blows separated the head from the body. Kopyion tore the amulet from around his neck. For a few moments he held the amulet in his hand, looked at the design, and then threw it on to the dead body.

'Evil against Evil,' he said.

Swarf had been sitting quietly, but this display frightened him. He ran out of the room. Although Bernice couldn't understand the savagery of the beheading, she knew that she couldn't let Swarf escape. She had a score to settle. He looked at her, and began to transform into a small brown insect. Bernice watched with fascination as the body seemed to turn inside out. She recognized the creature as a flying cockroach. It flew up out of her reach.

Bernice stopped.

'Bastard,' she shouted.

However, she was not the only one watching the shape-changer. A Hunter swooped down towards the escaping insect. The shapechanger saw it, but its getaway was too slow, and it failed to transform. The Hunter grabbed it in its claw, threw it into its mouth, and then ate it.

'Checkmate,' said Bernice.

She turned back to her friend. She didn't feel like talking, but she needed some answers.

'Doctor, why aren't we dead?' she asked.

The Doctor shrugged his shoulders.

The Georgian was walking around in a circle. He seemed tired and drained. He had been looking at the mangled and burnt-out machinery.

'The force of the explosion was directed at the other-world,' the Doctor said eventually. 'We just suffered the aftermath of the destruction of the machinery. But the effect on the otherworld must have been . . .'

'A holocaust,' said the old man.

'The otherworld?' Bernice looked puzzled. 'Do you mind me asking what precisely is going on here? Who are you? I'm getting just a little tired of all of this. I want something to eat. I want a good sleep.'

'I probably owe you an explanation,' said the Doctor. 'Someday . . .'

'How about now?' she replied.

271

'I think we had better be going,' said the old man. 'The Hunters are starting to swarm now they have tasted blood.'

Bernice looked up. The Hunters were gathering on the castle walls. They were framed against the morning sky, looking down at the four travellers. The creatures shuffled uneasily as they watched the activities going on in the ruined courtyard.

The old man started to walk out of the ruin. The Georgian stood still. He seemed to be in shock. The Doctor pushed him.

'Come on, it's time to go home.'

The Georgian seemed to smile.

'Be careful,' said the old man. 'Don't show that you're frightened.'

Bernice looked across at the Doctor.

'Is it over?' she asked, walking behind him.

The Doctor shrugged his shoulders.

She kept sneaking a glance at the Hunters. Their wings had started to beat faster, and they were showing an increasing interest in the goings on in the ruins. Two or three of the creatures were hovering above Ell's body. As the four travellers walked down the corridor, the mood of the Hunters suddenly changed and they began to attack the bloodied corpse.

The sky, for a moment, was darkened by the gathering of the scavengers.

Outside the castle, the morning sun was rising over the escarpment and casting long shadows across the plain. The red death was losing its grip on the vegetation. Life had returned to the world. The old man pointed towards the space station.

'I will return you to your TARDIS,' he said.

'It is over, then,' repeated Bernice.

He looked at her with eyes that penetrated to her soul. She didn't know who he was, or where he was from, but she saw into his eyes. He shook his head. But it would make no difference, for she had seen into his eyes and knew his answer.

'No. This was only a skirmish. They will be back. Someday. And next time, it will be full-scale war.

'This time they were only testing me. Seeing if I was still strong enough to resist them. And I failed.' The old man seemed terribly bitter. 'I showed that I would place one person's life above all else.'

'You saved my life,' said the Doctor.

'Yes. And I said the consequences would be grave. I will have to prove that even alone, I, Kopyion Liall a Mahajetsu, am prepared to stand up to them. Whatever the cost.'

'I don't understand,' said the Doctor.

'There's a bomb, in orbit around this world. It has been triggered. In a few hours, it will detonate and obliterate this solar system,' said Kopyion.

'What!' Bernice said.

'You don't need to do this,' said the Doctor.

Kopyion shrugged.

'How many will die?' Bernice asked.

'Several million – ' said Kopyion.

'But that's monstrous,' she continued.

'What would be monstrous would be the billions of people, the planets, the star systems and the galaxies that would be destroyed if they were ever to return. What are a few million people in the total history of the universe?'

'You can't allow it,' Bernice said to the Doctor.

The Doctor looked powerless. 'I wish I could do something,' he said, appalled.

'You can, Doctor. You must disarm the bomb,' Bernice replied.

'I can't.'

'Doctor . . .' She stared at him.

'No.' He shook his head. 'It was your idea that we visited this planet. You remembered the disappearance of the entire system. It has already happened. There's nothing we can do. We're part of history. We can't change it.'

Kopyion continued. 'All knowledge of the Althosian

system will be wiped from the matrix. The truth is too dangerous . . .'

They walked to the space station. They were strangely quiet. Bernice was seething with anger. Her friend must be able to prevent this genocide. The Doctor tried to explain, in his usual confused way, what had gone on over the last four days and why he couldn't interfere. But she didn't understand. She understood that it was something about the return of Monsters that had attacked their universe thousands of years ago, when the people of Gallifrey had fought a long, bloody war. She had been introduced to Blake, who rambled on about the eternal conflict between the forces of Good and Evil. But it didn't make sense to her. For once, she knew the Doctor had not been all-knowing, that even with his great age and status as a Time Lord he had been as confused as her. He looked sad, like a child who had found a penny but lost a pound. He seemed to want to say something, but it was lost and never said.

The ancient Gallifreyan had looked at the Doctor. Those burning eyes had stared at him.

'Don't get in my way again,' Kopyion said. 'If we meet again, I will kill you. Don't interfere in my work. It goes on.'

Epilogue

Bernice was tired. The conflict was over. For now. They had to return William Blake to his own time and place and then carry on wherever the fancy took them. Blake looked burnt out. The last week had taken a toll on the fifty year old man. Bernice was not really aware of his poetry or art, but knew that he was a mystic and artist. She would have liked to have had a conversation with him, but he was exhausted. He walked into the TARDIS and didn't even notice that it was larger on the inside than on the outside. He leant against the wall, and seemed to drain away.

'Do you still want to go and see the unknown?' the Doctor asked.

'I don't know what I want,' she replied.

Kopyion had taken them in his ship, across the planet. The planet that within a few hours would be destroyed. She had last seen Kopyion staring out of his space ship at the three time travellers. The Doctor had tried to say something to him, but Kopyion ignored him. The space ship had risen off the planet in a cloud of dust.

Back at the TARDIS, Bernice took a last look around. There was a breathless beauty to the jungle.

'Just have hope. Remember that we won this time, and it's possible that we'll win next time.'

'But it's not likely,' Bernice added.

The Doctor put his hand in his pocket and looked surprised. He slowly pulled out his yo-yo. He began to play with it, letting the weight fall to the floor and return to his hand. He smiled that idiotic grin, as if everything would be all right now that his toy was working.

They walked inside the TARDIS and closed the

electronic doors. The time machine seemed eerie. There was a coldness about it. It was almost menacing. The Doctor hadn't noticed. He started pressing switches and noting figures on the dials. The distinctive sound of the time machine dematerializing filled the air. The Time Lord was entranced by the machinery and began to fiddle with the console controls. He seemed to be ignoring Bernice.

'What are you doing?' she asked.

'We must return Blake to his own time.'

She shivered. She hadn't managed to shake off the vague feelings of unease that had disturbed her on the planet. Nothing had been sorted out. She didn't feel safe.

The TARDIS seemed to shudder.

The Doctor frowned. 'I am . . .'

'What?'

'Nothing.' He seemed angry. 'The TARDIS and I are perfectly all right. I was just thinking of the future.' He smiled inanely and turned away.

She had to take her mind off the events of the last few days. She saw the chess board.

'Do you want a game?' she asked. The Doctor ignored her.

'Do you play chess?' she asked Blake, still looking at the Doctor. He appeared bemused, staring at an array of instruments and lights as if uncertain how to proceed. 'It could be a while before we get you back home.'

She turned to the poet.

Blake lay on the floor with his eyes closed. He was fast asleep.

CAT'S CRADLE: TIME'S CRUCIBLE
Marc Platt

The TARDIS is invaded by an alien presence and is then
destroyed. The Doctor disappears. Ace, lost and alone,
finds herself in a bizarre city where nothing is to be trusted
– even time itself.

ISBN 0 426 20365 8

CAT'S CRADLE: WARHEAD
Andrew Cartmel

The place is Earth. The time is the near future – all too
near. As environmental destruction reaches the point of
no return, multinational corporations scheme to buy
immortality in a poisoned world. If Earth is to survive,
somebody has to stop them.

ISBN 0 426 20367 4

CAT'S CRADLE: WITCH MARK
Andrew Hunt

A small village in Wales is visited by creatures of myth.
Nearby, a coach crashes on the M40, killing all its pas-
sengers. Police can find no record of their existence. The
Doctor and Ace arrive, searching for a cure for the
TARDIS, and uncover a gateway to another world.

ISBN 0 426 20368 2

NIGHTSHADE
Mark Gatiss

When the Doctor brings Ace to the village of Crook
Marsham in 1968, he seems unwilling to recognize that
something sinister is going on. But the villagers are being
killed, one by one, and everyone's past is coming back to
haunt them – including the Doctor's.

ISBN 0 426 20376 3

LOVE AND WAR
Paul Cornell

Heaven: a planet rich in history where the Doctor comes to meet a new friend, and betray an old one; a place where people come to die, but where the dead don't always rest in peace. On Heaven, the Doctor finally loses Ace, but finds archaeologist Bernice Summerfield, a new companion whose destiny is inextricably linked with his.

ISBN 0 426 20385 2

TRANSIT
Ben Aaronovitch

It's the ultimate mass transit system, binding the planets of the solar system together. But something is living in the network, chewing its way to the very heart of the system and leaving a trail of death and mutation behind. Once again, the Doctor is all that stands between humanity and its own mistakes.

ISBN 0 426 20384 4

THE HIGHEST SCIENCE
Gareth Roberts

The Highest Science – a technology so dangerous it destroyed its creators. Many people have searched for it, but now Sheldukher, the most wanted criminal in the galaxy, believes he has found it. The Doctor and Bernice must battle to stop him on a planet where chance and coincidence have become far too powerful.

ISBN 0 426 20377 1

THE DOCTOR'S ADVENTURES CONTINUE IN DOCTOR WHO MAGAZINE

Every issue of *Doctor Who Magazine* is packed with new stories, archives, news and features about the world's longest running SF television programme. Special reports cover subjects such as new books — including the New Adventures — visual effects, design, writers and new merchandise.

For full details of the latest subscription details and other Marvel *Doctor Who* products, write to: *Doctor Who Magazine* Subscriptions, PO Box 500, Leicester, Great Britian LE99 0AA.